THE TIME OF THE FIREFLIES

THE TIME OF THE FIREFLIES

KIMBERLEY GRIFFITHS LITTLE

Scholastic Press • *New York*

Library of Congress Cataloging-in-Publication Data

Little, Kimberley Griffiths, author.

The time of the fireflies / Kimberley Griffiths Little. — First edition.

pages cm

Summary: When Larissa Renaud starts receiving eerie phone calls on a disconnected phone in her family's shop, Bayou Bridge Antiques, she finds herself directed to the river bank near her house, where a cloud of fireflies takes her on a journey through time to learn the secrets of her family's past — and save their future.

ISBN 978-0-545-16563-1 (jacketed hardcover) 1. Family secrets — Juvenile fiction. 2. Families — Louisiana — Juvenile fiction. 3. Time travel — Juvenile fiction. 4. Fireflies — Juvenile fiction. 5. Louisiana — Juvenile fiction. [1. Secrets — Fiction. 2. Family problems — Fiction. 3. Family life — Fiction. 4. Time travel — Fiction. 5. Fireflies — Fiction. 6. Louisiana — Fiction.] I. Title.

PZ7.L72256Ti 2014

813.6 — dc23

2013027396

10 9 8 7 6 5 4 3 2 1   14 15 16 17 18

Printed in the U.S.A.   23

First edition, August 2014

The text type was set in Calisto.

The display type was set in P22 Parrish.

Book design by Elizabeth B. Parisi

IN MEMORY OF MY TALENTED, CREATIVE,
AND LIFE-LOVING BROTHER, KENDALL,
AND FOR HIS MARVELOUS READER-BOYS KEITH, KOHNER, AND KYLER,
WHO KNOW THE POWER OF IMAGINATION, FAMILY, AND LOVE.

CHAPTER ONE

The second day of summer was a flapjack-and-bacon morning with enough sweet cane syrup to make your teeth ache. A glorious, heavenly day when you got no more homework due for three whole months.

It was also the day I got the strangest phone call of my life. Instead of my best friend, Shelby Jayne, there was an unfamiliar voice on the other end of the line. A girl's voice, breathy and whispery, just like a ghost's might be.

Nope, I didn't see no white figures floating up the staircase to the second floor. No moaning or chains rattling. No pockets of cold air that freeze you to the floor.

Just a voice on the phone. I'd never heard of ghosts waltzing around town making phone calls. Then again, I don't live in a regular house. My parents moved us into the Bayou Bridge Antique Store — a fact I do not brag about. It's embarrassing to admit I share the same space as musty, mothball-smelly furniture, dusty books, and teacups that dead people once drank from.

But Bayou Bridge Antiques boasts a LOT of telephones. An entire *wall* of antique telephones, and Daddy is always buying more at garage sales. He spits some shine on them, rewires the cords, and sells them to collectors, or folks who want to decorate their house in the "old-fashioned" style.

We have what's called "farmhouse" phones, which is a wooden box with a crank that a person had to wind up to make a call. And we have a whole slew of black "candlestick" phones. That's a phone that sits on a table with a fat tab people used to click with their finger to alert the operator.

We also have a couple dozen rotary phones in burnt orange, firehouse red, lipstick pink, and purple vomit. A rotary phone means there aren't any buttons. Folks had to stick their finger into a circular dial and push it around to get each number to dial up and connect.

Then there's also a fancy cluster of pretty Victorian phones, French provincial, Princess phones, and telephones my mamma calls "vintage" sitting on a sideboard with doilies and candlesticks and whatnot.

I never knew there were so many types of telephones floating around the world. You'd think they'd have been buried in a garbage heap long ago. I'd never paid them much attention until I was gulping down the last of my milk and a phone started to ring.

Mamma poked her head into the kitchen and shooed at me. "That isn't the store phone, Larissa. Must be our private line upstairs."

"I haven't finished my breakfast."

"That's because you're dawdling. Now go answer it. Hurry! I'm with a customer."

I figured by the time I ran up two flights of stairs the answering machine would have gotten it, but strangely, the ringing didn't stop. It just kept going, on and on and on. A peculiar ring, like a bell, but when I got to the phone sitting on the nightstand in my parents' room, it was dead silent. I lifted the receiver. Just a regular old dial tone.

But *something* was ringing. Getting fainter, like it was running out of steam.

I gripped the iron staircase railing and listened, knowing it wasn't the store phone or our private line.

The day was still early. Nobody was currently brows-
ing the second floor, although the sound of voices
floated up the circular stairwell, Mamma chatting to
a customer about a tea set from early-twentieth-
century England.

"Probably a country manor house set." Her voice
drifted upward. "Excellent condition, not a single
crack. Look at these miniature painted roses. . . ."

I played a game of Hot and Cold, trying to figure
out where the ringing was coming from. It got
fainter — colder — when I started down to the first
floor, but warmer when I ran back up. And loudest —
hotter — the closer I got to the wall of telephones in
the back corner.

A big, square walnut box was clearly ringing as I
approached. The two bells clanged furiously together,
like the phone had gone crazy.

Only problem was, *not a single one of those phones
was hooked up to an outside line*! None of them actually
worked. They're just for show, and most folks buy
them strictly for decoration. The metal bells clanged
away, and I wondered if my ears were working right.

I didn't remember Daddy hooking up the phone,
but maybe he'd run a line for a picky customer.
Somebody was calling this old phone!

A shiver whooshed down my neck as I lifted
the receiver and stuck it to my ear. The sound of

crackling came through, then silence deader than a graveyard at night.

A prickling rose on my neck. I heard *breathing*, and I was too scared to say a single word. The safest thing was to just hang up, but I couldn't get my arm to lift the heavy black receiver back on its hook.

The next moment a girl's voice softly said, "Hello? Anybody there?"

I was so shocked I dropped the phone. Quickly, I snatched it up again. "Um, hello?"

"Is this working?" the girl said as the murmur of static started up again in the background. "Did I get through?"

"I guess so. I can hear you," I told her.

"Who is this?"

I blinked in surprise. "Who are *you*?" After all, *she* called *me*. And I was pretty sure ghosts didn't actually talk. Or have voices. Or breathe. Maybe she wasn't really a ghost at all. . . .

"Larissa?" the girl asked softly.

I about jumped out of my skin when she said my name. "How do you know who I am?" I glanced behind me, but I was completely alone.

The girl said, "Doesn't matter how I know, but I need your help."

My voice wobbled. "Can't help you if I don't know who you are."

"Actually, Larissa —" She hesitated. "*You* need *my* help."

Nerves sizzled along my arms. There was something about her voice that was familiar, but I couldn't quite place it. "Is this a joke?"

"No!" she said quickly. "Never. This is completely serious. I need you to do something very important. And —" She paused. "It's a matter of life and death."

I let out a big breath, finally figuring out who it must be. My archenemy. "Alyson Granger, you are sick. Or stupid. I'm onto you. Don't know how you pulled this off, but I recognize your voice."

Touching the scar on my face with my free hand, I was about to hang up for real when the girl pleaded, "Oh, Lordy, girl. I am *not* Alyson Granger, I promise! Larissa, listen to me. You have to listen. Please, I'm begging you."

Her voice sounded like the big sister I never had. Cajoling, pleading, but stern, too.

I ran a finger along the edge of the white line of the scar I got last year. The year I hated myself. Hated my life. Hated every single kid in this town. "Just leave me alone," I finally choked out.

"Larissa, please don't hang up! I can't tell you who I am, but you'll probably figure it out eventually.

Right now, I'm afraid that if I told you, I'd lose you forever, and it was the biggest pain to get this phone to work. Because — because I have to be able to call you again."

She got the phone to work? What does that mean? I couldn't help being awfully curious, so I played along with her, imagining the revenge I'd wreak on Alyson if it was a huge joke she and Tara were playing to mess with my head. "Okay," I finally said. "I'm listening."

"I don't have much time, but —" She dropped her voice. "But remember this: *Find the fireflies.*"

"What in the heck are you talking about?" I spat out.

She started talking faster. "Find the fireflies. *Trust* the fireflies. You'll know what I mean when —"

Her voice was suddenly gone. Cut off. Disappeared into nothing.

I clicked the receiver tab over and over, but the phone was deader than a doornail. I willed her to come back, clanging on the bell with my fingernails to get it to ring again, but she was gone.

The second floor of the sprawling store was shadowy. Not many windows up here. The place was packed with stuff. An old blackened iron stove. Suitcases filled with dirt where I was planning on planting fresh flowers like I did last year. Shelby Jayne loved my daisy-and-petunia-garden suitcases. Only times they sold were to customers from out of state, like California or Vermont.

I didn't usually venture into the dark, creepy corners of the store, but across from the couches and desks, a rectangle of yellow fell through one of the small windows. Jumping around a bookcase, I ran over to gaze down on to the back of the house. Nobody was messing with the phone wires — or running down the dirt road playing a trick on me.

Returning to the wall of phones, I willed the metal bell to ring again. Not a peep. The only fingerprints in the dust were mine.

I lifted the long, frayed cord to the wooden schoolhouse telephone I'd been speaking into not three minutes earlier. It dangled in my hands.

I'd just received a call from a phone that wasn't hooked up — with a cord that went absolutely nowhere.

CHAPTER TWO

Next morning, I dreaded going downstairs. My stomach jumped in a squirmy, nasty way. Like I had grasshoppers swarming my gut. Or tarantulas with furry legs.

I stood in front of the round window overlooking the bayou, wishing I didn't have to leave my bedroom. Summertime meant no homework and no school. But it usually meant moving, too, and I was determined not to move again.

"I'll go live with Shelby Jayne in the swamp," I whispered to the window. "Or Grandma Kat in Baton Rouge."

Even though I was the peculiar girl at school living in an antique store, I had the best bedroom ever on the top floor — a bedroom created out of the domed cupola, painted sunshine yellow. Daddy had redone my furniture in pristine white, and yellow curtains fluttered at the window, showing off a view of the cypress. I could see all the way down the muddy Bayou Teche until it curved and disappeared.

Why couldn't my parents work at a bank or the post office? I'd attended five different schools and next year would be my sixth — just in time for seventh grade — if my parents didn't decide to move again. Especially after what happened last year. Mamma still couldn't talk about it without shaking with anger.

I'd never figured out why my parents uprooted us over and over again. Who knew what grown-ups were thinking? Didn't seem sane half the time. Parents could change up the rules on the spot when they didn't like how you'd dressed that day or if you had plans with your best friend.

"Breakfast, Larissa!" Mamma called up the stairs, her voice faint and tired. She was always tired these days. A condition like hers will do that to you.

I stood there, not budging. Thinking about the phone call and what the girl had told me.

"Now!" Mamma shouted again.

I touched a finger to the window as morning light filtered through the curtain's swirl of lace scallops. My bed was rumpled with pillows, blankets flung over in a heap, but I didn't want to make it. Fortunately, my mother almost never climbed the stairs all the way up here. Least, not recently.

"Girls who don't eat breakfast don't get no lunch, either," Mamma added.

"All right already," I muttered as I clumped down each step. There were fifteen to the second-story landing and another fifteen to the first floor.

The antique store wasn't a regular store in a strip mall, but a ratty, tumbling-down, three-story house — contents included. With a leaky roof. And a wrap-around porch with a caved-in step so you had to hop to one side and be careful your foot didn't fall through.

We had piles of old furniture, paintings and pictures, ceramics and figurines. Crates of dusty, yellowing books. Old farming equipment. Clocks. Toys. Garden tools. Games, playing cards, boxes of dice.

"You name it, we got it!" was my daddy's slogan.

While we ate breakfast, Mamma would jump up for easy access when the bell rang with an early-morning customer.

"Very convenient," she told me the first time the bacon burned.

"Saves rent," Daddy added, pulling his LSU baseball cap down over his eyes and chewing on the end of his unlit pipe. He'd quit smoking but had to chew on something. A toothpick wasn't near big enough.

We'd only been here a few months when I started suspecting the store was even stranger than I first thought. Broken junk was one thing. Haunted was something else.

Daddy said it was merely inconsiderate customers. Each night after closing out the cash register, he and I would walk through the store to straighten up (and check that nobody was hiding in the restrooms) before we climbed the stairs to bed. I took mental notes that everything was in its proper place, on its shelf or in its box. It was part of the ritual.

Next morning, a set of glass angel figurines would be sitting on a sofa. A rag doll hiding behind a stack of dishes. Or a stuffed bear sitting inside a rolltop desk.

I wondered what kind of game the ghost was playing. Mostly, I wondered what she wanted.

Ghosts always want something, right? Or they wouldn't be roaming around getting into trouble, or scaring folks.

I didn't know why Daddy didn't believe me when I told him that *stuff got moved*. He just shrugged.

"Must have missed it last night. I was tired." Or, "It was dark. The lights were already off in this corner." Or just: "I do believe you were dreaming, Larissa."

Except I was pretty sure I knew when I was dreaming and when I was awake!

"Who lived in the antique store before we did?" I asked my mamma as I slurped down my grits filled with a puddle of butter.

Her hair fell across her face as she bent over the skillet on the stove, blue gas flames licking at the bottom of the pan. "Don't know. Place was empty for a year when we bought it."

"Before that," I prodded.

She shrugged and turned on the water in the sink. "Doesn't matter, Larissa. Now finish eating so we can unpack the boxes that just came in."

But someone had reached out to me. I'd heard her voice with my own ears.

CHAPTER THREE

F*ind the fireflies. Trust the fireflies."* The words ran through my mind all day. Along with the bizarre fact that *I heard a voice on a* broken *phone.*

Grits never filled me up and lunch was only half a sandwich, so my stomach growled the whole afternoon as I fetched things for customers, and Mamma and I drew up For Sale signs and price stickers. I was pretty sure hunger could do peculiar things to your mind, so maybe I'd just been dreaming that whole telephone call.

That evening, the nightly routine with Daddy got even spookier.

Dusk had settled into the corners of the yard. Customers finally stopped peeking in the windows to see if we were *really* closed. Mamma had gumbo simmering in a giant pot and coleslaw chilling in the fridge.

"Let's start downstairs," Daddy suggested, taking off his LSU cap and smoothing down his hair.

"All that smoothing didn't help," I told him.

"What are you talking about, *shar*?"

"Your hair is all sweaty and clumpy."

"I had the proud honor of hauling several of our fine couches in and out of a truck, and then in and out of a house today for a new customer."

"Guess your weird hair was worth it."

"You got that right. If the summer stays as busy as today, maybe we can stay in the black this year." Daddy turned the OPEN sign to CLOSED and we set off, skirting the spiral staircase. "Make sure the restroom lights are off and it's got paper towels."

After I wiped down the bathroom sinks, took out the trash, and restocked paper products, we worked our way around the furniture, putting magazines back, dusting shelves, picking up toys and books and glass figurines that people had moved in their search for treasure.

The smell of okra curled out from the kitchen, and my stomach grumbled for the thousandth time today. "I'm starving."

"Got the upstairs still," Daddy reminded me.

I didn't need any reminding. I wanted to avoid that wall of phones. Especially when Daddy kept turning off lights.

He held my hand as we walked up the staircase, and then set me loose. "You go left and I'll go right and I'll beat you to supper."

"No fair! You got longer legs than me!"

I tried not to let go of his fingers, but he had already pulled away and was off, laughing.

"Daddy!" I said.

But he just laughed again. "I'm gonna get there first!" he threw over his shoulder.

"Don't turn off the lights until I'm done!" I yelled. I was twelve now, but I still hated the dark. Daddy made a sound like an evil mad scientist and disappeared into a far corner.

Everything appeared fine, just the normal chaos, dishes out of whack, some books upside down.

Through the far windows, night turned black as pitch. I tugged on the chain of a fake Tiffany lamp as I approached the wall of telephones and the light-bulb blinked on. The very next moment I turned *off* the lamp. If anyone was standing below the house where the meadow sloped toward the bayou, they'd be able to see me through the glass. I wished Mamma had put up some blinds. I felt exposed. What was more scary — spying creeps or haunted telephones?

Before I latched the doors of the tall Victorian wardrobe, I ran my hand over the taffeta and calico old-fashioned dresses.

Shelby Jayne and I loved to put on the flowing dresses, swishing the skirts around our legs; pin a hat on our heads; and strut around the antique store. It was our secret, and we only did it when no one was around. After all, middle school was coming up this year, and we didn't want anyone seeing us.

Some days I still wanted to turn back the clock to when we lived in Baton Rouge. Before the accident on the broken pier when I got scarred for life.

The year I died.

One minute I was standing on the broken bridge over the river, trying to stay upright as I inched to the edge, my toes gripping the rickety wooden planks so I wouldn't fall in.

The second minute, Alyson Granger's voice rang out: "You're cheating."

I stared at the black, eerie bayou water below the pier. My throat knotted up; my stomach was about to heave. The pilings swayed, loose and ancient, as wind tore at my hair.

"I'm not cheating!" I cried. I was merely taking

my time getting to the edge as I answered questions in their stupid Truth or Dare game.

"Wrong answers mean bigger steps, not baby ones," Tara Doucet added in her prissy, grown-up voice.

The third minute, my face burned as a few of the boys from my class showed up, laughing from their perches on the pilings. I was new in town. I didn't know what spots on the broken bridge were safe and which were deadly. Of course, the most deadly spot was where I was hovering, trying to stay on top of the wooden planks. The spot where the bridge dropped away after lightning had struck decades earlier.

The fourth minute I wobbled on the edge of the precipice over the frothing black water. Before I could answer another Truth or Dare question — or run away — I suddenly fell straight down to my death — pushed into the bayou by Alyson Granger, the sheriff's daughter, and Tara Doucet, the richest girl in town.

They'd followed me home from school, talking behind my back. I'd pressed my backpack tight against my chest trying to ignore them, but every word seared into my brain.

They were discussing the tea party Alyson's

mamma was giving in a few weeks to celebrate the first day of summer. The tea party I wasn't invited to. Leave it to my parents to move to a new town where school only had three weeks left.

"Did you get that new Victorian dress and hat to wear?" Tara asked.

"I can't wait to show you! I look five years older at least," Alyson said.

"The catalog picture looks perfectly divine," Tara said.

I rolled my eyes, waves of envy rippling through my stomach.

"Mamma's making orange-blossom tea and English scones with clotted cream. *And* finger sandwiches," Alyson went on. "And sugared fruit and iced lemon squares."

"Hope you pig out until you bust a gut," I'd muttered.

"What did you say?" Tara Doucet said, reaching out a hand to yank me to a stop on the bayou road.

My heart thumped a hundred miles an hour as Tara's big green eyes stared holes into my face. Her long, silky, waterfall hair swished around her shoulders.

"Nothing," I answered, wiping my sweaty hands on my shorts. "I didn't say nothing."

Her eyes narrowed like she could read my mind. "Hey, Alyson, let's show Larissa the bridge. She'll like that."

"T-Beau and Ambrose aren't here yet. We can't play Truth or Dare."

"We'll just do a little preview," Tara said. "Come on, it'll be fun."

As soon as I hit the water I couldn't breathe. Water filled my mouth, my nose. I couldn't see a thing.

My body collided with one of the pilings. My head crashed against the slimy, waterlogged beam, green with algae. The jolt shuddered down my spine. I didn't know which direction was up or down.

An alligator must have come looking for lunch because I was sure I felt his sharp, pointy teeth scraping against my face. Trickles of blood swirled in the water. I screamed and water rushed down my throat, cutting off the air I had left.

I was a goner.

Guess that was my punishment for choosing the wrong girls at school to try to be friends with. What kind of person talks about the best party of the summer right in front of the new girl and never invites her?

They were either clueless or the meanest girls in town.

When I fell into the bayou and saw the lights of heaven beckoning me — or the lights of the Gulf sucking me out to sea — I knew the answer.

And I vowed that if I lived, I'd never to speak to Alyson Granger again.

Blackness yawned before my eyes as I heard my daddy rustling with some furniture on the other end of the second floor.

"Stop being such a silly-nilly," I scolded myself, shaking my head to erase the memory of last year. "There's no such thing as broken telephones that can talk."

But then, why could I hear the girl's voice so clear and real in my mind? I knew deep down the voice didn't belong to Alyson Granger. The voice on the old telephone had been much more serious. Intense, not high and whiny.

I willed the wooden box phone with its metal bell on top to make a sound. I dared it to ring. *Dared it!*

It didn't make a peep.

"See?" I hissed at the phone. "You can't make phone calls! Your cord doesn't go nowhere!" I picked it up again, just to be sure, and the telephone wire drooped from my hand. Useless as a bent nail or a broken teacup.

I flung the cord away, shivers racing down my neck.

Then I froze to my spot on the hardwood floor.

I could feel someone watching me.

Slowly, I turned and scanned the windows, my neck prickling. My heart hammered at my throat so hard I thought I was gonna choke right then and there.

Far on the horizon a small golden moon rose above the cypress groves along the bayou.

There was nobody down below in the yard, but I could swear another pair of eyes was focused on me — and I couldn't seem to move my legs.

"Daddy —" I started to croak, but just then there was a sharp whine on the other side of the big room as he shoved a piece of furniture up against the wall.

The noise seemed to break me from my frozen state.

My gaze landed on the doll case where the most valuable dolls were locked up.

"Supper's ready," Mamma called from the foot of the staircase. "Where are you two?"

My stomach growled again as I skirted a bin full of bedding and a bookcase stuffed with ancient paperbacks.

Next to a massive cherrywood wardrobe, I kneeled down in front of the case overflowing with dolls: rows of chubby baby dolls, rag dolls, antique porcelain dolls, and stiff-legged Barbie dolls that were so old they were collector's items now.

In the center of the case sat the most exquisite porcelain doll we owned. Perfect features in a heart-shaped face and big blue eyes with super-long black eyelashes. She was amazingly beautiful in a rose-colored lace dress and a feathery hat tied under one ear with pink ribbon.

She had a tiny chip on her chin, but otherwise the doll was in perfect condition. A piece of cardboard sitting in her lap stated that she was about one hundred years old. In thick black marker, it also read: NOT FOR SALE. That was Mamma's doing. But she'd never tell me why. How could we have such a valuable doll and not let anyone purchase her?

Months ago, Mamma about lost her eyeballs when I told her Shelby Jayne was coming to our house to pay a visit and see the doll.

"That's Gwen's doll," she'd told me, all stiff and blinking.

"It's so beautiful," I said. "I want to show it to her."

Mamma pressed her lips together. "You leave the doll in the case and don't touch her."

I begged for a solid week, and Mamma finally let me and Shelby Jayne get her out — exactly once — to hold her.

"This doll is fragile and only for show," Mamma had told us sternly. After three minutes, Mamma placed her back in the case, stuck the NOT FOR SALE sign on her lap, and snapped the key in the lock.

Mamma's older sister, Gwen, had owned the doll. When she drowned in the bayou, Mamma inherited the antique, so she was like a family heirloom. Except I didn't know where she'd originally come from, or how Gwen had come to own her.

I crouched on the floor, my nose almost touching the glass.

For one crazy second, I knew that the doll's crystal-blue eyes had been studying me. She was staring at me that very instant. Her eyes locked onto mine, and I shuddered with the sensation of ice cubes on my skin.

Mamma always said, "When you get the shudders it means someone's been walking on your grave."

I usually ignored her silly superstitions.

"Anna Marie," I said, speaking the doll's name out loud. I didn't usually say it, but I knew what her name was. What I didn't know was whether Gwen had named her or someone else. I'd probably never know. Most likely, she came with that name from the store where she was purchased.

A moment later, the scar on my face began to burn something fierce. I rubbed my fingers along the ridge on my cheek as it throbbed. My eyes stung and I bit my lips to keep from crying. Guess I needed to put on some of that cream Shelby's mamma gave me to help it heal.

Still rubbing at my face, I started to turn away, and the doll's eyes seemed to move with me.

Quick as a flash, I jerked my chin to gawk at her again. The doll smiled a perfect, serene smile.

I'd never understood why Shelby loved this doll so much. Yes, she was beautiful. Yes, she was exquisite and lovely and her dress was made of real silk from India. But my dead aunt Gwen's doll gave me the creeps. Her facial expression made it seem as though actual thoughts were running through her porcelain brain. Under the flouncy dress and bows and pearls in the ringlets of her glossy blond hair, it was almost like the doll had a secret.

I shivered again as her icy blue eyes pierced mine. Almost like she was looking straight at me and was about to speak.

CHAPTER FOUR

I backed away from the doll case, my legs jiggly.

"It's only my imagination," I whispered under my breath. "Because of that stupid phone call. The one I probably imagined." Maybe part of my brain had exploded after all the homework and tests of the last couple of weeks of school.

Maybe I was just missing Shelby Jayne, who was in Paris with her grandmother Phoebe. But as I turned to run downstairs, I swore the doll's eyeballs were shooting needles into my back. I could *feel* it.

I was still rubbing at the scar on my face when I burst into the kitchen, bright and normal and ordinary.

Mamma was tasting the gumbo on a spoon, while a pan of corn bread sat steaming on top of the stove. She glanced at me, sweat dribbling down the side of her face, her hair tied back in a ponytail after the long day. Tendrils of hair escaped the blue elastic tie, flyaway and messy.

"Set the table, please, Larissa," she said, tsking her tongue at me.

"Why you tsking me? I ain't done anything wrong."

"You need to quit ducking your head every time someone looks your direction. I can hardly see your eyes most of the time the way your hair covers up your face."

I got out the plates and laid them on the table. "It hurts," I whispered.

"What hurts?" she asked, pressing a hand against her growing belly when the baby kicked. "I know my own legs hurt," she went on, not waiting for my answer. "All I want to do is fix sandwiches for supper and put my swollen feet up. But your daddy eats like a horse and always wants a full dinner end of the day. I suppose he's earned it," she added with a sigh. "Never get no time for a decent lunch."

I finished setting out spoons, and then mixed up a pitcher of frozen lemonade.

Mamma didn't want to hear that my scar hurt. She didn't like to be reminded. Not that she needed any reminding. That scar stared at me every single day of my life in the mirror — and every time Mamma looked at me, all she saw was the ugly scar.

The pot of gumbo went on the table with a thunk, and then Mamma brought over a plate filled with squares of corn bread.

"All shut up tight," Daddy announced as he walked to the sink to wash up. "Alarms are on, too. Not that I really think we need them. Not in Bayou Bridge."

"Hmm," Mamma said, collapsing into a chair.

Daddy laid his LSU cap on the tablecloth next to him, swigged down a whole glass of lemonade, and then clasped his hands for grace.

Soon as I mumbled an "Amen," Daddy was gulping big spoonfuls of the boudin sausage, okra, and rice in the gumbo fast as he could.

"I'll get the honey," I said, fetching it from the pantry in the corner.

"Thank you, *shar*. You read my mind."

Just like that doll, Anna Marie. She seemed to read my mind, too. I swallowed hard, wondering why I'd thought such an odd thing. Like the words popped into my brain.

While Daddy drizzled honey on his corn bread,

Mamma leaned over, tilting my face to the overhead light. "Let me see you."

I thought she'd forgotten about me, so I flinched at first when she ran her hand lightly down my cheek. "Does it really still hurt?"

I shrugged. "Not much now, but it did a little while ago. When I was upstairs with Daddy closing up."

A frown creased her brow. "How often does that happen?"

"Maybe I bumped into something without knowing it."

She studied my face, brushing back my hair. "It's a bit red and swollen. More than I've seen in months. Maybe I need to take you to the doctor."

"Don't want to go to the doctor. I stopped using Miz Mirage's medicine cream. I'll just start up again."

"Hmm." Mamma touched my chin. "You're a pretty girl, Larissa. Don't forget that."

"Mammas have to say that. It's a rule to love your own children." I draped my hair over my face, staring down at the lumps of rice in my bowl.

Mamma drew in a breath. "I don't love you because of any rule, Larissa! And you *are* beautiful. I just wish you'd stop hiding your face. Stand up to those bullies."

I set down my spoon, bracing for the argument we'd had a million times. "They don't bother me anymore. I've told you that over and over again. It happened once. That's it."

Mamma pushed back her chair, her eyes wild. "Once was more than enough! Luke," she said, addressing my daddy, who was buttering his third piece of corn bread.

He eyed her. "What, Maddie?"

"I told you we should have moved. This town protects those kids. Kids who push other kids into the bayou. They still play that stupid game! Ever since I was little and Gwen drowned —"

"Can we talk about this later?" Daddy glanced at me, then back again at Mamma.

"You always say that! And we never do! Here we sit, pretending it never happened. We should have pressed charges. Written editorials in the newspaper. Brought all those kids to justice. This is unacceptable. Our daughter is scarred for life, and we pretend it never happened!"

I inhaled and a piece of bread plugged up my throat. My eyes turned watery and I started coughing. Daddy reached over to rub my back, then got up to get me a glass of water.

"You're making Larissa feel worse," he said, his

voice low. "The way you go on about it. Will you just be quiet? At least at the dinner table?"

Mamma made an angry noise, and then flung a dish towel across the counter. "You're always too tired to talk later. I am, too, but at least I care."

"Talking about it won't undo the past, Maddie. It won't bring back your sister, and it won't take away what happened to Larissa. You planning on hating everybody here for the rest of your life — even folks who had nothing to do with Larissa's accident? Is that your plan?"

Mamma gasped and her face turned red. I pushed away my plate, sick to my stomach. Third day of summer, and all the ugly memories from last year washed over us again like a tidal wave from the Gulf.

"We should never have come back to Bayou Bridge!" Mamma said, bending over to cradle her big stomach.

"You said you wanted to come back to Bayou Bridge. Try to make peace with Gwen's death. Do something about your parents' old house across the bayou. Your family was here for almost two hundred years, but that property is about to get condemned. The authorities have only given us a little more time to do something about it. Tear it down, sell it, what-ever. Don't matter to me."

Mamma's face got splotchy. "Bad luck follows us wherever we go. You just don't seem to care!"

"What do I gotta do to show I care? Take my shotgun and go wave it around? Get hauled off to jail?" My daddy's voice kept rising, louder and louder.

"I'm not saying that!"

"Then what are you saying, Maddie?" Daddy's neck turned crimson, the pulse in his throat beating hard.

I covered my ears with my hands. "Stop it," I said, but my parents didn't hear me.

"We could sue. Hire a lawyer —"

"With what money? We're barely bringing in enough to cover groceries and the light bill."

"Then I want to move again," Mamma said, staring so hard at the salt and pepper shakers I thought she was going to make them explode with her eyes.

"We can't afford to move again!" Daddy spat out, slapping a hand against the table. "We got a mortgage and a big, fat loan on this store, and I'm not going to do bankruptcy. Not gonna do it —"

"But, Luke! Those kids — they just got away with — my own sister died because of that awful game —" She flung her hands up, pressing them against the sides of her head as her reddish-brown hair flew helter-skelter, held back by stupid, ugly, black pins.

Across the kitchen, I saw myself reflected in the dark glass of the window. The same flyaway hair, the same black bobby bins. I was almost the spitting image of my mamma, except for the scar. The big, ugly, white ridge of scar slashing down my face.

"I can't stand it," I whimpered, feeling like I was going to be sick.

"Sit down, Larissa," Mamma told me.

"No," I said, and I was shocked to actually say that to her. I'd never disrespected my mamma before.

"You will sit down and finish your supper before I tie you to the chair, young lady!"

"If I eat another bite, I'm gonna throw up!" I said, blinking back the tears seeping out my eyes. "In your heart, you do think I'm ugly. The scar will never go away, and I'm sick of you always telling me to brush back my hair, hold my head up high, and show it off!"

I started backing toward the door. I felt trapped in the kitchen. Mamma's shame and grief were going to drown us all.

"She's got a point, Maddie," Daddy started to say.

"I'm sick of talking about it!" I yelled. "Sick of thinking about it! Sick of you fighting about it!"

Lunging for the back door, I yanked it open. The muggy evening filled the doorway, heat smacking me in the face. I pounded down the stairs, flew off the last step, and ran across the grass as hard as I could.

CHAPTER FIVE

The screen door slammed behind me. I could hear Mamma's voice. "Larissa's running off again." Then Daddy, his voice rising. "Do you blame her, Maddie? You gotta leave her alone about the accident. You gotta deal with your own ghosts and get past this."

Ghosts. What kind of ghosts was Daddy talking about? It was the same argument I'd heard for a year. Mamma just *had* to move to Bayou Bridge. And now Mamma wanted to move again. Didn't matter where. Just not here.

Maybe my father was talking about Mamma's sister, Gwen. But she wasn't a ghost. She was lying peacefully in the town graveyard. She'd never lived anywhere near the antique store. I knew almost nothing about her.

A narrow alley ran behind the stores on Main Street. I dodged garbage cans and freight pallets behind the stores and shops. Raced past the post-office trucks. Another block down, I smelled the fragrance of yeast and cinnamon behind Sweet Ellen's Bakery where sometimes Mamma gave me a couple of dollars to buy cinnamon swirls when she got a sugar craving. She said having a baby did that to her.

I'd hoped my parents' arguments would stop when we moved to Bayou Bridge, but it got worse ever since my accident. I worried they didn't love each other anymore. And I worried I'd be listening to them fight about money and my scar until I left for college. Or ran away to live with Grandma Kat in Baton Rouge, although that would mean leaving Shelby Jayne, my best friend.

Shelby Jayne was lucky that she got to spend so much time with her grandmother Phoebe, who doted on her something fierce, although we both wished we had brothers or sisters. Maybe that's why we'd become such close friends. We both needed a sibling. And we'd both been tormented by the kids on the broken bridge. Our mammas knew each other, too. Turned out Miz Mirage, Shelby's mamma, had been best friends with my aunt Gwen who drowned so many years ago.

Drowning was the worst way to die. Especially in the muddy Bayou Teche where you couldn't see the bottom. A shudder ran down my spine every time I relived falling into the river last summer, ragged nails gouging my cheek that I'd have sworn were alligator's teeth chomping on me, water filling my mouth. I could still feel the sensation of the swaying broken pier as I hung on for dear life — and pictured my own blood swirling in the water.

My eyes burned with the memories — and I tripped in the dark alley and fell flat down to the ground. Pain throbbed at my elbows and knees as I rolled over.

Glittery stars smeared across the evening sky. A slice of moon shimmered above the trees, hanging like a white jewel. Frogs croaked and belched. Crickets and cicadas hummed in the air.

Then I heard the soft gurgling of water and knew I was near the bayou.

Bayou Bridge Antiques was on one end of town. Alleyways lay behind the Main Street businesses and a couple of neighborhoods sat diagonal to Main, bordered by sugarcane fields. After running through the alleys and then cutting down a side street, I was on the long road that fronted the Bayou Teche. It was kind of crazy to come down here. The first time was accidental, but now I couldn't stop myself from returning to the place where the accident happened, the place where my life changed forever. It was like teasing at a loose tooth. Or picking off a scab. It hurt, but you couldn't stop yourself.

In the twilight, shapes were just shadows, the edges of the world blurring. Streetlights flickered on near the houses set back off the road. The cemetery was just up ahead, too, and I did *not* want to end up there without a heavy-duty flashlight and Shelby Jayne by my side.

The ground sloped toward the water's murky edge, and I skirted the shrubs and a few cypress knees to sit on the edge. Wrapping my arms around my bent legs, I saw that I was sitting almost directly in front of the broken-pier bridge. The pier that used to connect the town to the deserted island across the bayou. Something about the bridge lured me, haunted me.

When we first moved here, Daddy had taken Mamma across the water in a boat to see her old house. I remembered her saying that it was in terrible condition. Roof and porches sagging, weeds as high as her shoulders. The walls stained and moldy, floors ripped out.

Far as I knew, Mamma never went back. She said it was too painful to know how beautiful the island used to be with a mansion house her great-great-great-grandparents had built when they owned most of the sugarcane fields around here. Back when Bayou Bridge wasn't even a full-fledged town yet. Mamma said ships used to travel down Bayou Teche and pick up the harvest. Boats stacked tight with tons of cane to transport to the mills for making into sugar and molasses.

Strange how a family could be so rich at one time, and now here we were — the same family two hundred years later — so poor. Well, not dirt poor, but money was tighter than a stuck crawfish trap. Our truck rattled like a pair of dentures in a skeleton. Daddy had to use a lot of gas when he went to garage sales and flea markets and estate sales searching for good stuff. Mamma and I held down the fort, then spent days unpacking and tagging each item.

I sighed and perched on the edge of the bank, keeping an eye out for slow-moving red alligator eyes. The evening was quiet, ripples barely stirring the surface.

Down the road, I heard the sound of kids jumping on a trampoline in their yard. A woman calling her children into supper. Were my parents looking for me, or were they still fighting?

Laying my scarred cheek across my knees I could pretend my face wasn't mangled up. I could pretend my skin was smooth and perfect. If someone were to walk over and see me sitting here in this position, they'd never know unless I raised my head.

I wanted to call Shelby, but we'd said good-bye on the last day of school. She'd already flown to Paris with her grandmother Phoebe for two weeks to visit art museums and eat snails drenched in garlic. I missed her, especially when I heard all those kids in the distance talking and laughing as they trooped into their house. The door banged shut and the night fell still again.

Sitting here pretending I didn't have a scar lasted for about five minutes before tears started stinging my eyelids. I lifted my head and wiped at my eyes.

Lightning bugs gathered just down the bank a little ways, where the cypress knees grew dense, jutting out of the water at the steps of the broken bridge.

The swarm of crazy fireflies multiplied, growing thicker.

Like dancing stars.

Flying yellow lights.

Buzzing pieces of glowing magic.

My breath caught like an ache in my throat as I watched the beauty of the fireflies in the dusk. I stood up, brushed off my shorts, and moved across the damp, grassy bank. My foot slipped as I hit a patch of mud, but I grabbed the branch of a cypress and hung on until I got my balance again.

The number of fireflies seemed to keep growing as I skirted a patch of leafy elephant ears. The fireflies became a spinning yellow cloud. Wispy and weightless, fluttering through the dusky, humid night.

I'd never seen so many lightning bugs at once in all my life.

I wished I had a jar to catch some. Wished I had my camera, because the lightning bugs weren't just flying; they were dancing and floating, elegant and graceful. A silent, beautiful light show.

I took another step toward the cloud, hoping they wouldn't fly off and disappear. But just the opposite happened. The fireflies came closer, swarmed me, and then enveloped me inside their cloud.

I lifted my arms out to my sides and turned slowly, like a ballerina on top of a music box. Golden light shined on my face, and I could feel their tiny wings lightly touch my arms and hands and cheeks.

I wanted to laugh and cry at the same time. It didn't seem real or possible that they would wrap me up in their cloud of light, but it was actually happening.

The cypress and tupelo and shrubbery fell deeper into shadow, but I almost thought I could lift off and fly with them.

Maybe I was dizzy from dancing, maybe I was dreaming, but I knew deep inside I wasn't. This was really happening.

All at once, my foot sank into the bayou as I slipped into a mud hole. "Ack!" I squealed, jerking my knee up. My sandal was soggy, my toes gooey with slime. The fireflies had brought me right to the steps of the broken bridge.

In the twilight, the pier was gloomy and menacing. After my accident last summer, I swore I'd never go on that bridge again. Even if someone bribed me with a suitcase full of money.

The cloud of lightning bugs stopped, hovering in the air at the steps to the bridge. Then, all together, those hundreds of dancing lights moved forward across the first few wooden planks.

Halfway out the bridge ended in blackness where it lay broken. There was a huge gap of at least twenty feet before the bridge picked up again on the far side. The spot where the planks of the bridge had fallen in was scary and dangerous, with jutting, broken boards and rusted nails, water rushing fast as ocean waves.

"I'm not going out there," I said, stopping on the first plank. I gave a nervous laugh, and my legs shook. I was talking to a swarm of fireflies!

My head ached, and I put a hand to my forehead. My brain seemed to turn to mush. My vision filled with the thick swarm of fireflies, and I couldn't see the bayou in front of me any longer. The tiny flying creatures lighted along my arms, touched each of my fingers, tugging at my shoulders, urging me forward. How very peculiar.

I couldn't seem to think straight. What were they doing? Luring me into the water? If I fell in, nobody would ever find me in the dark. Nobody would even hear me scream. I'd drown like Gwen. Only worse. She'd been found. I might never be seen again, but pulled out to sea for real this time.

The moon rose across the murky waters, a thousand ripples silently moving across the surface.

The fireflies danced faster, thick as heavy syrup, the light blinding and beautiful. I was in a tunnel of light, and yet, I wasn't scared. They didn't want to hurt me. Only wanted to — to show me something. Maybe I was dreaming! Or going crazy.

The girl on the phone had told me to *find the*

fireflies. Were these the fireflies she was talking about?

I took two more steps forward. The fireflies were right there with me, kissing my cheeks, my hair, propelling me forward.

The bridge shimmered under the moonlight, and all at once the edge where the planks had collapsed into the water had miraculously been fixed. The rusted nails were gone. The broken, empty space filled up with brand-new planks, tight and strong and sure. The bridge stopped shuddering as I stepped closer to the middle of the river. Protected by the fireflies. Like a miracle.

I rubbed my hot neck as the image of the perfect bridge wavered like a mirage in front of me.

Then, out of the darkness, a scream sounded behind me. A girl was yelling my name. Feet pounded the bridge. I held out my arms so I wouldn't fall down, but the sudden flailing scared the fireflies. The tiny yellow lights spun off into the night, disappearing into the trees and darting under the elephant ears. "Where are you going?" I cried out. "Don't leave!"

Someone yanked on my arm. "Larissa Renaud? Is that you?"

I whirled around. My head spun and my stomach

lurched like my dinner was about to come back up. Through the twilight, I stared into the face of my mortal enemy. The girl who'd almost drowned me a year ago. The girl who'd scarred my face forever.

Alyson Granger.

CHAPTER SIX

My eyes locked onto Alyson's eyes, just as it began to drizzle rain. Her hair dripped, long strands of brown sticking to her forehead.

She ogled me like I was a crazy person. "What are you doing out here?"

"What are *you* doing out here?" I spat right back at her.

"You were gonna jump, weren't you?"

"No, I wasn't!" The words flew out of my mouth just as my stomach shot into my throat. I willed myself not to throw up. I felt like I'd just been yanked back from a different dimension, a different time. . . . I'd seen the bridge whole and new. Was it the future? The thought made my head spin furiously.

"Look!" Alyson yelled, pointing. "There's the broken end of the pier right there. If I hadn't grabbed your arm, you would have gone right in!"

I gazed down at my feet. Water rushed past the pilings not a foot away. I had no idea I was this close to walking right off the end into the bayou. Prickles of heat raced up my neck. What had I been thinking?

"The fireflies . . ." I began. "They were just here."

In the dim light of dusk, I saw Alyson frown. "There were a few lightning bugs along the banks as I came down the road, but they never last long."

"But the bridge —" I tried to see beyond the trees and water. I'd seen the bridge whole and unbroken just a minute ago. As though it had never been torn apart. No rotting planks submerged with rusted nails for teeth.

I reached up and touched my face. My scar was still there, and my hair was going frizzy from the drizzle. Goose bumps crawled along my arms. I was cold, my fingers stiff, like I'd been standing out here for hours.

"What time is it?" I asked, and then I stiffened. I was talking to one of the two girls I hated most in the whole town.

"Almost eight thirty," Alyson said.

I *had* been out here a long time. Supper had been at six. Just a minute ago I'd been dancing with the fireflies, whirling right in the middle of their cloud of shimmering light. . . .

Alyson's hand came toward me like she was going to touch me, then she pulled back self-consciously. "You were going to fall in. If I hadn't stopped you, I mean."

My chest tightened. "No, I wasn't. I know where I am. I have eyes, you know!"

Alyson took a swipe at her soggy hair, which just made it stick up funny on her forehead, and shrugged. "I know what I saw."

I pressed my lips together. "I bet you wish I had fallen in again. Just so you could make fun of me."

Alyson's mouth dropped open and her eyes widened. "No, I don't," she said in a low voice.

"Yeah, right. Just keep telling lies."

"I'm not lying. You don't understand —"

I started to shake. "What don't I understand? That I got this scar on my face for the rest of my life — because of you!"

"That wasn't supposed to happen. It was an accident!"

"Some *accident*." I heard my own voice laced with hate. Tears bit at my eyes and I blinked to hide them.

She wasn't going to get the satisfaction of seeing me cry. Not this time. This summer I was older, smarter. I wasn't going to let anyone hurt me again, ever. Right now, I wished she'd move out of my way. "Where did you just come from?"

Alyson glanced off to her right. "Tara's house."

That's what I was afraid of. "Thought so. Now, if you'll excuse me, you're blocking my way. Unless you came out here to push me off the bridge again. Although you probably need Tara to help you." My words were like spitting darts.

"You're wrong, Larissa. That's not why I ran out onto the bridge. You were about to go in. I mean it! I — I was scared for you."

"Ha!" My voice sounded mean to my own ears, but I couldn't stop. I wasn't going to believe anything Alyson Granger said.

She took a step back. "I'm not your enemy. At least I don't want to be."

I didn't want to hear it. "You ruined my life!" The truth came out in harsh, jagged pieces. Like a knife in my throat. "Just go away. Leave me alone."

Alyson's pale blue eyes went wide, and her lips trembled. She turned and ran down the bridge toward the road, her feet pounding the old wooden planks so hard the bridge shook.

Once she hit the bank, she sneaked a peek at me over her shoulder, but I didn't move. I just waited for her to get out of my life, hopefully forever. I'd spent all school year pretending she didn't exist. Her and Tara Doucet both. They thought they were better than everybody else. They thought they owned this bridge. Thought they could get away with torturing and bullying new kids.

Anger bubbled up into my throat as I brushed away hot tears. Rain came down harder, and my fingers were like ice. Puddles formed on the slippery bridge planks. My parents were going to have a fit.

I'd never said hateful words like that to anyone before. I wanted to hurt Alyson, but I never expected her to look so shocked. Upset, even. Words might hurt for a few minutes, but what they'd done to me was a *thousand* times worse. I pictured Tara Doucet in her rich house with a fire and silk pajamas. Sipping hot cocoa from a champagne glass, carried in by the butler on a silver tray with a doily.

I gulped back the lump in my throat. Funny how, only a few minutes later, the feeling of satisfaction was gone. All I could see were Alyson's eyes, distressed, like she was going to cry. But I've cried a million tears over the last year, I reminded myself.

The current of the bayou kicked up as the wind rose. Waves whipped into froth, rushing downstream. Black cypress branches swayed along the shoreline of the island as wind tossed leaves from the ground.

I slipped up the slope back to the road. Alyson was long gone, and the dark road was lonely and deserted. Hugging myself, I ran, my toes gripping my sandals so they didn't fall off. I was wetter than a drowned rat.

When I got to Main Street with its old-fashioned streetlamps and hanging flowerpots, I couldn't stop thinking about the fireflies, the way they'd swarmed me. Had they really been leading me down the bridge so I'd fall off — maybe truly drown this time? That seemed impossible, but I couldn't shake the feeling that there was something more I was supposed to know. Something I'd missed.

I'd seen the bridge whole and new, hadn't I? Was it just a trick of the moon — the trick of a thousand lightning bugs? I remember being dizzy, almost sick, like being in a tunnel, traveling, and picking up speed.

I reached the edge of our soggy front lawn and my feet skidded. Caught my balance right before my bare knees hit the stone walkway to the front door. My clothes stuck like glue; my hair dripped in fat clumps. Mamma was gonna yell at me. Daddy would ground me for the rest of the week for taking off like I did. And for yelling at them and staying out so long. When I pushed open the kitchen door and saw the clock, I gulped. It was almost nine.

"Larissa?" It was my daddy from the kitchen.

I shut the door behind me. "Um, yeah."

He came around the corner and stopped at the cash register. Rubbing a hand over his bare head, he crammed his baseball cap back on top of his messy hair, then retreated back to the brightly lit kitchen.

I followed him, shivering so hard from the rain and my encounter with Alyson that my teeth chattered. "Is Mamma super mad?"

Daddy scratched his chin, a shadow of stubble along his jawline. "She went to bed already. Being on her feet all day wears her out. Getting worse now that the baby is getting closer."

I nodded, chewing on my lips.

He gave me a parental stare. "I was just about to get the rescue squad out to look for you. You look like a drowned nutria, *shar.*"

Water trickled down my neck, rain or tears, I wasn't sure. "I didn't mean to stay out so long. Two hours went by like ten minutes."

"That so?" The kettle started screaming on the stove, and he reached over to turn off the gas, then leaned back against the counter.

"I'm not lying. It's true."

He cocked his head at me, and his deep brown eyes seemed to see right into my mind. I squirmed, tugging at my damp shorts. "Guess time doesn't mean much when you're twelve. Here and then gone, but there's no rewinding the clock to make up for being out past dark."

"Is Mamma gonna . . ." I started. "Will she ground me?"

"Don't think so. She doesn't realize just how long you were out all by yourself." His eyes pierced mine. "But where you been, Larissa?"

"Just down to the bayou," I said vaguely. "I saw lightning bugs, too. Before it started to rain."

"Maybe they'll be back tomorrow and we can take a jar to catch some." Daddy reached over to rub my arms. "Let's hustle you into a bath and then bed. Customers come mighty early in the summer."

Upstairs, we were both smothering yawns while I started the water. The sound pounded into the porcelain tub as I grabbed my nightgown from my room.

"Wind's coming up," Daddy said, thumbing through the stack of towels in the cupboard. He handed me one and shut the window tight. "Come say good night when you're done."

I nodded, breathing a sigh of relief for not being in too much trouble. I peeled off my wet clothes and dumped them in a pile. The heat of the water steamed the mirrors, and the bath rug was cozy under my toes.

After I climbed in, I leaned back, shut off the spigot, and closed my eyes.

A whirl of images floated through my mind. Lightning bugs dancing along my arms. Shadowy trees. The shimmering bridge under the moonlight. Alyson Granger, her eyes big and round and spooked.

Why would she believe I would jump into the muddy, creepy water? Alyson was crazy, that's what. She probably *hoped* I was going to jump and came over to spy on me so she could report back to Tara and the rest of them.

My parents' earlier fight rumbled through my head, so I sank deeper into the water. All I could hear was the swooshing, echoey sound the bathwater made. Soon my knees got cold because the tub was short, so I washed my hair and ran the faucet again to rinse it clean.

After wrapping myself up, I dried my hair with a second towel, and then leaned over the sink toward the mirror. My hair was getting long, way past my shoulders now. I'd been growing it for months on purpose. If I turned my head just so, you couldn't see the scar at all.

I had pretty much perfected my posture, but Mamma was always nagging at me to forget what happened. Trim my hair. Style it. Stand up straight and look folks in the eye when they talked to me. She drove me crazy. She was such a hypocrite. I could only hope the new baby would distract her from nit-picking so much.

Leaning into the mirror, I ran my finger along the folded pleat of skin and winced. I wondered if plastic surgery could hide it or fix it. My stomach did a jump as the image of T-Beau from school came into my mind. I dropped my curtain of hair around him, too, even when he tried to talk to me during algebra. I forced myself to hate him. He had come along with the other boys the day of that stupid game of Truth or Dare, and sat on the pilings and watched. The day Alyson and Tara pushed me in. The day I became "that girl with the scar."

Some days it was hard to hate him too much when he glanced over at me in class — and then pre-tended he hadn't.

I pulled my nightgown over my head, drained

the tub, and combed out my hair. When I got to my parents' door, Daddy placed a finger on his lips. "Mamma's asleep; let's leave her be."

That was fine by me; I didn't say anything as Daddy hugged me good night. He dropped a kiss on my head. "Better dry your hair before you go to sleep, *shar.* Don't want to catch cold."

I lifted my chin, biting my lips as I asked him the question I'd wanted to for so long. "Do you think my scar is very ugly? Do you think a doctor could make it disappear?"

He gave me a sideways smile. "I know you're the prettiest girl in town, *shar.* Besides Mamma, of course."

I thought about their argument earlier. "You're paid to say that."

"Hey, nobody pays me much of anything, girlie." He leaned against the doorjamb. "Scars do fade a bit. But maybe down the road you won't want it to go away. It'll be a memory of the person you were, the person you *are.* You're not gonna be afraid of anything. And you're not vindictive. That scar is a badge of honor."

"There's one thing you're forgetting, Daddy."

"What's that?"

"Girls aren't supposed to have scars."

"Who says?"

"Everybody!"

"I'd like to know who everybody is. I'd like to meet them someday."

I rolled my eyes. "You're so predictable, Daddy."

"Larissa," he said, turning serious. "That scar just proves you're a warrior. You can get through anything. There are worse things in life than a little bitty scar."

"But it's not small at all —"

My daddy held up a hand. "You'll understand one day. And one day, that scar will hardly be noticeable. Because there're so many other things that will be more important to you. I can promise you that."

"I'm going to hold you to that promise."

He grinned at me. "Come back and talk to me when you're thirty," he said, teasing me, but dead serious, too. "And we'll see where you are."

I shook his hand, hard. "It's a deal. But I probably won't wait until I'm thirty to talk to you again."

He scratched his chin as he stared up at the ceiling. "Yup, tomorrow'd be nice, now that I think about it. Seein' how you're my favorite daughter."

"Oh, Daddy. I'm your *only* daughter."

He waggled his eyebrows. "See you in the morning for our rounds."

After he closed the master bedroom door, the antique store settled into night. A little creaky, but mostly quiet. Once inside my own room, I couldn't hear anything except raindrops splattering the window ledge. Pinpricks of light from Bayou Bridge's neighborhoods pierced the black night. I imagined the lightning bugs hiding out under the elephant ears in cozy nests during bad weather, sleeping while recharging their light batteries.

Jumping on the bed, I rubbed down my hair with the towel and tried to imagine what it would be like to have a baby brother. Mud pies and dump trucks and sandboxes. Wrestling matches and boys in the front yard playing Kick the Can. On the other hand, a sister meant dolls and dressing up and experiment-ing with hairstyles. Squealing slumber parties and baking cookies on a rainy day. I guess I could like either one. I was sure Daddy wanted a son. Did he wish I was a boy? I'd never thought about that before. He said the scar didn't matter, but I knew it would matter less on a boy than a girl.

Pressing my cheek into the pillow, I pictured Alyson Granger's baby-blue eyes in my mind. Wild in the storm. Scared, too. She didn't seem mad. She didn't seem like she hated me. But maybe that was just her faking me out, getting me to trust her so she and Tara could be mean again.

I could still feel her fingers on my arm. Had she really been yanking me back from the bayou's swirling waters — or did she have ulterior motives?

The voice on the telephone floated through my mind. *"Find the fireflies."* I held my pillow to my stomach, knowing I'd found them. Or *they* had found me. The rest of the girl's instructions flooded over me, the strange intensity in her voice when she whispered, *"Trust the fireflies."*

Throwing off the blankets, I stuck my feet on the floor, staring out the window. What in heck did that mean? *Trust* the fireflies? How do you trust a flying insect?

I pictured the lightning bugs earlier this evening, dancing among the elephant ears. Their lights a thousand tiny golden lamps. A delicious shiver rushed down my spine when I thought about what it felt like to walk among the fireflies.

I had to go back to the bayou. Back down by the creepy broken bridge. Tomorrow. As soon as the sun started to sink.

CHAPTER SEVEN

Half an hour later, I still lay flat on my back, rigid as a board, thinking about how much I did *not* want to go down to the broken pier again, even if I knew I had to. I dreaded the shadows at dusk and the giant cypress trees that whispered in the night. What if Alyson showed up and got the rest of the kids from school to hide out and scare me all over again?

I rolled over, burying my head in my pillow. The voice of the girl on the phone kept slamming into my brain. *"It's a matter of life and death."*

What was she talking about? That seemed crazy. But the girl had seemed so urgent, even frantic. She told me to trust the fireflies. She seemed so confident, like she knew things I didn't know. But didn't she know about the accident where I almost died? Didn't she know I was terrified?

Besides, how did we even know each other? Over the phone it was hard to tell how old she was, but she was definitely older than me. I couldn't think of a single older girl from school or town that I knew. She'd called on a disconnected phone and refused to tell me her name.

My pillow grew hot. If this was some kind of trick, I didn't want to be the biggest baby in town, but there was no way in heck I was going to be pushed off the bridge again.

I'd have to be prepared. If someone tried to push me, I'd have to grab their arms or their shirt and pull them in with me. I knew I could do it. I'd be ready for them.

Thunder rumbled in the distance along the bayou.

A dog barked in someone's backyard.

I swallowed hard, wishing I'd grabbed a drink of water, but I just pressed my eyelids tighter as the sensation of falling hit me once more. The heavy, murky river water rushing up my nose, burning my throat as I sank into the sickening darkness.

Later, the night of the accident, I'd woken up in a

hospital bed, Mamma and Daddy staring at me, white gauze wrapped around my head. Their faces floated in front of my eyes, and then Daddy put a hand on my forehead. His lips moved, saying something I couldn't hear. Water clogged up my ears, sloshed inside my brain. I wanted someone to fix it, but I fell asleep again.

Next time I opened my eyes, a nurse bustled in with a stack of food trays.

"So," I asked softly, pushing myself higher in bed as she fluffed my pillows. "Was it an alligator?"

The nurse blinked, puzzled, then her face cleared. "You mean that cut you got on your face? No, wasn't an alligator. It was the old, rusted nails on those ancient pilings that got you good. Doctors stitched you up, gave you a tetanus shot, and you'll be good as new. Right as rain."

She set down my lunch tray and I gazed at the cold milk carton, the red squares of Jell-O quivering in a glass bowl. Nails had ripped at my face like knives. A whole mess of nails sticking out of the broken pilings. The pain had been unbearable. I remembered hearing voices shouting and yelling, but it was all a blur as I'd sunk my way to the bottom of the bayou.

The next day, I was helped into a wheelchair and came home.

I never knew what Daddy had said to me when I first woke up and realized I hadn't died. I wanted to know, but I felt stupid asking him. Like I was a little kid that needed reassuring.

Once I was alone in my bedroom, I pulled off the white bandage, piece by sticky piece. My hair had dried ratty and greasy, but Mamma said we'd wash it the next day.

"Don't mess with it," she'd told me. "We can't get the stitches wet."

But once I was in my nightgown and she was finally gone, I got a mirror and peeled back the gauze. I just *had* to see.

I could hardly breathe when I saw the angry black stitches. My cheek had swelled up like a balloon. Purple-and-green bruises covered my skin like I'd been punched in the face. The scar was repulsive, and I was hideous. For weeks after the accident, I cried so much I thought I'd be sick.

One night when Mamma hadn't shut the bedroom door tight, I could hear my parents talking. I peeked through the crack. Mamma was in a fury over the kids who'd taunted me on the bridge. She'd said the kids deserved to be arrested and put in juvenile detention. Daddy had tried to calm her down, but she refused to be soothed.

I didn't know whether Mamma's anger made me feel better or not. Mostly, I just wanted her to be quiet and stop ranting. Let me cry in peace. Let me hate them all on my own.

I didn't know I'd fallen asleep until Daddy burst in the next morning. "Wake up, sleepyhead! Sun's shining and it's getting hotter than firecrackers already."

My throat felt thick and my eyes were crusty. "I'm tired," I said, pulling the sheet up over my head.

"It's late, *shar.* We got customers in ten minutes. Had to open up shop all by myself."

"Why didn't you wake me?"

"You were snoring to beat the band. Figured I'd let you sleep since it's summer vacation, after all. We're not going to work you like a horse every single day. Just every other day." He laughed at his own joke. "Well, hurry up and get dressed. Mamma's not gonna be happy keeping your breakfast hot. Besides, cold *pain perdu* isn't good for the soul. She has a doctor appointment today, so you'll have to do the cash register for a couple hours while she drives into St. Martinville."

I raised my arms and let them drop limp again. "See how tired I am, Daddy. I can hardly move."

He lifted an eyebrow, then winked. "Up and at 'em, Larissa. We're on a tight schedule today."

"Okay, okay!" I rolled out of bed as he went downstairs, stubbing my toe on the corner of the bed as I whispered, *"Find the fireflies. Trust the fireflies."* I could tell it was going to be a peculiar day.

When I got downstairs, the OPEN sign was turned out, the front door unlocked, and Mamma was drying the breakfast dishes.

"Six weeks left, Luke," she said as my daddy drained the last of his coffee. "What're we going to do when I'm tending the baby and Larissa is back in school?"

"Maddie, can this conversation wait until tonight?"

"You're always putting me off. We can't afford part-time help. This baby is coming at the wrong time."

Daddy put his hand on her shoulder as she slumped at the sink. "Babies aren't usually convenient, are they?"

I glanced sideways to watch them, wondering if they were still mad or what. You can never tell with parents.

Daddy went on, "Babies come when they come. We sure been waiting a long time. We'll just make the best of it."

"*You*, Luke Renaud, are the most optimistic person I ever met," Mamma said.

I could tell she wanted to stay mad. Or at least she didn't want to shake off her pessimism. Mamma was a glass-half-empty sort of person and my daddy was the opposite. Everything to him was half-full — even if it might be barely half-full when we didn't get a single customer into the store some days.

I thought about the two baby boys my mamma had years ago that didn't live past a few hours. I remembered Mamma locking herself in her room, hearing her crying when I came home from school. All those trips to the doctor. Friends coming over. I ate a lot of chicken soup and there were plates of cookies all over the house.

"Are you going to find out if it's a girl or a boy?" I asked now, spearing a piece of the fried cinnamon bread with my fork and soaking it in syrup.

"Larissa!" Mamma cried. "I swear, sometimes you sneak around like a ghost. What're you doing listening to our private conversation?"

"Just obeying you by eating breakfast."

"No sass, my girl." Mamma raised an eyebrow at me. "I'll leave the sink plugged in so you can do your own dishes when you're done eating. Think we got potential customers coming down the street."

I nodded, my mouth full so I wouldn't have to answer her.

"Polish off the grits in the saucepan," Mamma added, running a hand through her flyaway hair. I hoped she wouldn't pin it back. I knew she got real hot when she was working, but still, it made her so dowdy.

"And, Larissa," Daddy added, heading out the kitchen door, "finish opening up the second floor, would you?"

"Thanks for leaving it for me."

"Just stick close. Mamma's doctor appointment is at ten."

After I finished eating, I washed up the dishes, rinsed and dried, then ran upstairs.

Opening up the second floor meant some light dusting, checking for cabinet keys, fluffing dolls' dresses, rolling back the lids on the desks, and double-checking that everything had a price tag within easy sight.

I found a few stuffed animals tucked behind some glassware on a shelf. Several old-fashioned hats scattered here and there. A red-and-white-checked apron left on the floor near a bookcase. Leather button-up shoes inside a crate of holiday lights and ornaments.

And the sliding glass door to the doll case was open a crack.

"Huh?" Had Mamma unlocked it and forgotten? Some of the dolls were left out on top of the glass. The rag dolls and the Barbie dolls, ones that weren't as valuable as the antique dolls.

I crouched down to slide the door closed and searched for the key. The porcelain doll's piercing blue eyes caught mine, willing me to look at her. A shiver crawled along my shoulders, like a spider's legs scuttling across my bare skin. "You are beautiful," I whispered. "But why do you give me the creeps?"

Her blue eyes seemed to flash, and I blinked. Then her gaze seemed to grow darker, like she was angry at my words. Her mouth froze into an eerie smile. The scar along my face began to itch. I reached up and scratched at it, feeling the welt rise. "Ouch!" I lifted my hand and there was a smear of blood on my fingers. I rubbed at it some more, but it only got worse, so I found a box of tissues and held one tight to my face to stop the bleeding.

At last I spotted the key sitting on the window ledge. A tremor of movement caught my eye as I locked the case. I would have sworn the beautiful antique doll had moved ever so slightly. But that was crazy. I'd probably bumped into the case when I reached for the key.

I backed away, my eyes locked onto the doll, an ugly, prickly feeling washing over me.

"This is stupid," I finally muttered. "It's just a doll."

A sudden pain in my cheek made me double over. "Dang, that hurts!"

I hurried to the bathroom mirror. Sure enough, my scar was swollen and angry, a streak of blood where I'd scratched too hard. It was my own fault. I needed to leave it alone. Now Mamma was gonna be fussing at me. I'd just have to stay out of her way today. I pressed a cold, wet washcloth against my cheek to get the swelling down.

Instead of putting my hair into a ponytail and clipping back all the stray flyaway hairs, I left it hanging down. I knew I'd get sweaty later, but I brushed my hair down over the right side of my face, covering up part of my eye, too. Didn't want to scare off customers when my parents took off for the doctor appointment.

I spent most of the morning reading a book and staring out the front window by the cash register. It was a slow day for some reason. Maybe we'd get more tourists as June got better under way.

By the time Mamma got home and made lunch, my face looked more normal.

"Does the doctor know whether it's a boy or a girl?" I asked, trying to distract her as she spread mayonnaise and mustard on a row of sliced bread. I laid out slices of turkey and ham, then got out a pitcher for lemonade.

"We pretty much decided to be surprised," she said, refilling the paper towel dispenser. "But since — since we've had trouble in the past, they insisted on an ultrasound so they could see the baby and what's going on."

My mouth went dry. "It is okay, isn't it?"

"Of course. The baby is growing perfectly normally. You have nothing to worry about."

But I knew that sometimes there were things wrong that you couldn't see. Things inside that made a baby sick. Or made them die after birth. The lungs or the heart.

"You could tell, right?" I pressed her.

"I'll let Daddy tell you."

"Is it another boy? Think I'll finally have a brother?"

Mamma smiled mysteriously. "Go take this sandwich to Daddy and let him tell you."

I grasped the plate with the turkey-and-ham sandwich and a couple of dill pickles and headed to the front counter.

A customer left, clanging the bell. Daddy said, "Perfect timing, *shar*. I'm starving."

He wolfed down a big bite, then picked up his glass of lemonade.

"Spill it!" I demanded. "What are we having? A boy or a girl?"

Daddy chewed some more and all the while he kept grinning at me.

I stuck my hands on my hips.

He finally stopped eating. "Larissa, in six weeks you are gonna be a big sister."

"I know *that* already!"

"You're going to be a sister to a little baby sister. We're having a girl!"

A girl. A girl? Never thought that would ever happen. Not after two lost baby brothers. "Doesn't seem possible."

"It was clear as day on the ultrasound not two hours ago."

"Did you want a boy?" I asked, almost afraid to say it.

"You kidding me? I love my girls, and I can't wait to see if she's as pretty as you."

"She'll be prettier," I heard myself say. "You'll forget all about me."

My daddy set down his sandwich. "Now where'd you get that idea?"

"You'll have me fetching diapers, making bottles, giving her a bath, doing extra chores. Guess you can call me the new maid."

Daddy winked at me. "I suppose you're right, *shar.* But it's gonna be a whole lot of fun."

I shrugged my shoulders, not sure if it was going to be much fun or not. Two older women with gray hair and big black handbags came through the front door. Daddy nodded at them and said, "Good afternoon." Then he said to me, "Hopefully, two daughters will be quieter than a rowdy boy."

"Girls squeal and scream, Daddy. Believe me, I know," I told him, sudden tears biting at the corners of my eyes.

"As long as I can count on your advice and expertise," he said, finishing up his lunch real quick and heading off to answer any questions for our new customers.

"A sister," I whispered, heading back to the kitchen. My eyes swam with the most peculiar emotion. My throat felt funny. I had a bubble of excitement imagining a real sister to play with. Someone who'd look up to me. But I felt lost all of a sudden, and the feeling stuck in my throat like a prickly burr.

I was used to having Daddy all to myself. I pictured him cuddling the new baby, holding her hand as she learned to walk — and me standing off to the side, watching my family being happy again.

All year long I'd wanted Mamma to stop bothering me about my hair and my scar and not making any friends except Shelby Jayne. Pretty soon she'd focus on the new baby instead of me. I'd become not only an invisible girl at school, but right here at home, too.

A whimper choked at my chest, and I gulped past the pain. At least I had a secret of my own. The clock ticked by slow as molasses as I waited to go down to the bayou, my secret growing bigger and more special with each hour. But after eating my plate of fried shrimp and leftover coleslaw, I worried about leaving the house. Especially after I'd run out last night.

Daddy came out of the office with a stack of bills and invoices for mailing. "Would you walk all this down to the post office, *shar*? Stamped and ready to go. Just put it in the slot for Outgoing Mail and it should get picked up first thing in the morning."

It couldn't have been more perfect.

I traded my sandals for socks and sneakers so I could run fast if I needed to. Or at least fast*er*.

I left my parents sitting on a couple of settees on the second floor, their feet resting on a pair of boxes, while they discussed the pros and cons of rearranging stock.

As I passed the side street where the county sheriff's office resided, Alyson Granger's face popped into my mind. Even if I wasn't jumping up and down with joy about having a new sister, I wouldn't let any of the kids in this town hurt her.

I pushed through the heavy glass post office door, shoved the pile of mail into the slot, and then jogged down to the main intersection and turned left.

The sun nestled against the tops of the cypress trees, sending out streaks of orange and red. I slapped my arms as the mosquitoes came out and picked up speed.

Find the fireflies.

Trust the fireflies.

The smell of barbecue dripped through the still air, making me hungry, even after a big supper of my own.

Down at the water, the evening was motionless and still. Not a person in sight. I walked along the bank, skirting elephant ears, studying the forest of cypress. When I reached the broken bridge, I gazed across at the even denser trees that engulfed the deserted island. My mamma had lived over there when she was young. They'd moved away when her sister, Gwen, drowned.

I'd always wanted to see the deserted house. We didn't own a boat, and Miz Mirage, Shelby's mamma, always said to leave the place alone, to let it rest with its memories and sadness.

Crouching down, I hugged my knees, careful not to sit on the damp mud. Mamma would know right away where I'd been. She was afraid of the water. Just like me. And yet the bayou fascinated me, drew me to it like a magnet.

The air grew more humid as the sun shivered along the tops of the cypress forest on the island. Not a whisper of a breeze. Only water shushing against the shoreline, kissing the cypress knees that stood in uneven rows above the waterline.

I glanced down the empty stretch of road that ended at the sugarcane plant, thinking I should probably start back. But when I pushed myself up from the ground, that's when the lightning bugs arrived. A huge swarm rose up out of the elephant ears and tupelo leaves, as if they'd been there all along, hidden behind a trick of the light or a magic mirror.

I moved toward the cloud of fireflies slowly, not

wanting to scare them off. They were so beautiful, so otherworldly.

"Okay," I whispered aloud, creeping closer. "I found the fireflies. Now what?"

The tiny lights dazzled my eyes; their little wings spun around me. I reached out and wiggled my fingers, feeling them flicker and bounce off my skin.

I was walking *inside* the cloud of fireflies. Hundreds of lights pricked at my eyelids, lit up the sky around me, circled me like a halo. It was incredible. It was magical.

The column of lightning bugs moved forward, with me right inside the deep golden light. They were darting, zooming, and I practically felt like I was flying. Not a second later, my eyes dropped, and I gasped. My chest tightened and my palms turned sweaty. I was standing in the danger zone right where the broken planks of the bridge began.

"What are you doing?" I cried to the fireflies. "Don't take me out there!"

I stepped back to return to the safety of the bank, but the fireflies swarmed me again, blocking me from fleeing, urging me forward instead. They wanted me to follow them off the edge of the bridge into the water? That was unthinkable. Horrifying. What had I gotten myself into?

A moment later, the bridge began to shimmer. I held my hand above my eyes where the sinking orange sun peeked through the cypress trees. I'd swear there were lights coming through the trees on the island. More lightning bugs — or real electric lights?

Gulping, I tried once more to return to the safety of the bank, but I was at least twenty feet from shore now. How did that happen? I yelped, but my voice sounded small and pathetic. Strangest of all, the planks of the bridge were firm under my feet. They weren't swaying or rocking. The bayou water swished calmly around the now-sturdy pilings.

"I — I have to go back," I moaned, but the fireflies wouldn't let me.

They darted like wild things, touching my arms and legs and hair, like they were trying to pull me forward. "I am *not* falling off this dang bridge ever again, so just let me go!"

"Trust the fireflies," the voice came to me. I twisted my head, wondering if the girl on the antique telephone was there, but of course, I was alone. Except for the fireflies.

"Okay, I'll go a few more steps and that's it."

Nervously, I stepped forward. Every single plank was there and locked into place. I shook my head, baffled.

A last ray of sunlight broke through the trees, and I couldn't believe my eyes. The bridge crossing the water was glowing in the golden sunset, but it wasn't broken anymore. Each plank was firmly in place — not a single one missing — all the way to the opposite shore. I shook my head, hoping I hadn't gone a touch crazy.

I couldn't look down. I just focused on the cloud of fireflies guiding me across. One step at a time. If the lightning bugs suddenly disappeared, I swore I was going to race back home as fast as I could. My heart thudded with terror. If a single plank disappeared I'd crash straight into the bayou. If that happened, I was a goner. Nobody knew I was here. Nobody would ever find me.

I nearly turned around for the third time, but gritted my teeth and kept going, the swirly column of fireflies carrying me across. Two steps later, I was on the muddy bank of the far shore and I thought about kissing the earth in relief.

The fireflies dipped and danced, releasing me from their protective cloud. For several moments, all I could see was a sky filled with thousands of lightning bugs, but seconds later they were disappearing under the leaves, burrowing into the mud, or whatever fireflies did.

It was muggy and hot, and my stomach felt strange, but I'd miraculously made it across in one piece. Along the shore to my left was a dock, small but sturdy, the wooden planks painted a clean, fresh white. Tied to the moorings, several boats bobbed on the quiet water.

Wiping my hands on my shorts, I took a deep breath and peered through the trees along a winding overgrown path straight ahead of me.

That's when I heard the sound of voices up ahead.

CHAPTER EIGHT

The voices were indistinct, but definitely human.

I crept along the narrow path, searching through the trees for No Trespassing signs, but I didn't see any.

When the path opened up, I was standing at the edge of a clearing, staring at a huge white house on a sloping rise in the middle of the crowded cypress.

The voices were louder, but still no sign of anyone. I circled the edge of the woods, keeping out of sight. Shelby Jayne and my mamma always said how run-down the old house was after being abandoned for twenty years. Broken windows, sagging porch, and gaping holes. Stained and mildewed walls and floors.

That wasn't true at all. *This* house was spectacular. Pristine white paint gleamed under the slanting evening sun. Columned porches looked brand-new. Curving steps led to a grand double front door. Perfect flower beds hugged the house. And a pond, including a waterfall, gurgled in the far corner of the yard. A sweep of emerald grass ran all the way to the banks of the bayou on the far side of the island.

I kept circling the house from the safety of the cypress woods, but all of a sudden, I halted. There, only a few feet ahead of me, were the owners of the voices.

A girl about my age sat on top of an overturned bucket. She had her chin on her fist as she scrutinized an older man wearing cotton overalls and a striped work shirt. He was digging with a shovel into the soft dirt between the lawn and the woods. The girl studied his work intently and every few moments she'd lean over and inspect the hole he was digging.

She was wearing the frilliest, most girlie-girl dress ever. Her hair curled in dark ringlet sausages, smoothed back from her forehead with an array of butterfly hair combs studded with gemstones. That fancy hairstyle must have taken hours to create.

I blinked, crouching down into the damp leaves, unable to take my eyes off her.

The girl shifted her feet and I saw that she was wearing button-up shoes. Just like the ones I'd returned that morning to the trunk of old-fashioned clothes we kept in the store. This girl was the essence of an overdressed mannequin from the Edwardian era. Was she dressed up for some kind of costume party? Halloween was still five months away.

She was probably the most beautiful girl I'd ever seen. Prettier even than Tara Doucet. Her eyes were big and a deep blue color with long black eyelashes; her mouth and lips were cute, showing white teeth that didn't need braces; her nose was the perfect size without a single bump. She had a creamy porcelain complexion, perfect flawless skin. I ran a finger against the ridge of my scar and wanted to hate her just a little bit.

"Now remember, Mister Lance," she said, leaning closer. "This is our secret. I'm counting on you."

The elderly gardener shoved back his straw hat and scratched his head around a thinning patch of gray hair. "Aye, Miss Anna. Mum's the word."

He rocked back on his heels, surveying the expanse of lawn stretching clear around the house. Magnolia trees dotted the yard, as well as pink blossoming crab apple trees and giant oaks. I spied several outbuildings in the distance, a barn painted red, a shed, and a roof over an open space that might have once been an outdoor kitchen. There were also a couple of out-houses as well as a long row of weathered shacks that probably housed slaves back in the olden days.

The air was steamy, like a damp rag, and Miss Anna surreptitiously swiped at the sweat along her forehead.

Gazing along the line of trees closest to me, I glimpsed holes dug up next to the cypress and oaks. What the heck were they doing? The older man rubbed at the stubble sprouting on his chin. "You sure we lookin' in the right place, Miss Anna?"

The girl nodded firmly. "That's what my grand-mother told me. That the silver forks and spoons got buried in the yard. When they got wind that the Yankees were coming. The Yankees stole everything, you know. All the local folks' money, their chickens, even their silverware. She said they were lucky they didn't burn down the house."

Mister Lance's demeanor grew wistful. "True, that. Most houses got burned to the ground. Y'all was lucky them soldiers used your house as their headquarters."

Miss Anna nodded primly. "Grandmother Sophronia said it was because the barges and ships could come right up the Bayou Teche. We had a good dock back then. Before the war, they loaded sugar-cane right down at the water. After the war Grandmother said they had to sell off some of their land, just to keep body and soul together."

Mister Lance clucked his tongue and tried to hide a smile at her little speech. "Is that right?"

Miss Anna nodded from her makeshift bucket stool. "See all that land across the bayou where the road leads into town? Used to be owned by our family."

"I surely did know that, Miss Anna. Been working for your family since I was a youngster myself."

The girl in the blue dress and white pinafore ruffles composed her face into a regal expression. "That's why we simply *must* find the buried treasure — I mean, the silver. It will save my family from going to ruin."

"That ain't likely, Miss Anna."

"But the silver will make *certain* we have security for generations to come."

"You're probably right about that. But ain't it about quittin' time, Miss Anna?" Mister Lance hinted, shading his eyes.

Miss Anna spun on her patent-leather heels as she surveyed the yard. "It's just *got* to be here, Mister Lance. Let's do one more tree. Mind you, just the oldest ones. The newer trees weren't even here fifty years ago, so they couldn't have hidden the family silver there, of course."

"Smart thinkin'," the old man said, smothering a yawn. "But how come you're so sure it's still here? Maybe your grandpappy already found it and used it up after the war."

Miss Anna widened her eyes. "I believe I'd have heard the story from Grandmother Sophronia. But perhaps the person who buried it died during the war and the secret location died with them? That's my theory."

The old man pursed his lips. "Hmm. Could be, I guess."

"Besides, if they'd found it, they wouldn't have had to sell off all the sugarcane fields."

Mister Lance considered this. "You've got it all figured out, Miss Anna. You'd probably do something mighty splendid if you went to university when you get all grown up."

Miss Anna primly placed her hands in her lap. "This is 1912, you know, and ladies are getting more educated all the time. Mamma says women will soon get the vote, too."

I almost fell straight into a patch of weeds. Did that girl say 1912?

Time seemed to stand still. It was peculiar. More than that, it was downright spooky. My ears heard Miss Anna say the words, but I was hoping I hadn't understood her correctly.

Nineteen twelve? Really? *This was the year 1912?*

Impossible! That was over a hundred years ago!

I shook my head, reflecting on how much she reminded me of Tara Doucet from school. The same way of carrying herself like she owned the world. Miss Anna was a plantation girl just like Tara was. Well, like Tara's ancestors. The Doucet Mansion wasn't a working plantation anymore, of course. No fields, just the regal mansion house still standing on the Bayou Teche where it curved on the far side of town.

My mind whirred. This island used to belong to my mamma's family . . . but who was Miss Anna? And what happened to this beautiful columned home? When my mamma lived here as a girl with my grandparents, there wasn't any fancy plantation house.

Mister Lance mopped his face with a handkerchief, then stuffed it into his pocket. "All righty, Miss Anna. We'll do one more dig. Lead the way." He picked up two shovels and a spade, gave the hot sun a grimace, and then looked longingly into the thicket of trees where I crouched.

I froze, my legs fixed to the earth. I swear he was staring right at me. Could he see me in the shrubbery? I didn't move a muscle, not even an eyeball.

Finally, Mister Lance shook his head, wiped at his eyes with the back of his shirtsleeve, like they were watering, then trudged after Miss Anna.

The girl strode to another towering cypress tree about twenty feet from where I was hiding, her skirts flouncing, ringlets bouncing in perfect rhythm. "I'll bet this tree is a hundred years old," she pronounced, running a hand along its gray, stringy bark. "Which means it was planted long before the Yankees invaded Louisiana."

"You're probably right, Miss Anna." The gardener exhaled noisily as he surveyed the ground. "Looks rock hard," he muttered, stomping on the shovel. The sharp edge bit into the thick grass.

I sat stone still, wrapping my arms around my knees to make myself as small as possible. Was there really buried silver on the property? I felt like I was watching a movie right in front of my eyes. The sun lowered, and I kept an eye out for alligators and wasps and stinging ants.

While Mister Lance dug, sweat dripped like rain down his face. Miss Anna peered into the growing hole. Cicadas buzzed in the trees, and I flinched as one dive-bombed straight for me. Don't move, I told myself. But the cicadas with their hard shell bodies made such a racket I was pretty sure Miss Anna and Mister Lance would never hear me even if I wiggled or crunched a twig accidentally.

Crazy thoughts bounced around my brain. *How* in the world did I get here? *Why* was I here?

Find the fireflies.

Trust the fireflies.

The voice on the phone knew something I didn't know.

I saw myself walking step by step across the broken bridge inside the swarm of fireflies. I saw the bridge shimmering in front of me, rock steady — as if it had miraculously fixed itself.

But nope, that hadn't happened at all. I'd actually slipped back to the time *before* the bridge had been struck by lightning and broken into pieces. I'd passed into a time when the bridge was new and whole and horses and buggies probably crossed it to drive into town.

My eyes flew wide as a new voice entered the yard. A boy's voice with a thick Louisiana accent.

"Miss Anna, Miss Anna!" he called. He was wearing cotton work overalls, too, but without a shirt, and his dark skin glistened with sweat as he came running around the back of the house.

Anna walked briskly forward, shading her eyes. "What are you hollering about, T-Paul?"

The pile of soft black soil had grown, and the way Miss Anna walked, her spine rigid, I knew she didn't want the boy to see what she and Mister Lance were doing.

"Miz Normand's come home! Back from New Orleans!"

"Oh, drat!" I heard Anna exclaim softly, quickly smoothing at her dress. "I mean — how wonderful that Mamma is home!"

T-Paul halted on the lawn, his feet bare. "Carriage arrived not ten minutes ago, and she's brought your uncle with her, too!"

Miss Anna gasped. "You mean Uncle Edgar? He's really and truly here? How marvelous! There will be games and talk tonight. You know he's just returned from his trip to New York City. I've saved all his postcards from around the world."

"I'd love to see those international stamps, Miss Anna, if you'll oblige me sometime," T-Paul said shyly.

Miss Anna didn't hear him. Or pretended not to, as she inspected the dust on her shoes and retied the sash at her waist.

"What's your mamma ordered for supper?" T-Paul

asked. "Bet it's something special — one of Mister Edgar's favorites."

Anna waved at the boy to go on to the house. "I hope you already unpacked Mamma's trunks from the carriage. Have the horses been seen to?"

"Yes, miss!" I heard T-Paul shout as he ran toward the back porch.

Anna glanced over her shoulder at Mister Lance, who straightened, staring after her. She gave a quick furtive wave to tell him to put away his tools and get out of sight.

I could hear the gardener's bones creaking as he rubbed his spine, then flexed his fingers, pulling off a pair of gardening gloves.

Miss Anna's and T-Paul's voices faded as they scampered up the steps to the house. I'd never seen anything as lovely as that back porch. It boasted beautifully polished pine planks. White wicker chairs were placed strategically along the length of it. Tubs of summer flowers bloomed in colors of pink and yellow and purple.

"No silver here," Mister Lance said out loud to no one, startling me. He stuck the point of the shovel inside a hole about two feet in diameter. "But I'll bet my last dime she'll be wanting me to dig 'round the whole tree tomorrow. And every tree in the dadgum bayou."

I covered my mouth to keep the laugh from slipping out.

His head shot up as if he'd heard me, and I shut my eyes so he couldn't see them glittering in the sunset. I prayed the shadows would hide me. Guess it worked, because Mister Lance pushed the soft dirt back into the hole, picked up his tools, and made his way back to the shed in the far corner of the property.

Aware of all the dark, empty windows of the house, I got up, too, hurrying back to the bayou while keeping under cover of the trees. Branches scratched at my arms, and I skirted a red-ant hill swarming with the lethal creatures.

A whirl of thoughts crashed around my mind. Miss Anna Normand lived right here in this very house in 1912.

I had to find out who she was — and why I'd slipped into the past in the first place.

CHAPTER NINE

Yellow light lit up the windows of the mansion house as I took the path back to the dock. I tried to imagine the Normand family inside. Candles on the dining table? Servants dishing up plates filled with delicacies? Polished sideboards with ceramic hot plates from Europe? It was a life I could only dream about. A life long gone into history books.

The fireflies were miraculously waiting for me at the bank. They rose into the air in a golden swarm of light, escorting me back across the bridge.

As I stepped onto the firm, muddy earth, I got chills realizing that Miss Anna was a girl who had already died. If she was about twelve in 1912, that meant she was born in 1900, right at the turn of the last century. I wanted to know a whole lot more about Miss Anna and her family. There must be a reason why I'd been able to walk across that broken bridge.

I'd seen a different time period — without a time machine, or a special potion, or a magic set of shoes. Maybe time was constantly going on all around us. And we could catch tiny glimpses now and then.

From what Anna had said, her family was the original owners of the plantation, back before the Civil War. I wondered if my Grandma Kat knew who Anna Normand was. 'Course, my grandmother lived on the island fifty years after Anna's time, and Mamma's maiden name was DuMonde. The Normand family must have lost the house or had to sell it.

Later that night while Mamma was doing the dishes and Daddy was in the storage shed searching for candlesticks for a customer, I locked up the second floor by myself.

I straightened the baskets of old *Life* and *National Geographic* magazines. Got out the Pledge and a dust rag for the bookcases. Then the window cleaner to wipe customer fingerprints off the glass cabinets of china and figurines and mantle clocks and dolls.

I froze when I heard a phone ring behind me. I tried to ignore it. Mamma would get it any second now. But the ringing kept on, and Mamma did not answer it.

I knew the ringing was closer than the kitchen downstairs. Much closer.

I stared at the back wall of phones, my pulse thudding in my throat. This time it wasn't one of the farmhouse phones with its clanging old-fashioned metal bells. It was one of the Princess phones. The pink one.

After ten rings, I finally snatched it up.

I'd barely said hello when a girl's voice said, all in a rush, "You have to go back. . . ."

I could hardly swallow. "Go back where?"

"To 1912. You must follow Anna Normand."

"You mean stalk her?" I thought about how I'd hid in the woods secretly watching the girl and the gardener. "But I wasn't purposely spying on her! And how do *you* know her?"

"I don't know her exactly," the girl admitted, her voice low.

The phone crackled. I switched hands, but it wasn't much better.

"I don't have much time," she added. "This connection is always tenuous, you know."

"Actually, I do know that," I said. "After all, the phone line *isn't even connected to the wall*! And why should I go back? What if I get stuck?"

"You've got to. Remember, it's a matter of life and *death*."

Those words made spiders crawl up my neck.

"And find the Bible," she added.

"What are you talking about? This is crazy. *You're* crazy!"

"Am I crazy?" she said, not taking offense. "But — La — Larissa, think about it." She stammered as though it was difficult to say my name. "Haven't I been right so far?"

It was true, she'd been right about the fireflies. But why was I supposed to go back to 1912? What was so important or special about Anna Normand? So I could *know* how awful my own life was? So Anna or somebody like Alyson Granger could rub it in for the rest of my life?

But I had to admit I was curious. And this girl on the phone seemed so serious when she talked about life and death. "Where do I find the Bible?" I asked.

All of a sudden I realized I was talking to myself. The phone had stopped working. The girl was gone.

*   *   *

The next day was Sunday. I pulled on my church dress and nicest sandals, melancholy rising. Birds were singing in the cypress on the side yard. I was missing Shelby Jayne. Two weeks without my best friend loomed like a giant black hole.

It was time to search for the Bible.

As I searched the second floor, my bare legs brushed the hem of my dress. The hair on the back of my neck rose like fingers crawling along my skin. Eyes seemed to follow me, but I sucked down a whimper. With my other hand I rubbed at the scar on my cheek. It felt twitchy and achey.

The afternoon sun glinted off the glass of the doll case, and in the halo of light all those blue and green eyes sparkled like real eyes and not glass. "Aah!" I choked out. The dolls appeared alive sitting behind the glass. "Jeepers," I finally breathed, trying to get my heart to stop racing.

We had tons more bookcases than I remembered. They seemed to have multiplied like rabbits. There were ten bookcases on the second floor and five more on the main level.

It took an hour to scan all those books.

The cases contained old classics, books about budgeting your money or quilting or the Civil War. There were a few children's picture books, like *Mike*

Mulligan and His Steam Shovel and *Goodnight Moon*; the whole collection of Louisa May Alcott novels; plus the set of Anne of Green Gables; and books by the author Elizabeth Goudge. My favorite of her books was *The Little White Horse*, even though I'd never had a horse and probably never would.

Finally, I checked the bookcases downstairs. Dull science books. Fat novels like *War and Peace.* A few Sherlock Holmes books. Agatha Christie mysteries. And two full shelves of Nancy Drew that I'd read twice through already.

I plopped into an armchair, yawning so hard my jaw ached. Instead of giving up, I rose once more and maneuvered through rows of dishes and tea sets, skirted the staircase landing, and then wiggled through the stacked desks and furniture until I reached Daddy's office.

It was more like a closet than a real office. A rickety table where he did paperwork and invoices. There was also a swivel chair, dust everywhere, and filing cabinets that never quite closed. A second door led to a small space where my parents spent an evening twice a week boxing up items for shipping.

The office was tight, and the smell of turpentine clogged up my nose. Sometimes Daddy refinished pieces of furniture when they were particularly scratched up or peeling.

I lifted the lids of the boxes, peered at the labels, and found only two boxes with books that hadn't been inventoried yet. Bending back the flaps, I lifted out stacks of used and new books and laid them on the floor, my knees getting dirty from the dust. Sticky spots from old duct tape pinched my skin.

I scanned the spines with my finger. Isaac Asimov and Robert Heinlein science fiction, and somewhere Mamma had found a set of Harry Potter novels, mostly in good shape. Those would probably sell fast.

After reading each book's title and placing it back into the last of the boxes, I became aware that I was done. There wasn't a single book that was remotely a Bible. What if we'd sold it? What if I was too late? If that was true, then the girl on the phone was too late.

Was I reading book spines and poking through boxes for absolutely nothing?

"Larissa, you are plumb stupid crazy," I muttered as I went into my bedroom to check my own bookcase. It was only four shelves, and I'd never seen a Bible there, so the task seemed futile, but I figured I could check it off and know I'd tried my best.

Daddy always let me have first pick of the kids' books when he bought them for the store. After I was done reading, Mamma would get after me to let her stick price tags on them and bring them downstairs.

"What's the point of reading a book twice?" she'd say. "We could make some money off those."

"A few quarters ain't gonna break the bank," Daddy would argue back.

"I want to keep my favorites," I'd try to explain to Mamma.

Pretty soon she'd forget about it. Until we had a few days without any real sales and the cash register was getting empty.

All during church services, my mind raced. I even flipped through the Bibles stacked in the Sunday school closet. They were all alike, no markings, nothing unusual.

On Sundays the antique store was closed. After we ate a big Sunday lunch, Mamma put her feet up with a book, ice cubes clinking in a glass of lemonade, while Daddy went over the accounting ledgers.

I ate so much lunch my stomach was full and I got super sleepy. I curled up on one of the Victorian settees on the second floor and read *The Little White Horse* until the book dropped and my eyes closed.

Not five minutes later, I felt eyes burning into the back of my head.

I rolled over, my pulse pounding in my ears. Goose bumps broke out on my arms.

I sat on the edge of the couch, and then my eyes swung to the doll case. Seemed like every one of those dolls was staring at me, studying me.

"Stop it," I told them sharply. "Stop looking at me!" It was totally stupid to talk to inanimate dolls, but I felt spooked. Their eyes followed me as I got up, picked up my book from the floor, and went to find Mamma. I wasn't gonna sit there with all those eyes on me.

Her growing stomach seemed to be getting even bigger as she leaned back in the recliner.

"Does the baby kick much?" I asked her.

"More and more all the time as he's growing."

"What do you mean *he*? Daddy said it's a girl."

"Well, we actually don't really know. The ultrasound *looked* like a girl, but you never know. Doctors get it wrong all the time, and I don't want to get my hopes up either way. I just used the word *he* because my — our other babies were — well —" She stopped, her voice dropping. "Our other babies were all boys in the past."

I changed the subject. "Do you know if we have any Bibles stored away somewhere, like maybe the shed?"

"Did you already go through what we have in the store?"

"Yes, ma'am. Not a single Bible anywhere."

"If we don't have any on the bookshelves then we don't have any at all. We don't keep books in storage. All our stock gets placed on a shelf." Mamma took a sip of her lemonade. "So why you got a yearning to see a Bible all of a sudden? Did they give you a reading assignment during Sunday school today?"

I hadn't thought of that, but she'd given me the perfect excuse. "Um, yeah. They want us to read the story of Noah and the Ark."

"Well, the only Bible we got on the premises is the one I keep in my closet. Top shelf next to a box of family photos and papers."

"You have a Bible?" I tried not to appear as surprised or shocked as I felt.

"It's an old family Bible, actually. My mamma gave it to me when I got married. It's really old."

"Can I look at it?" I wiped my hands along my shorts, sweaty and excited. It just had to be the Bible the girl on the phone was talking about!

"You gotta be careful. The pages are getting thin and brittle." Mamma pushed herself up and waddled to the closet. "Grab that stool, will you, Larissa?"

I hurried to obey and then I stood on the stool, stretching my arms to grab a cardboard box with *Family Pictures* scrawled on the side in black marker.

"There are some hand openings on the side. Use those," Mamma instructed.

Half a minute later, I had the box on the bed, and Mamma lifted the lid.

It was a mess inside. A few photo albums and a bunch of loose papers and individual pictures, plus manila envelopes stuffed with more pictures that needed sorting.

Mamma said, "Our more recent pictures are on the computer, so most of these are photos of me when I was growing up, and my parents and grandparents. Some cousins, aunts, and uncles." Mamma snorted as she held up a snapshot. "Look at how funny those flowered pants are. And my hair was always ratty. What a mess I was at eleven."

As I riffled through the albums and unsorted pictures, I noticed that some of the pictures dated back to the 1940s and 1950s when my great-grandmothers dressed in pencil-thin skirts and white gloves, their hair lacquered with hair spray.

"Funny how times change, huh?" Mamma murmured. "Oh, here's the Bible." She lifted it out, and the book wasn't as big as I'd thought it might be as she placed it in my arms. "Now go do your reading. I'll be napping until supper."

"What's for supper?"

"Leftover sandwiches and a cold salad. Too tired to do much else. But I made a lemon pie and it's in the fridge for dessert."

My parents always napped on Sunday afternoons, so I was free for a couple of hours. I lugged the Bible into my bedroom and laid it on the bed, carefully cracking open the cover. There was a Table of Contents with the Bible books all in a long column, Genesis, Exodus, Leviticus, and so on. Written on the flyleaf were a few words inscribed with thin, spidery handwriting. The kind of writing people used to do with a quill pen and a bottle of ink.

This Bible presented to Miss Julianna Landry on her wedding day, April 19, 1898, in New Iberia, St. Martinville Parish, Louisiana, by her loving parents. Wedded to Mr. Blaine Normand of Bayou Bridge, owner of The Island.

Lightly, I ran my finger over Julianna Landry's name. How pretty! I wished there was a picture of her.

"Wait a minute," I blurted out. My stomach thudded straight to the floor. Quickly, I turned the cover of the Bible back to the front. Stamped in faded gold lettering were the words *Family Bible.* My *mamma's* family Bible!

My fingers couldn't move fast enough. I flipped through the thin, brittle pages, but there was nothing more about the Normand family.

Julianna Landry married a guy named Blaine Normand. . . . Normand was Miss Anna's last name. If Julianna Landry was married in 1898 and Miss Anna was about twelve years old in 1912, that meant she was born in 1900. Julianna Landry Normand had to be Miss Anna's mother! Right? I supposed she could be an aunt or a cousin, though.

Idly, I turned the blank end pages. This Bible *didn't* end with the Book of Revelations like I first thought! The last few pages had genealogy charts filled with names and dates, as well as a picture of a tree with branches representing the descendants of Julianna and Blaine Normand.

I gulped, tracing all the names with my finger as I read them out loud.

"The first child of Julianna and Blaine was Anna Amelia Normand, born March 3, 1900, which means she recently turned twelve years old just like me.

"When Miss Anna grew up, she married a man named Charles Prevost, and they had a daughter named Daphne in 1925. Daphne married Henry

Moret and they had two children, the oldest was a boy named William, and a daughter named Katherine Prevost Moret in 1952."

The name Katherine was familiar, but I couldn't figure out why, so I just kept going.

"Katherine married Preston DuMonde in 1975 and had a daughter named Gwen." My voice started to shake. "They also had a girl named Madeline who was born in 1983! Maddie DuMonde married a man named Luke Renaud!"

My brain seemed to whirl with names and dates. "Maddie is my *mamma* and Luke Renaud is my daddy!" I exclaimed. "And Katherine — that's — she's my grandma in Baton Rouge! Which means . . ." I counted back the generations. "Daphne is my great-grandmother, which means that Miss Anna Normand is my great-great-grandmother."

Miss Anna. I *was* related to her! I read the names of the family tree again. My name wasn't there under Maddie and Luke Renaud, but I knew it should be. None of the baby boys, my brothers who'd died, were there, either. Mamma hadn't kept the family Bible going, which made me feel left out. Was she just lazy? I felt my lips trembling, but I tried to brush it off and do some more figuring in my head as I studied the dates.

Julianna Landry's and Blaine Normand's parents must have lived during the Civil War. I wondered when my first ancestors had come from France.

I squinted my eyes, trying to remember what I'd seen when I'd crossed over the bridge — when I was still back in 1912. Sugarcane fields as far as you could see. My great-great-great-grandparents had owned a sugarcane plantation. They'd built that fancy mansion house once upon a time.

I tried to wrap my brain around the fact that Miss Anna Normand was my great-great-grandmother. I had to find out what happened to her. And there had to be a reason I was able to travel back to 1912. Maybe we were supposed to live in that house again. Maybe my family was supposed to fix it up like it used to be. We could live there instead of this ratty old antique store.

Unless Mamma balked. She was a good balker. After all, her sister died on that broken bridge. Maybe I was just a big dreamer, but I couldn't help thinking about that beautiful house from long ago. I ached to see it again, and I ached to live in it, just like Miss Anna did.

CHAPTER TEN

I raced downstairs for the box of old clothes. There was still the danger of the broken bridge, but I couldn't think about that — and I definitely couldn't look like a girl from the future in my shorts and sandals.

After tossing stacks of clothes around the floor, I finally found a dress that wasn't too big or too long. Anna had been wearing a dress that didn't quite hit the tops of her stylish button-up boots. I held up a faded creamy white dress that was starting to yellow. It had long sleeves, which were hot for summer, but nothing else would fit.

I kept digging until I found a ribbon to tie around my waist. It wasn't as wide and satiny as Miss Anna's, but it would do.

I tried to curl my hair, but gave up after a couple of attempts to make my bangs *do* something. Besides, the curling iron was so hot it made me sweat. Stringy strands stuck to my forehead and chin. I found some clips and pulled it back, although my scar was bigger and uglier without my hair covering it.

It didn't matter. I wasn't planning on being seen. The costume was just in case something went horribly wrong and I was caught. I'd say I was an orphan. Or some lost cousin from Houma visiting relatives in Bayou Bridge.

I found some stockings deep in my dresser drawer and put on the pair of black button shoes I'd come across a few days ago. They were a little big, so I stuffed some tissue into the empty toe space and practiced walking. The heels weren't *too* high. Hopefully, I wouldn't trip. If dresses had been longer in 1912 I could have worn my sneakers or sandals and hidden them with the hem.

Sunday afternoons in Bayou Bridge were quiet, Main Street almost deserted. Only the gas station was open, and I crossed the street before I got too close so my clothes wouldn't be conspicuous in case someone pumping gas saw me.

I was so focused on getting to the bayou I nearly jumped out of my skin when St. Paul's church bells started to bong five o'clock.

As I got off Main and was passing some of the neighborhood houses, I could hear kids' voices in the yards. An older couple sat on their porch reading a newspaper. A woman raised her hand at me and I lifted mine in a half wave.

Walking faster, I ducked down along the scraggly bushes hugging Bayou Teche. The lace at my neck was itching and my hair clung to my face in sweaty tendrils.

All of a sudden, I ran smack-dab into someone. A girl with brown hair and a stupid smile on her face. A girl named Alyson Granger.

"What in the heck are you doing out here?" I crossed my arms in front of my chest, pretending I could hide the old-fashioned dress I was wearing.

"I'd say the same for you," Alyson said stiffly. For some reason she was still wearing her Sunday dress. With white rolled socks and black Mary Janes.

"Just minding my own business. Now go away."

"This is public property, and I can be here if I want to."

I swept my hand out impatiently, wishing I could make her disappear into the earth. "Go somewhere else that's public. There's miles of it around."

"I'm running an errand for my mamma," she said, indicating a plastic bag.

"What's in there?" I asked, curious in spite of myself.

"My mamma's famous gingersnaps."

"Since when did they become famous?"

"Everybody adores my mamma's cookies. She could open a bakery if she wanted to."

"We already have one. It's called Sweet Ellen's Bakery, in case you forgot." I shook my head and tried to pass, but she stepped in front of me.

"What's your problem?" Alyson asked.

"Isn't it obvious? You're my problem. The biggest problem of my life. You're just too prissy for your own good. All dressed up delivering cookies in a stupid plastic bag, of all things. Why not a pretty plate?"

Alyson bristled, but didn't bite at my question. "Some folks *like* plastic bags. Maybe it saves 'em from washing and returning a plate. Besides, look at you all dressed up for Halloween or something. You're five months early."

"I *know* when Halloween is."

She smirked. "Could have fooled me."

"I think I could fool you on just about everything in the gol dern world!" My voice rose to a near shout. I hadn't wanted to see anybody, and now here was the worst person to run into.

Alyson's eyes traveled down my yellowing dress, the black sash, the buttoned-up shoes. "You are one peculiar girl, Larissa Renaud."

My whole body turned hot. I was pretty sure my face was getting red, too, and when it does, the white ridge of my scar stands out even more. I wanted to yank Alyson's perfect brown hair and throw her cookies into the bayou, but instead I clenched my teeth. "I. Am. Not. Peculiar!"

As soon as I said the words, I ran down the bank, hoping she'd leave me alone — for the rest of my life. But my ankles were so wobbly in the shoes, I had to slow down. I sneaked a backward look. "Dang!"

Alyson was still staring at me, clutching her stupid bag of cookies. Did she offer me a cookie? No. 'Course, I'd have thrown it into the muddy river and let the alligators snack on it. Actually, I'd like to see an alligator snacking on Alyson Granger's toes. "Go away!" I yelled.

She finally wheeled around and continued marching into town. Once she turned the corner, I saw the lightning bugs straight ahead. They were more beautiful than ever as they danced and spun in dripping trails of light. When the fireflies formed a halo of golden light around me, I walked slowly across the bridge as they guided me to safety.

When they disappeared under the elephant ears, I ran up the path, scurried into the thick woods, and headed toward the house.

Not two minutes later, I heard voices and the sound of gaiety. Ribbons of cooking smoke rose like tufts of clouds. Next, the mouthwatering scent of barbecue spiced the air. Grilled chicken, links of sausage boudin, and pork cracklings spattering in their grease.

Keeping low to the ground, I brushed past shrubs of azaleas with their falling petals, staying close to the dense tupelo and low-hanging Spanish moss.

Finally, I found a spot where I could rest against a cypress trunk. Peering around a hedge of manicured shrubbery, I could see a summer party in progress on the lawn.

The whole family was there. I didn't see Mister Lance, but I did see T-Paul in a pair of cotton pants that were too short for him and a buttoned-down shirt, his hair slick and wet. He stood near the banquet tables spread with white linen and loaded with salads and soft breads and cut-up watermelon. The boy stealthily grabbed a fresh hush puppy from a plate and popped it into his mouth.

I pulled my knees under my chin, mesmerized.

Several women sat in lawn chairs or chaise longues. Big hats decorated with ribbons and bows perched on top of their upswept hair. The hairstyles reminded me of the Gibson Girl hairdos I'd seen in old magazines in the antique store. Their dresses were satin with an overlay of lace and rear cascading ruffles, in shades of lavender and green and yellow.

One young woman held a white parasol over her shoulder, twirling it in her gloved hands. All the men, young and old, wore white shirts with rolled-up sleeves. A couple of them had suspenders or half-buttoned vests and they were playing catch with a baseball.

My stomach rose like it was floating on fizzy water. I wished I could join them instead of hiding in the bushes like a homeless girl or a spy.

Sudden shouts pierced the air as one of the men dropped the baseball and had to run for it across the lawn. The ladies clapped at the men's successful plays, chattering together, their Southern voices drawling with charm and culture.

"Mamma!" Miss Anna called as she stepped off the porch. She planted a quick kiss on her mother's cheek, nearly knocking her hat off. So that beautiful woman in the pale lavender must be Julianna Landry

Normand. I gaped at her until my eyes hurt. "Uncle Edgar's coming outside now!"

"At last," her mamma murmured, smiling at the other ladies.

The sun skimmed the trees, painting the sky with pink and red. I spied Mister Lance walking the perimeter of the yard, reaching up to light a series of lanterns hanging from the porch with a long stick lit with a flame.

Miz Julianna rose from her chair, calling out to the men. The baseball game ended with a burst of shouts and clapping when one of the men crossed home plate.

"Time to eat!" T-Paul said with a whoop.

There were two men dressed in white aprons manning the barbecue pit. I could see deep red coals, catfish and chicken and boudin sizzling on a grate above. My stomach growled and I pressed my hand against it, although nobody could hear me in the cypress grove.

The chefs brought platters of steaming meat over to the tables and set them down among the salads and hush puppies and cakes.

A woman and a young girl about my age stood behind the food tables wearing starched aprons and shooing flies away with straw fans. The girl was dressed just like the woman, so I figured she was probably her daughter. They both wore their hair in braids tied in a round bun on the back of their heads.

The Normand family talked and mingled with their guests, urging them to fill their plates. The amount of food was enormous. Anna plucked a piece of watermelon with her fingers when her mother wasn't watching and stuck it in her mouth. Behind the table, the servant girl's forehead puckered in a tiny frown. Anna caught it and glared at her. The serving girl quickly smoothed back her features when her mother observed the exchange.

"Mind your manners to Miss Anna, Dulcie, girl," her mamma said.

"Yes, ma'am," said Dulcie softly. "May I fix you a plate, Miss Anna?" she added.

Anna shook her head. "I'll do it myself. Then I can pick just what I want to eat without you giving me a plate of nasty brussels sprouts."

"As you wish, Miss Anna," Dulcie's mother said. "But as you can see, there ain't any brussels sprouts on the menu today."

Miss Anna gave a sly smile. "That's because Mamma ordered all of Uncle Edgar's favorite foods — all my favorites, too."

"You are a blessed young lady, and much loved," the woman told her.

"Now where's my favorite girl?" A tall man roared as he jumped down the porch steps and strode across the lawn. He had sunburned skin, a full mustache, and bright red suspenders. He caught Anna up and swung her around.

"Uncle Edgar!" she cried. "I'm so glad you're finally back home!"

"And I saw that, you little watermelon thief," he chided, tugging on her green hair ribbon.

Miss Anna spun in her lace party dress, a swirl of color in the breeze. "I can have whatever I want, Uncle Edgar, and you can't stop me."

He rocked back on his heels, amused at her sassiness. "Is that right?"

Anna lifted her chin. "I've been waiting all day for the barbecue to start, and now I'm going to have one of everything. Or two!"

"You'll get so fat we'll have to roll you upstairs to bed," her uncle told her, grabbing a plate and beginning to load it with barbecued pork.

The sound of talk and dishes grew louder as the family and their guests crowded the tables to load their china plates. Then the men sat on blankets spread around the lawn, talking about the weather and the price of sugarcane, while the women perched on chairs under a wide tent awning, eating daintily with forks and knives.

"Where's my fan?" Miz Julianna asked. "It's getting quite hot, isn't it?"

"The humidity rises as the afternoon lingers," one of her friends said. "A true sign that summer is here to stay."

Dulcie's mother came over with a fan and opened it for her mistress. "Thank you, Beatrice," Miz Julianna told her, quickly waving the fan, which set the wisps of curls around her face to dancing. "At least the sun is beginning to set. There will be shade soon."

"I don't know how the boys can run around playing ball," the young woman with the white parasol remarked, glancing at Uncle Edgar, who had started talking about his travels. She set down her half-eaten plate on the table. "Mr. Normand, if you're going to tell stories, you must regale the entire group. We all want to hear how you survived the jungles of South America. Or Africa. Or Arabia. I declare I never know where you're going next."

"Miss Sally Blanchard," Edgar said with a small dip of his head. "This time I visited the islands of the Caribbean. I danced half dressed with the natives and then hollered like I was possessed by a banshee when we danced for their voodoo ceremony."

Miss Sally's eyes grew wide. So did Anna's. Mine did, too, actually.

"I'm trying to picture you wearing nothing but a grass skirt, Edgar," one of the men said with a laugh. The two men looked quite a bit alike and I wondered if he was Anna's father. "I've seen folks do that down in Jackson Square in New Orleans. Dancing until they're exhausted, and then smashing their brandy bottles on a tree."

Miz Julianna shook her head at her husband. "Oh, hush, Blaine. Not in front of the children."

"But I want to hear, Daddy!" Anna burst out. Her mother raised her eyebrows, and Anna sank back into her chair, but her blue eyes were alive with curiosity as she drank up every word. "Is that really what they do, Uncle Edgar?"

He nodded. "The tribal people do, especially in the countries of the Dominican Republic where they practice the religion of Vodou, as they call it. They believe they receive spiritual power if the spirits possess their body during the wild dances. They have the potential to see visions and gain wisdom. It's quite enthralling, actually."

Anna practically fell off her chair. "Did you see visions or spirits, Uncle Edgar?"

He cracked a grin. "Only the spirits of too much liquor, I'm afraid."

Julianna Normand gave her husband a meaningful look. "There are children present," she murmured again.

"Did you like living on the islands, Mr. Normand?" Miss Sally Blanchard asked.

Uncle Edgar snapped his suspenders. "The beaches are stunning, the culture fascinating. But I left because the islands are rather dangerous at the moment. They speak French like most folks do here in Louisiana, but the Germans and British and French are fighting each other for occupancy, and an entire group of Syrian Arabs are living there and wanting to control the government. There was a plot that resulted in the Presidential Palace being destroyed, so I finally came home. My hide is worth more than lying on a beach watching the pretty native girls."

There was a twitter of embarrassment from the women, and Miss Sally blushed, ducking her head.

"Time for seconds!" Anna's father declared.

Uncle Edgar added, "Nope, I do believe it's time for presents!"

Anna ran over to tug on his arm. "I was hoping you'd say that!"

I was enthralled with this family from a hundred years ago. Getting on my knees, I leaned forward to make sure I didn't miss a single thing.

"Look, there's Mister Lance with the cart now," Uncle Edgar said, rubbing his hands together.

The elderly gardener pulled a cart decorated with flowers and ribbons and bearing a huge stack of wrapped gifts across the lawn.

Edgar rushed over to begin handing them out. "Something for everyone!"

"This is the best part of all your trips," Anna told him.

He tugged at her hair again. "You're so mercenary, my little *cher.*"

Anna swished her dress, her ringlets flouncing. "No, I'm not! I just like presents, especially from exotic countries."

"Since we don't get to travel with you, Edgar," her mother added, "it's like you bring a piece of it home with you." She turned to the women and added, "My house is becoming very cosmopolitan with statues and trinkets from around the world. Every corner table and nook."

"I'd love to take a tour sometime," one of the women said.

"Our home is going to be on the Garden Club Christmas Tour this year." I could tell by the excitement in Miz Julianna's voice that she was thrilled.

Her friend laid a hand on her arm. "You had better start your list-making now, my dear."

"It's going to be quite a job, Charlotte," Miz Julianna admitted. "But an honor."

Uncle Edgar grabbed three more packages. "It's Christmas in June!" he bellowed.

Miz Julianna sputtered with laughter. "Oh, Edgar, you are just too much and too good to us!"

Edgar Normand truly did have a gift for everyone. Cuban cigars and brandy for Anna's father, a beautiful hand-painted tea set for Miz Julianna, embroidered handkerchiefs and shawls for all the women, including Miss Sally and the servant Miz Beatrice. A ball-and-bat set for T-Paul.

A black dress suit for Mister Lance with matching suspenders. "I can wear this to church — or the next funeral," he said, and everyone laughed.

Miss Anna ripped off the lid to a white box and reached in for a stunning pink dress with deep mauve ribbons. "Oh, my, Uncle Edgar even got me grown-up white gloves!" she exclaimed, holding the soft kid gloves to her cheek.

"The dress is very pretty, Anna," Miss Sally told

her. "And the gloves fine, indeed. Your uncle has good taste."

"Well, the saleswoman does!" Uncle Edgar said, waggling his eyebrows.

The sun began to lower, and Miz Beatrice and her daughter Dulcie started removing the plates and platters from the table and carrying them into the house.

"Not so fast!" Uncle Edgar declared, holding up a hand to stop them from leaving. "I've saved the best for last."

"What, there's more?" Anna demanded, closing up the crisp white lid to the dress box. "Show me!"

Uncle Edgar raised his eyebrows and there was a twinkle in his eyes. "I decided there were too many empty stalls in your barn, Blaine, dear brother."

"What have you got up your sleeve?" Anna's father said, putting his hands on his hips.

Uncle Edgar ordered, "Mister Lance, go ahead and bring her out."

Anna bounced on her toes, her hands clasped together. "Bring out who — what?"

The gardener disappeared around the side of the house for a moment, and then returned leading a chestnut-colored pony by the halter.

Uncle Edgar squeezed his niece's shoulder. "This little beauty is called Dixie, and she's a two-year-old filly from one of the Caribbean diplomats who wanted to sell her to someone returning to the States. I'll help your father break her and teach you to ride."

"Oh, Uncle Edgar," Anna breathed. "Truly? For me? I've always wanted a pony of my very own. Father only uses his horses for farmwork, and I've always longed to ride all over the parish and feel the breeze in my hair — and pretend I'm Lady Godiva —"

"Oh, Anna! Really!" her mother said, shaking her head at her daughter's dramatics.

Miss Sally hid a smile. "You've been reading too many novels, Anna dear, but I think I grasp your fancy picture."

Anna threw her arms around her uncle's neck, and he picked her up off her feet, reminding me of something my daddy used to do. I brushed at my eyes, trying to remember the last time he'd done that. Picked me right up and held me so tight I thought I'd burst for air. I couldn't remember.

I'd already pinched myself several times, but the scene in front of me never melted away. I don't know what Miss Anna was or what I was seeing. An apparition, a dream, or ghosts from the past?

What was time doing on this island? Had I gone to the past or had they come forward to my future?

"And before you hurry off, Miz Beatrice," Edgar said in a louder voice before the servant rushed off again with an armload of table settings. "I have one more thing for your daughter, Dulcie. If you don't mind a gift from a vagabond."

Miz Beatrice wiped the sweat from her face. "Oh, Mister Normand, sir, you are too kind. These beautiful shawls are more than Dulcie and me ever expected. A thousand thanks to you, truly."

Uncle Edgar waved her words away. "I don't have more boxes of fancy dresses or any more ponies hidden away, but I did find something I think your little Dulcie will enjoy. I got to visit a special island where dolls are made and treasured. The locals really love their dolls and show them off on a place called the Island of the Dolls. It's becoming quite a tourist spot. The craftsmanship is remarkable, and the dolls are shipping to Europe and Canada. I brought one back with me in this last box for Dulcie, if she'd like it."

Miz Beatrice pushed at her daughter's shoulder. "What do you say, Dulcie?"

"Oh, thank you kindly, Mister Normand," the girl

said, her face lighting up like a parade. "Thank you ever so much!"

"You haven't seen it yet!" he told her with a chuckle. "Maybe you'll hate it and say it's silly and too babyish for a young lady like yourself."

From under the wagon's blanket, Edgar Normand withdrew a final white box tied in a cluster of purple ribbons and handed it to Dulcie.

While the girl untied the ribbons, my eyes darted toward Miss Anna, who was petting her pony and trying to pretend she didn't have her eyes fixed on the servant girl opening the very last present, even though she was surrounded by boxes full of lovely things of her own.

When the lid dropped away, Dulcie gasped. She gazed at Uncle Edgar in adoration as she lifted a porcelain doll from the box. Shiny blond ringlets ran down the doll's back and framed her lovely face. She was dressed in an elegant mauve dress with layers of lace, even on her pantaloons. Black high-heeled shoes decorated her feet. A hat of silk and ribbons sat jauntily over one eye. A parasol perched in her delicately formed porcelain hands. The doll was simply stunning, and simply perfect.

I had to cover up my mouth so the group on the lawn wouldn't hear me gasping in shock behind the shrubbery. The doll in Dulcie's arms was the very same doll sitting in the case back at the antique store. That was my mamma's doll. The doll she wouldn't let me touch because it was over a hundred years old. The doll that had once belonged to her dead sister, Gwen.

CHAPTER ELEVEN

I sank back on my heels, holding in a terrible longing to examine the doll up close. Did she have those same blue eyes? If Uncle Edgar gave this doll to Dulcie more than a hundred years ago, how in the world did Mamma's sister, Gwen, own her?

Crazy thoughts jumped inside my head like a frog on a skillet. "Remember the family Bible!" I whispered to myself. "Miz Julianna and Anna are linked down through the century straight to my own grandmother and mother."

That's why the girl on the phone told me to find the book. She wanted me to come here. She wanted me to find this place and this family — *my* family.

I blew a breath up at my flyaway bangs. My hair wasn't thick and rich like Miss Anna's hair. No silky waterfall locks passed through the generations to *me*, but I truly was related to Miss Anna.

I tried to get ahold of myself as I rocked back on my heels, plopping onto the ground in my old-fashioned dress. My mind whirled. This plantation mansion with its columned porches and miles of sugarcane fields — my family used to be rich. One of *the* families in St. Martinville Parish.

Goose bumps broke out on my arms. The sweat on my skin turned cold.

"Come lead your new pony to the barn," Uncle Edgar said, holding out the halter to Anna.

As I peeked through the shrubbery, a funny look passed over Miss Anna's face. She held a hand to her head and wilted into the nearest wicker chair, darting a glance at Dulcie, the servant girl. "I'm afraid I'm suddenly feeling so very tired."

"Oh, dear," Miz Julianna said, pressing a hand to her daughter's forehead. "You *are* a bit hot and damp."

"She's been in the sun all day," Miss Sally spoke up. "Poor dear, it's probably all the excitement. It's not every day a girl gets her very own pony."

"Perhaps I need to rest so I can ride him tomorrow," Anna told her uncle.

"Indeed," Uncle Edgar said with a nod. "I shall be here the next few weeks and we'll have a lesson every morning."

"Teach her to take care of it properly, too," her father added with an amused expression that made him look just like his brother, Edgar. "You do know, Anna, that you'll need to muck out the stable, brush him down, and feed him twice a day —"

"Oh, Blaine," Miz Julianna said, rolling her eyes. "You do go on."

"I just want her to learn responsibility," Mr. Normand said, but his mouth quirked up and everyone knew he was teasing.

"I'll help her," Dulcie piped up. "I've taken care of horses before."

"Is that right?" Mr. Normand said. "You are a talented young lady."

Miz Beatrice pinched her daughter's arm and hissed, "Mind your manners, my girl. Don't speak unless spoken to."

"She's all right," Miz Julianna assured Beatrice. "I'm sure she could be a big help to our Anna."

Miz Beatrice gave another small push at Dulcie. "Show Miss Anna your new doll and keep her entertained for a moment. I'm almost finished up here, ma'am," she said to Miz Julianna. "Then I'll start the washing up inside."

"Thank you, Beatrice. T-Paul, be sure there's plenty of hot water in the kitchen."

"Yes, ma'am." He snapped to attention, and then ran toward the metal basins sitting by the water pump at the corner of the house.

Something funny was going on. I felt it in my gut as Dulcie reluctantly handed over the gorgeous porcelain doll, and Anna seized it in her arms. She ran a finger over the doll's silk clothing, the satin ribbons streaming from the hat, the soft feathers, and the dainty rosebud mouth. "What will you call her?" she asked Dulcie, who stood by helplessly watching.

Dulcie swallowed. "Think I'll give her my favorite girl name. Anna Marie."

"Why, that's *my* name," Anna said. "How wonderful of you."

Miss Sally's face beamed from her chair. "It's lovely to see such friends."

"I'll share my pony if you share this doll," Anna said, fluttering her eyelashes at Dulcie. "After all, if she's going to be my namesake, I have a right to hold her, don't I?"

Dulcie licked her dry lips. "Of course, Miss Anna."

Uncle Edgar rubbed his hands together. "Well, that's all settled, and I hope everyone enjoys a piece of the Caribbean. Next time there'll be elephant tusks from Africa, for I'm determined to snag some ivory and make a new set of piano keys for my sister-in-law."

"You're such a braggart, Edgar," Miz Julianna told him affectionately. "But such a thoughtful braggart thinking of me."

"Africa, how utterly wild!" Miss Sally's eyes lit up. "A real safari with motorcars and guns and everything?"

Uncle Edgar tipped the brim of his hat. "You'll be the first to see the photographs upon my return, Miss Sally. Now, Blaine, let me practice my batting swing again before it's completely dark."

I think I was the only one aware that Miss Sally's face was crestfallen as Uncle Edgar strode across the lawns to the batting area. I was pretty sure the young woman was hinting that she would like to *go* with Uncle Edgar on his African safari. Which meant she was hoping for a more permanent relationship. But Edgar Normand didn't seem to get the hint. It gave me a delicious feeling knowing Miss Sally had a secret crush on Uncle Edgar.

The hanging lanterns glowed brighter as the sun sank behind the cypress, disappearing altogether. The island grew darker, more shadowy.

I stretched out my stiff legs, cramped from sitting

tucked between the tree and the bushes. My parents were going to be frantic I'd been gone so long. Maybe they'd even ground me. Last time I was here, it wasn't near this dark. I'd stayed way too late.

"Oh, look, Mamma," Anna said, the doll sitting snug in her arms. "The lightning bugs! They've come out."

"Today was especially humid," her mother said, not paying much attention as she directed T-Paul to take down the tables while Dulcie folded the linens. "That's when the fireflies usually come out to play."

I crawled forward a little more. Dulcie stared unhappily at her gift from Uncle Edgar still sitting tight in Anna's arms while she had to go off and clean up. The servant's daughter would probably never own anything so lovely ever again in her life. I felt sorry for her.

"The lightning bugs are dancing in the trees over there!" Anna cried out. "I'm going to catch one. Bring me a jar, T-Paul!"

I jerked my head up. Anna was staring directly at the thicket in which I hid. She was going to find me! If I stood, she'd see me for sure. Oh, why didn't I leave five minutes ago!

I started to crawl on my hands and knees, keeping low. The shrubbery seemed so noisy, crackling and snapping as I scrambled around the trees.

The long dress wrapped tight around my knees and I lurched forward, dive-bombing into the dirt and leaves nose first. "Ouch!" Jerking at the tangled old-fashioned dress, I began crawling again, but Anna was right behind me. Running toward the cloud of fireflies — fireflies that belonged to *me*. Fireflies I *needed* to get across the broken bridge. I didn't want Anna scaring them off or scattering them. I really did not want to spend the night out here.

The lightning bugs buzzed around my head, making me dizzy. How long could I stay in the past? Any second now, the year 1912 might dissolve right in front of my eyes. I could be stuck over here in the dark all night long!

"They're so pretty!" Anna called out, much closer now. At first she was behind me, and then she was to my right. I figured if I kept going left, I'd eventually reach the bridge, if my knees didn't give out. They were scratched and burning worse every minute.

I was probably shredding the old-fashioned dress, too. Mamma was gonna kill me if I ruined it. The price tag said fifty bucks.

All of a sudden Anna's crashing and running stopped. "There you are!" she whispered, her voice right above me. I heard the sound of a lid on a jar.

Before I could stop myself, I let out an "Ah!" and then clapped my hand over my mouth. Anna was standing right in my path. She skidded to a stop.

In the final moments of twilight, Miss Anna Normand blinked at me real slow. In one hand she held a jar with a firefly buzzing frantically up against the glass, glowing like it was made of spun gold. With her other arm, she cradled Dulcie's doll tight against her, the beautiful porcelain straight from the Island of the Dolls in the Caribbean.

"Who are *you*?" Miss Anna demanded, her eyes big as saucers. "Are you a thief? Do you have a gang of hoodlums waiting to burgle our home?"

I crouched on my knees, holding still as a statue. I was still stupidly hoping she couldn't see me, so I said nothing.

Anna cleared her throat. "I spoke to you, girl. Who are you? Now answer me! Before I scream. Are there more of you hiding in the trees?"

Finally, I shook my head.

"Rise to your feet," she commanded, and I gulped, slowly standing. Leaves crackled under my buttoned black shoes. "Where did you come from?"

For a split second, I considered pretending I was deaf or couldn't talk, but I figured that might be too complicated. "I'm from — from Bayou Bridge."

"You're a town girl, or a servant girl, or what?"

I shook my head to all of her questions.

"Your dress is despicably dirty. And torn along the hem."

I nodded, feeling completely foolish.

"What's on your face?" She reached out to touch the scar on my cheek.

"Don't!" I shrieked, pulling back. For several long seconds we stared at each other, me all dirty and torn and scarred. I even had shreds of Spanish moss snarled in my hair. I'd hoped Miss Anna would assume I was some poor, ugly girl and let me run away.

"Your face has got a terrible scar," she finally said, curious. "How'd it happen?" Then Miss Anna Normand lifted her finger and connected with my cheek. There was a faint brush as her skin grazed my chin and ran along the ridge of my white scar.

But the moment we made contact, our two worlds collided.

I jerked backward like I'd just got hit by lightning. Falling straight down, I hit my head on the ground. Tears sprang to my eyes and pain radiated out from my skull.

Anna let out a bloodcurdling scream — and then the scream cut off and she was gone, vanished. Just like that. The whole thing happened in a split second.

I groaned in pain and tried to move. I was lying on my back in the dirt and leaves and moss, still wearing the old-fashioned dress, but the sky was lighter than just seconds ago.

Glancing around, I let out a breath. Anna Normand was gone. Disappeared into thin air.

Up ahead, I could make out the chimneys of the old Normand Mansion. Chimneys crumbling and blackened with age. I was back in my own time, the sun hovering on the edge of sunset. As if time hadn't passed at all.

Slowly, I rolled over, stroking my face where Anna had touched me. The feel of her fingers, her skin against mine, had been so bizarre.

Inch by inch, I got on my hands and knees and pushed myself up. A twig snapped. I heard the rustle of a leaf. My stomach shot into my throat.

I was staring straight into an alligator's beady red eyes.

CHAPTER TWELVE

A real live alligator.

I gulped down a nasty taste in my mouth. Willed myself not to scream or throw up.

I could lose a hand or a foot, if not my head. I could end up scarred up one side and down the other.

My eyes darted back and forth. It was a good thing it wasn't quite as dark as when I'd left 1912. The alligator was sitting in a pile of brush waiting for prey — me. The reptile appeared sleepy, it hadn't stirred yet, but I knew it had the potential to move *fast*.

I estimated ten, fifteen feet between us, which meant I had a fighting chance. My paw-paw had always told me that alligators were shy and more scared of me than I was of them. At that moment, I wasn't so sure I believed him. I'd never been *this* close before.

Move, I told myself. But I was glued to the ground, terror gushing up my throat.

The gator's eyes shifted toward me. That's all it took. I let out a wild scream and raced for the bank.

Wind tore at my throat as my legs pumped like a madwoman's. I leaped through the brush until I hit the dirt path. I swore the gator was right behind me, tail slithering, jaw snapping, about to come down on my heels any second. He'd pull me into the deep bayou waters and roll me around until I drowned. I'd seen it on *National Geographic*. Heck, I'd heard my mamma and daddy read about it in the newspaper right here. I was about to die! But I didn't dare take the time to look behind me; I just ran and ran and ran and ran.

The sound of gasping was raw in my ears, and I was about to burst into sobs when I turned back around wildly, wishing I had a thick tree limb to use for a weapon. No sign of the gator.

I finally slowed, but stayed on the cleared path. I swiveled my head back and forth, but all was quiet. No red eyes. I began to consider that I may have startled the gator as much as he startled me. Should have remembered that while dusk was the perfect time for lightning bugs, it was the worst time for gators and other critters.

Keeping a sharp eye, I stumbled toward the broken bridge, and my stomach dropped like a rock. The fireflies were gone. They'd disappeared before I could get back across!

Yesterday I'd floated back across the bridge, easy peasy. What was different this time?

Miss Anna Normand had touched me, that's what was different. The past and present had crashed together. Two worlds that weren't supposed to see each other, let alone touch. As soon as her finger met my face, I'd been instantly zapped back to my own time. In the very same spot I'd been standing in 1912.

Horror shot down my back. "That means —" I gulped. "That alligator was there all the while I was hiding behind the cypress during the barbecue, and I didn't even know it."

The broken bridge was still broken. It was getting dark. I was stranded.

Hot tears stung my eyes. I felt like a baby, but I knew I was stuck here for the night. With alligators hiding close by. Which meant I had to walk myself back up to the deserted house with its moldy walls and caved-in staircase. With dirt and mice droppings and no dinner.

I stared across the water and tried to stop bawling, tried to come up with a plan to get home.

I wondered what Anna told her family when I disappeared in front of her eyes.

Maybe we were all living in some sort of parallel time warp.

Then I wondered if it really *was* the fireflies that had taken me to the past. Or could I see the past because I lived in the antique store? Maybe I was tainted by unseen spirits clinging to the old furniture and tea sets and porcelain dolls. To the old-fashioned dress and shoes I was wearing.

The girl on the phone had told me to come. She *knew* something I didn't know. Next time she called she had some explaining to do! I didn't know what I was supposed to do back in 1912, although obviously, I wasn't supposed to interact with my ancestors. I could still feel the whisper of Anna's fingers along my cheek.

I whirled on my toes, thinking hard as I paced the dock. The girl on the phone had said, *"It's a matter of life and death."*

"So why don't you just *tell* me?" I burst out. "Next

time I'm gonna get myself killed. Next time I'll be *sitting* on an alligator's head!"

Twilight settled, and the broken bridge disappeared with the darkness. I could barely make out the shoreline and the dirt road beyond. Tiny pinpricks of neighborhood lights. It wasn't really that far, but it seemed like miles.

It was time to do the only thing I could do. Scream bloody murder and hope the sound carried. "Help!" I yelled. "Help! I'm over here! Help me! Please help me!"

Pretty soon, nobody else would be able to see me, either. I'd be hidden behind darkness. Stuck here all night. And if I was, I couldn't sit here on the bank. I'd have to find my way back to the deserted house without a flashlight. Without any kind of light *all night long.*

"Heeeelp!" I screamed, waving my arms like a crazy person. "Somebody please help! I'm over here!"

Then, like a miracle, I heard a faint voice give a shout in return. Heard the slosh of waves, a shadow on the water.

My eyes bugged out as I strained to see, and all of a sudden a rowboat bumped against the partial dock. A girl sat inside, thrashing the oars, trying to maintain her position as a small wave hit the pilings.

"Grab the rope!" she called. In the dim light, I tripped over the torn hem of my long dress as she threw me the rope.

The girl had brown hair, and her eyes were just a little bit frantic as the boat banged against the pilings. It was Alyson Granger, again. *Of course.*

But I was relieved to see another human being, even if it was my mortal enemy. "What are you doing here?"

"Don't you remember?" Alyson said, hanging on to the piling with one arm. "I passed you a while back. After I delivered Mamma's cookies I came back to see if you were still lurking around the cypress knees."

"I wasn't *lurking*," I said, my face going hot.

Alyson shrugged. "Then I heard shouting, and I could tell it was coming from across the water. That's when I saw you dancing on the bank."

"I wasn't *dancing*, either! I was jumping up and down and waving to get someone's attention."

"Whatever. You're lucky I have good hearing."

I nodded, both grateful and wary at her showing up to rescue me.

"So what are you waiting for?" Alyson said. "Get in and grab an oar. We need to get back before it's pitch-black."

Alyson held the boat against the dock, keeping it steady while I scooted myself over the edge of the pier and slid into the boat. She handed me an oar. "You stroke right, and I'll stroke left and steer."

"Whose boat is this?"

"My older brother's. He left it tied down there a ways closer to our house."

"Did you have to get permission?"

"Probably, but I knew there wasn't much time. Hey, row faster, okay? I don't like to be out on the water when it's getting dark."

"Well, me neither!" My heart was going a hundred miles an hour. I was grateful to be rescued, but annoyed that Alyson Granger was my savior. She'd probably tell the whole town how dumb I was. We fell silent as we bumped into the opposite bank a few minutes later.

"Jump out first," Alyson instructed, "and tie us up on that tupelo trunk right there."

I did as she said and made a knot so the rope wouldn't loosen.

I was impressed with Alyson's boating skills. Guess she'd done this before, like most every bayou kid. But I was surprised she'd come out so quickly to get me. She didn't run home to get help or permission. Never knew mousy follower-girl Alyson Granger had it in her.

After we were standing in the soft dirt along the bank once more, I tried to catch my breath, brushing back my sweaty hair. Then I realized I was exposing my scarred cheek. Quickly, I turned away to climb up the bank's incline to the road.

"Larissa," Alyson said behind me in a quiet voice.

"What?" I said impatiently, not wanting her to gawk at my face. "Guess you want my daddy to pay you for rescuing me?"

Her eyes flew wide. "What are you talking about? You think I'm that much of a creep?"

I shrugged. If the shoe fit . . . who was I to say differently?

"I just — I just wanted to ask you if that scar — well, I mean, does it hurt?"

"No," I said fiercely, waiting for her to make fun of me. I paused. "Least not much. Sometimes."

"I'm sorry," Alyson apologized. "You know that day last summer? I never meant for you to get hurt. Really, I didn't. I hope you'll believe me. I *want* you to believe me. Because it's the truth."

I shrugged again, not giving her satisfaction either way. But a tiny part of me was glad to hear her say that. Words I never thought I'd hear her say in a million years. "Gotta get home," I finally said.

She nodded. "Yeah, me, too."

We stood there for another few seconds.

"My mamma's gonna kill me for missing supper."

Alyson nodded conspiratorially. "Mine, too. And now my brother will, too, if he ever finds out I took his boat."

"Then I hope he never finds out." I felt my mouth working up into a half smile and I quickly stopped it.

"Thanks, Larissa."

"Um, yeah. Thanks for coming to get me. Guess if our parents found out we'd both be in a huge heap of trouble."

"That's for sure."

Silence hung again and I finally started down the road, the only light coming from a few backyard lamps beyond the fences.

Alyson reached out to touch my arm. Real fast. Light as a firefly. I jerked, remembering when Miss Anna had touched me: so soft, like a quick breath of air. "Just wondering . . ." Alyson said, playing nervously with the ends of her hair. "How'd you get over there anyway? The bridge is broken. There's a huge gap of at least fifteen feet of broken planks. Or no planks at all. I don't think anybody with half a brain would swim it. Besides, you ain't wet."

I bit at my lips. She'd deem me certified crazy. Off

my rocker. "It's hard to explain," I said in a low voice. "You wouldn't believe me."

"Hmm." She didn't press me, but her eyes were intense as she studied me.

I didn't want her probing any deeper so I picked up my skirts and raced for home. After a minute I sneaked a glance over my shoulder. Alyson Granger's shadow had disappeared into the night.

CHAPTER THIRTEEN

This town is cursed, I tell you, Luke," Mamma was saying as I walked in the door.

Daddy was clearing the supper dishes and Mamma leaned against the sink, arms folded across her chest, belly protruding like a beach ball under her balloon-like blouse.

"Why did we ever come back?" she sniffed. "Everything bad that ever happened to my family happened here in Bayou Bridge. I must have been crazy to agree to buy this store." Then Mamma saw me and pounced. "Where have you been, Larissa? I was about to call the sheriff! We waited for supper and you didn't show. I called around to the neighboring shops and a couple girls from school and nobody'd seen you!"

"I'm fine," I said, chills running down my arms when I remembered those red, sinister gator eyes. If my parents knew, they'd never let me out of the house again.

"I even called Shelby Jayne, but Miz Mirage told me she was gone on a trip with her grandmother Phoebe."

"I *told* you that already," I said. "You never listen to me."

"Of course I listen to you, but you can't just waltz in and out however you please. I needed your help with the cooking. And Daddy had a million phone calls about some delayed shipments we've been waiting for on special order."

Daddy ran a hand through his hair and sighed. His eyes were puffy and tired. "I got paperwork to do. Tomorrow's Monday, a brand-new week of problems."

"Don't you care about your own daughter?" Mamma said, her voice shaking. "Where she's been, what she's been doing?"

" 'Course I do. You know that. I was about to go looking for her when she walked in the door." He turned to me and rubbed a hand along my arm. "Yep, it's really her. In the flesh."

"Don't you get sarcastic with me, Luke Renaud."

"Not being sarcastic, honey, just trying to lighten the mood. I'm tired and gotta stay up late again in the office. Larissa is here and perfectly fine. Although a little dirty."

"So *where* have you been, young lady? And wearing one of the store's antique dresses?" Mamma asked.

I blinked at my mother, the overhead kitchen lights harsh and bright.

"Um." What was I supposed to say? That I'd been following fireflies back to 1912? Almost got eaten by a gator? "Um, I was with Alyson Granger." That was true, actually. At least for the last thirty minutes.

"Guess if we'd called Sheriff Granger he would have known where she was," Daddy said.

"Not funny," Mamma said, her eyes narrowing. "Since when are you friends with the enemy?"

"Maddie!" Daddy winced.

Mamma sucked in her breath, guilt on her face.

"Since when do you call a little girl the *enemy*?" Daddy went on. "You gotta stop this kind of thinking. It's making you angry and bitter all the time."

Mamma's voice shook. "I got a right to be angry and bitter. My family has practically been destroyed by this town and the people here."

Daddy shook his head. "I don't know what to say to that. Your family survived. We'll survive. We haven't been *destroyed*. These accidents were horrible and unfortunate, but you've got to get rid of the hate in your soul, *shar*. You've poisoned yourself — and now you're going to poison Larissa."

Mamma whirled me around to stare straight into my eyes. "Are you going to stand there and tell me that you're really and truly friends with Alyson Granger?"

My stomach dropped. "'Course I'm not friends with her! I just saw her on the road. I'll never be friends with her! I hate her just like you do, and I always will! Are you satisfied now?"

My mother let out a cry, then whipped back around to the sink full of soap and dishes. Her body trembled, as if she was holding in a flood of emotion.

I was beginning to believe my mother about Bayou Bridge. This town was cursed. Maybe we did need to move and go somewhere safer. If we hadn't moved back, I wouldn't be scarred. I'd still have my old friends, my old house, a normal face.

A sick sensation spread through my stomach and up into my throat at everything I'd lost. 'Course, worse things could happen, I guess. I could get eaten by a gator. My parents could lose the antique store. They could sit me down one day and tell me they hated each other — and pull me apart in the process.

Daddy slammed dishes off the table and into the sink. "Did you hear that, Maddie? You just proved my point. Larissa not only has a scarred face but a scarred heart. What do you think we can do about that now?"

"It's this town," Mamma repeated quietly, her voice low and terrible.

Daddy threw up his hands. "That's ridiculous. It's not the whole town. An accident. Two accidents, I guess, but accidents. Nobody was trying to permanently maim or kill Larissa. A prank by a bunch of *kids* that got out of hand. We have to forgive and forget and move on."

Mamma's hands shook, but I wasn't sure if she was boiling mad or still crying. "Gotta get rid of my ghosts," she finally muttered, her voice raw as a skinned knee.

Stiffly, Daddy walked over to her and put a hand on her shoulder. "Baby."

She brushed him off. "I need to be alone for a while."

He turned to me and said, "Grab a plate of food and skedaddle off to your room, Larissa. Give us some time, okay? And next time call us when you're out somewhere, especially after dark. It makes us worry."

"Okay, Daddy." Hurriedly, I grabbed a ham sandwich, a bowl of salad, and a slice of lemon pie. I was so relieved I had permission to go upstairs to peace and quiet.

"Wait a minute," Mamma told me, stopping me with her hand.

I tightened my grip on my plate. Was she gonna take dinner away from me?

"Don't look so scared, Larissa. Just got a question for you. Besides ordering you to clean that dress."

"What, Mamma?"

She chewed on her lip. "Have you been messing with those dolls upstairs lately?"

A shock of surprise ran through me. I was not expecting that at all. "You mean the dolls in the glass case? The one that you keep locked?"

"That's the one." Her dark green eyes held my gaze tight to hers.

"No, I don't open it without your permission."

"You sure? You don't need to lie. You're not in trouble. I'm just — just wondering because . . ." Her voice trailed off, a frown between her eyes.

"You think someone's been messing with the lock?" Daddy asked.

Mamma shook her head. "No, the lock's fine. It's just, well, I can't explain what I mean exactly. Just a funny feeling."

"I promise I haven't opened the case. Sometimes I look at the dolls and, of course, I dust the case, but that's all."

"Well, if you promise," Mamma said, but she didn't sound completely convinced.

"Must be the baby coming so soon," Daddy said. "You got nerves and jitters."

Mamma nodded. "Guess so."

But she didn't seem satisfied. I wondered what was on her mind. Did Mamma suffer bizarre thoughts every time Anna Marie's chilling blue eyes followed her around the second floor? I'd always thought it was just me.

I took my plate, went upstairs, and shut the door. I was safe in my cozy room. No dolls' eyes. No strange phone calls.

Besides, I had to mull over the fact that the fireflies had escorted me back in time. Time slipping like sand through an hourglass. I'd just visited the summer of 1912. It was powerful. And perfectly real.

I could still see Miss Anna taking the porcelain doll — minutes after Dulcie received her as a gift. I replayed the moment when Miss Anna, clutching the doll in her arms, touched me — and I was zapped back to my own time.

Miss Anna wasn't nice to take the doll and walk away with it. She hadn't just admired it and given it back. She'd snuggled with it. Pressed that doll tightly in her arms like it belonged to her. She got a *pony,* for crying out loud. Anna probably already owned a whole room full of dolls. Dulcie was lucky to have a rag doll with strands of yarn for hair.

Miss Anna was a little bit selfish. And Dulcie couldn't say a thing because she was a servant. I hoped Miss Anna had given the doll back later that evening. But I wanted to *know* if she had really returned her to Dulcie. I was dying to know what was happening in 1912 right this minute.

"Right this minute," I repeated, laughing out loud and falling back on the pillow. "I want to know what happened this very moment in 1912, but it was more than a century ago. It's already *history.*"

I fiddled with the eyelet on my bedspread. Deep down, I already did know. Miss Anna never gave the doll back. Anna Marie remained with the Normand family. Passed along to my grandmother and my mother. Sitting in our very own doll case right below me.

It gave me a terrible feeling knowing my own great-great-grandmother was so mean. A little thief. Hopefully, she'd grown up and gotten past her self-ishness, but I'd never know.

I was just finishing my last bite of sandwich and

licking my fingers when I heard a phone start to ring.

My heart beat fast inside my chest. I could tell that the ringing was coming from the main floor, not my parents' room. It was the girl. I knew it. But did I want to talk to her?

Two seconds later, I bolted off my bed. I ran down the narrow stairs and dashed on to the second floor. The phone continued ringing.

The sound was coming from one of the black candlestick phones. The telephone rang twice more, and then I finally snatched it up. "Hello?"

"Larissa? That's you, right?"

"Yeah, it's me."

"I — you sound so young over a phone line. Well, I guess you are young. Just turned twelve, right?"

"Yeah," I slowly answered. How did this girl know so much?

"Of course you just turned twelve. That's why I'm calling. Because this is *the* summer. The summer you have to save your family."

"What do you mean by that?"

"I mean your mamma. Your baby sister."

"I don't have a baby sister."

"Not yet, but you will."

"Are you some kind of fortune-teller? Maybe it's a boy. The ultrasound could be wrong, you know."

"Nope, it's a girl," she said firmly.

"How do you know so much, smarty-pants?" I was irritated by this mysterious, know-it-all girl. Irritated by my parents. Irritated by Miss Anna.

"It's hard to explain right now. Besides, even if I told you I doubt you'd believe me. Maybe you'll figure it out eventually."

"I will," I said defiantly. "You don't have to make me feel like a dummy."

"You're anything but stupid, Larissa. And, well, you know you have to go back."

"I was just thinking that before you called. I want to know what happened to Miss Anna. But why can I see her — why can I see all of them?"

There was a pause. "I'm not sure, but I think it's got something to do with the curse."

"You mean the town curse?" I gulped. "It's true that Bayou Bridge is out to get our family?"

She didn't answer that directly. "Let's just say that I'm not joking when I say it's a matter of life and death. So you *have* to go back. If you want to save your little sister. Just don't let anybody touch you — and watch out for alligators."

"No kidding. Wait — how do you know about

that? You got some kind of crystal ball?" I paused, wondering if someone truly had been spying on me as I crossed the bayou in the cloud of fireflies. It was too creepy to consider. The girl's last words burst through my thoughts. "Hey, what do you mean save my little sister? What's going to happen — ?"

There was silence. I tapped the phone. Nothing. Jiggled the metal tab up and down. But it was no use. She was already gone.

How could I save my little sister when she wasn't even born yet? And, in a cruel and twisted way, it felt like history was repeating itself. My mamma had been the little sister when her older sister drowned. Maybe there was a connection and maybe there wasn't. Either way I knew I was going back.

The girl on the phone didn't have to convince me. Not one little bit.

CHAPTER FOURTEEN

A few nights later, Daddy declared he was going to take Mamma out to dinner. Get her away from all the store's worries. Mamma tried to protest, saying we couldn't afford it, but I could tell she was glad to leave.

Which meant I was free.

Fast as I could, I got through the routine of closing up the shop. Dusting, rolling down the desks, straightening pictures, and wiping fingerprints from the glass cases.

I liked seeing the store pretty at night when it was clean again, all the lights blazing and making the china glow. Normally, I would have set myself up on a couch with a book and a bag of popcorn, but I had to take advantage of the time.

I ran all the way to the bayou. It was a hot and heavy night. Summer was in full swing now. The lightning bugs were swarming, flying fast as if they were waiting for me.

My feet squished in the mud as the tiny golden lights swirled. I stepped up onto the bridge. Crossing the broken bridge always made my stomach roll over like I was gonna throw up. What if it didn't mend itself brand-new? What if I fell in again?

I gritted my teeth and took the first slow, careful step. If I wasn't supposed to slip through time, then why did the girl keep calling me? The idea had crossed my mind that the girl might be Miss Anna Normand. What if she was calling me *from the past* after she saw me hiding in her bushes? There were phones in 1912. What if one of the phones in the antique store was an old Normand telephone? But how would she know who I was or where I lived? The girl who kept calling knew about my family, my unborn sister. And she sounded so urgent when she told me I needed to go back in time to save my baby sister from dying. But that made no sense! Why was my sister in danger? From what, or from who? And who would *know* that anyway? Who cared enough and was motivated enough? The whole thing was a puzzle with too few pieces to fit together.

A sudden shout behind me made me jerk around.

A girl with brown, billowing hair ran toward me. I groaned. I guess Alyson lived down this road, but she was getting to be a nuisance.

I didn't want to answer her prying questions, so I ignored her shouts, ran down the wooden planks of the bridge, and was caught up in the lovely procession of dancing fireflies. It helped if I didn't look down at the rushing water, and I hoped Alyson was too far away to see what I was doing.

A thin spiral of smoke rose from one of the chimneys when I got to the clearing, but there was no sign of the Normand servants or family.

I circled the whole yard, staying hidden in the woods, pausing to admire the grand white columns along the front of the house. Ivy and rose trellises climbed the walls. A humongous vegetable garden spread across a tilled clearing behind a gate. Perfect rows of leafy vegetables, probably weeded and hoed by T-Paul and Mister Lance.

Every once in a while my feet disappeared into a mound of soft dirt near the biggest and oldest cypress trees. Looked like Mister Lance was still following Anna's orders, digging up tree after tree as they searched for imaginary long-lost Civil War silver.

After I circled the perimeter from the safety of the woods, I wiped at the sweat along my forehead, longing to sit in one of the rocking chairs on the porch. Have someone bring me cold lemonade. There was no movement anywhere. The coast was clear.

I got to my feet, ready to spend ten minutes on the back porch, pretending I was a rich lady in 1912, when Miz Beatrice and Dulcie opened the back door. Quickly, they swished through, their long skirts sweeping the polished planks of the porch.

I shot down behind a bush. That was a close call! Would I be jolted back to the present if they touched me as Miss Anna had? I didn't want to find out.

The mother and daughter strode across the lawns, their shoulders square and stiff like they were mad at the world, as they headed into one of the outlying buildings. Turned out the building wasn't a shed or an outhouse but rather a summer kitchen. The windows didn't have glass, so smoke and heat could escape. Rows of glass canning jars and a stack of big kettles sat on wooden shelves. Stacked underneath were frying pans for cooking large quantities during harvesttime when extra hands were hired.

The open windows allowed me to hear everything. It was perfect. I hunkered down under the rear window.

"Now we need this Dutch oven for baking the pineapple upside-down cake," Miz Beatrice said, as if consulting a list. "Dulcie, fetch me some baking potatoes from the root cellar."

"But there're spiders and snakes down there."

"Land sakes, child! It might be dry as a bone, but there ain't no snakes. They stay down at the river for water."

"What about spiders?" Dulcie said next. "I hate spiders with a passion."

"You're getting to be as melodramatic as Miss Anna." I heard a trapdoor squeak. A pause, as if Miz Beatrice was peering down. "All I see is a few cobwebs. Tomorrow, I'll get T-Paul to clean 'em up with the broom, but nothing is moving at the moment."

"Mamma!" Dulcie let out a grump.

"I'll shine the light and you get me an apron full of big potatoes."

"Why potatoes? It's blazing hot to bake potatoes."

"Miz Julianna says she's got a hankering to have them for supper tonight. Although why not a good, chilled potato salad is beyond me. We got us that new icebox contraption."

I heard the clip-clop of footsteps going down, then footsteps coming back up.

"Got ten big ones, Mamma."

"They look good. Now that wasn't so hard, was it?"

I wiped my face with the hem of my shirt. Dulcie was right. It *was* blazing hot.

Softly, Miz Beatrice said, "Think I know what's still bothering you, sugar."

There were tears in Dulcie's voice as she slowly said, "Mister Edgar gave *me* that doll."

"It's not like we can march into Miss Anna's bedroom and just take that doll out of her case."

"Why not? She belongs to me!"

"Because we'd be accused of stealing, that's why not," her mother said indignantly. "We're only servants, in case you forgot." Miz Beatrice added hopefully, "Maybe she'll give her back when she's done with the doll."

"That'll never happen. Miss Anna says the doll is safer in her room. Soon she'll forget it was ever mine."

"Try to put it out of your mind, darlin'."

"I never owned anything like that doll. Never will, either. I hate her with all my heart."

Miz Beatrice gasped. "Don't be talking about hating, child."

"She gets everything she ever wants," Dulcie said darkly. "Makes me want to cut off her ringlets."

"I know it seems that way, sugar. But there ain't nothing we can do about it. Just pray Miss Anna will remember us and grow some kindness. Meanwhile, we will forgive and forget, and maybe one day you'll get another doll just as pretty."

"Not a doll from the islands. They're rare."

"That's probably true, my girl. How often does someone go to the Island of the Dolls and bring back a trunkload to pass out?" Miz Beatrice laughed softly at the thought.

But her daughter began to weep, and my heart tugged at her loss of something so wonderful and beautiful. Snatched away so quickly. I knew what it felt like to be treated so badly that all you could think of was revenge. You had to do something — anything — to turn that nasty, bitter feeling into something sweeter. I figured revenge could be like chocolate. Rich, dark chocolate mousse, with juicy strawberries and whipped cream on top. My mamma had wanted revenge on the town this past year and it had turned her sad and angry. She hadn't been happy in a long time. I didn't want to be like that, but I knew I had been, and I wasn't sure what to do about it. Pain was real and it took time to heal. Just like the scar on my face.

There was a rustling noise as if Miz Beatrice had pulled her daughter into her arms to comfort her. "There, there," she murmured. "One day you and that smart brain of yours is going to college if I have to work the skin off my hands. You're going to be happy. A doll is just a thing. Something nice and pretty, but not something to live and die over."

I bit at my lips, trying to think of the last time my own mamma had hugged me. *And*, Mamma owned the doll now, which made me feel guilty and peculiar. Miss Anna Normand had been cruel to Dulcie, and for no reason.

CHAPTER FIFTEEN

The next instant, Miz Beatrice and Dulcie left the outdoor kitchen and walked briskly back across the lawns to the house. I rocked forward into a crouching position, ready to run into the trees if they turned around and saw me.

As soon as they entered the back door, I followed, quiet as I could, exposed as I ran across the open lawns toward the house.

Three seconds later I stood at the door, panting. I counted to five, and then twisted the door handle and peeked inside.

No sign of anybody. The hall was empty — and gorgeous. Without a sound, I stepped through, drinking in the sight of high ceilings, crown molding, and ivory wall panels. Paintings hung everywhere. Fancy crystal lamps perched serenely on hall tables. And this wasn't even the front entrance!

Quickly stepping behind a coatrack to hide, my foot caught around the leg of a side table. A painted ceramic bowl filled with pink dahlias trembled precariously, and without thinking I grabbed the edge of the hall table to keep the bowl of flowers from crashing to the floor.

My stomach dropped. I'd touched something in the past! But nothing happened. I frowned, confused. Maybe I was only thrown back into the future when I touched a living person.

A second later, three fireflies came buzzing down the hall, heading straight for me. "What are you doing here?" I whispered. "How did you get into the house?" There must have been a window open somewhere. Before I could figure it out, the lightning bugs danced and whirled around my head. Instantly, the house turned dark, just as the sound of brisk footsteps headed straight for me.

"What was that?" Miz Beatrice's voice came out of the fuzzy blackness. "Must be the missus. Hurry, now, Dulcie! Skedaddle!"

Their voices faded, and the world fell away.

The next moment I was plummeting wildly,

tumbling through space, crashing past a set of stairs. But that was strange because I wasn't near a staircase.

I landed with a sharp thump, but I wasn't hurt, just dazed. Slowly, I moved my arms and legs. They seemed to work fine, not even a sprained ankle. I swung my neck back and forth. No bumps. No headache.

Studying my surroundings, I realized that I'd landed in the upstairs hall. How did that happen? I'd fallen *down,* not *up.*

More hall tables and gilt mirrors floated past my eyes. Several closed doors led to bedrooms, I assumed, but there was one thing I noticed right away. The furniture was more worn, like the house had suddenly aged. Or I'd been flung *forward* in time. Chills ran down my arms. "What happened to 1912?" I whispered.

At least I was alone in the hallway. But somewhere I could hear a woman crying horribly, wailing. Then the sobs turned to forlorn weeping, like the woman's heart had broken.

I knew I should run away, but instead I crawled toward the sound. It was coming from the last bedroom at the end of the hall.

The door swung open, and a man emerged wearing

a doctor's coat and stethoscope. His face was grim and he was obviously distracted by the weeping female voices — more than one now, I'd realized — giving me a split second to crawl into the next room, which was thankfully empty.

This room was a nursery, all done up with a freshly painted crib and stuffed animals and painted giraffes on the wall. Sunlight streamed through the window, past white-and-pink gingham curtains.

The crib was empty. So was the rocking chair. And there was a doctor in the house who seemed very disturbed. I swallowed hard, dreading what would happen next.

From behind the nursery door, I watched the doctor give orders to a nurse. She pressed her lips together, her eyes bloodshot. "I'll send for the coroner from the downstairs telephone," he told her. "Stay here, and I'll be back in a few minutes."

His footsteps sounded on the stairs, and the nurse returned to the very last bedroom down the hall. I crept forward, my mind full of questions. Who had died? Miz Julianna Normand? Miss Anna's father? Why was the house so quiet?

From the doorjamb I peered inside the master bedroom. A sitting area was first and then a large bed on the far end near a bank of windows. A man stood at the bed holding an infant wrapped in pink blankets in his arms. It only took a moment to realize that he was weeping silent, dreadful tears.

Another woman, someone about my grandmother's age, immaculately dressed, lifted her face to the crying man. Her gray hair was pinned into a sweeping hairstyle and sprayed in place like a helmet. "Let me have the child, Hank," she said to him.

"Are you sure, Miz Anna?" he choked out.

She nodded, her face strained. "My wailing is done for now. See to my daughter — your wife. Take care of Daphne."

It hit me that the young woman lying in the big bed was dead. Her face was chalky white and quickly turning gray. She lay there so very, very still, but her blond curls were damp from childbirth. The bedclothes were stained, and the nurse was about to strip the soiled sheets and blankets.

Instead, she took a step back, averting her eyes as the man named Hank dropped to his knees beside the dead woman and pressed his face into her side. He clutched her hands with his own and his shoulders shook in silent sobs.

A second nurse appeared from the bathroom area. She plastered a stiff smile on her face and held out plump arms. "Let me see the babe and check her and weigh her, Miz Prevost," she said in a thick Cajun accent.

"I — I — wait," the older woman said, straining to sit up in the armchair. "The baby — my granddaughter — is fine for another two minutes, Nurse. Hank!" she said, speaking loudly to get his attention. He finally lifted his head from his dead wife's cold, lifeless hands. "Hank, what did you and Daphne —" She paused to take a breath, as if grasping for composure. "What did you and Daphne decide to call the baby? You had a name chosen, correct?"

Hank looked bewildered. "A name? Oh, yes. Yes. Daphne and I — Daphne especially wanted to call her Katherine. Katherine Prevost Moret. We planned to call her Kat."

"A darlin', lively name," the nurse said soothingly, picking up the pink bundle from the older woman's arms and cuddling her. "You'll have a fine life here, Kat, with your daddy and your grandma Anna, won't you, sweet baby?" She carried the newborn to a table where a tub of warm water was ready to wash her. Stacks of cloth diapers sat in rows, as well as several baby nightgowns and knitted booties.

My throat was tight like I was going to cry, too. A funny pain hurt inside my chest and my eyes burned.

Daphne Prevost Moret had died only moments ago, while giving birth to her daughter.

Her husband, Hank, jerked his head up, glancing toward his mother-in-law, the older woman with pretty silver hair, all dressed up, as though that was her usual daily wardrobe. Miss Anna Normand, now Miz Anna Prevost, in later years.

Miz Anna gave Hank a grim look, and then buried her face in her hands, crying with a sudden fierceness, "No, no, no. Not my Daphne. She can't be gone. This can't be happening. Not after Charles —" She broke off and quickly wiped at her face, as though ill at ease to show such strong emotion. She pointed to the green marble mantle where a porcelain doll sat prettily in her pink silks and ribbons. "Get me my doll, Hank," she demanded. Then softer. "Please."

Pressing his lips together, Hank rose, crossing the room slowly. He retrieved the doll and handed it to her, stumbling into the footrest of a wooden wheelchair sitting close by. How strange. Where did that come from? I wondered.

The older woman stroked the doll's lacy dress, and then placed it in her arms, rocking the doll with a peculiar expression on her face. So Miss Anna — now Miz Anna Prevost — still owned the doll. She never gave it back to Dulcie. My uncomfortable suspicions had been right all along.

Footsteps thumped back up the staircase. The doctor was returning! And I had no time to scramble back to the nursery and hide.

Squeezing my eyes shut, I boldly, or foolishly, placed both palms flat against the flowery papered walls and sucked in my breath, as though bracing myself for the impact of a car crash.

Nothing happened, and my stomach dropped, knowing I was about to be caught. Darting this way and that down the hall, I tried to figure out the best escape route when a small swarm of fireflies suddenly surrounded me. Before I could react, I was whirling again. The sounds of weeping echoed in my ears until silence and darkness overtook me again.

When I opened my eyes again, I was still in the house. Disappointment crushed me. This time the mansion house was darker, shadowy. No crisp gingham curtains. No sunshine. It smelled funny, too. Like sour milk and mold.

The furniture was not the antique Edwardian-age pieces any longer. Much more modern, but shabbier with frayed edges. Any afternoon sunlight was closed off by heavy drapes in the downstairs living room.

For a minute I worried that I'd fallen through time into a different house altogether, but I recognized the staircase. The same scrolled wood, scratched and badly in need of sanding and varnishing. Since I sometimes helped Daddy refinish a table he'd bought at an estate sale I recognized the signs of age and dark patina.

The rest of the house was completely different. Smaller, more homely, without any of the grand ceilings and moldings and furnishings. A prickle ran up my neck as I wondered what year it was, and what had happened to the original mansion. The doctor was gone, as well as the baby and Hank and his dead wife. But once more, I heard the sound of weeping.

Quickly, I backed myself into a corner under the staircase. The only light came from two table lamps on the opposite side of the room. Two small couches and a fraying armchair had been shoved against the walls. A faded carpet lay in the middle of the wood floor.

Then it occurred to me that the furniture had been moved and the room cleared because a table was in the center of the room with an open coffin lying on its surface. On the white satin pillows lay a girl about twelve years old. Her blond hair rested in waves against the pristine satin.

Her spirit was clearly gone, her eyes closed, the lids an unsettling gray.

I desperately wanted to know who she was, but I didn't dare move from the safety of my corner. The parlor was stuffy and hot. Drops of sweat formed on my neck and under my arms.

Down a short hallway, light spilled from a doorway, including the sound of clattering dishes, water running, and women's voices. The scent of food wafted through the house: casseroles, steeping tea, fried shrimp.

Neighbors who brought food for the wake. Because that's what this was. A wake with a dead body smack-dab in the living room. A dead *girl*. It was so wrong, so horribly sad.

A woman in shorts and a pink blouse, wearing white sandals on her feet, came down the hallway. I shrank behind the chair's stuffing trying to squeeze myself smaller.

"Here we are," the woman murmured, carrying a steaming cup of tea. She set it down on the table next to another woman I hadn't noticed because she'd been sitting like a statue in a corner of the couch. She must have been the one I heard crying when I crashed into this new time period. "Oh, Kat, you gotta drink something."

I slapped a hand over my mouth so I wouldn't make a sound. Kat was short for Katherine. Katherine Moret DuMonde — my grandmother. I recognized her, and it was like a knife in my own heart.

"Can't," she choked out. "Not when Gwen will never —"

"Ssh, ssh," the woman in the pink blouse whispered, putting her arms around her friend. "You can't think like that. Sweet Gwen is with our Lord. You gotta keep that in your mind else you'll go crazy."

Gwen was my mamma's dead sister. I started to sweat even more, and I felt like I had razors for eyelids.

"Now take a sip," my grandmother's friend ordered. "It's hot, so be careful."

"Where's Maddie?" Kat whispered, and I knew she was talking about my mamma.

"She's with my daughter, Jenny. They're upstairs playing quietly. Don't you worry, Kat, she'll be fine. Kids are resilient."

Kat shook her head. "They said it was lightning — they said —" She broke off, and I saw her red-rimmed eyes, balled-up tissues and handkerchiefs littering the couch beside her.

My Grandma Kat's hairstyle was different so many years ago, longer, blonder, without any gray. No crow's-feet wrinkles around her eyes, although her arms and hands were wrinkled, just the way I'd always seen them my whole life. That was strange because Kat had to be young in this time period. She couldn't be much more than thirty-five. I recognized her sharp green eyes, the way her head tilted when she listened to her friend. And I recognized her voice, even though she'd been crying so hard she had gone hoarse from the grief.

My grandmother took a sip of the tea and set it back down. She squinted at the light from the lamp, clearly exhausted. "Where's my husband?"

"On the bayou with my Zachary checking out the bridge. Making sure folks can get out to the island with all the planks broken up like they are. The weatherman was saying on television that it was the worst storm of the decade." She stopped, flustered, like she'd said too much. Gently, she added, "People will be showing up soon. Can I get you anything else? Got so much good food in the kitchen."

My grandmother rubbed her palms down her slacks, shaking her head. My eyes traveled along the floor and I saw that she was barefoot. Grandma Kat always kicked off her shoes when she came into the house. Hardly ever saw her wear shoes. But she didn't respond to her friend's questions, just stared at the casket in a daze.

"Just sip on that tea and I'll be back again in a minute. Got something for you." The woman peeked through the front drapes, clucked her tongue, and returned to the kitchen.

My grandmother's weeping tore at my throat, paralyzing me in my hiding place, but I needed to get out of there. It was time to leave my safe corner. I worried about crossing the bridge in the dark and the lightning bugs deserting me. Alligators and bobcats hunting me down.

Before I could move, my grandmother's friend came down the hall carrying a shoe box. She perched on the couch, biting her lip, as though she was nervous to speak.

"What is it, Marla?" Grandma Kat asked.

"I hate to show this to you. Knowing what it means to your family and all, I mean."

My grandmother snatched the shoe box and flipped off the lid. She gasped as fresh tears rolled down her face. "Oh, no!" she cried out. "I promised Miss Anna I'd take care of her for the rest of my life."

I couldn't take my eyes off them as Kat lifted the doll, Anna Marie, from the box. She was bedraggled and dirty, her ringlets tangled. The fancy mauve dress was sodden, the black shoes muddy. "What happened to her?" my grandmother asked sharply.

Her friend Marla reached out a hand toward the doll, and then folded it back into her lap. "They found her washed up on the bayou bank. Near the bridge. With —" She stopped and closed her eyes for a moment.

Grandma Kat clutched Anna Marie to her chest, rocking her like a baby. "She's ruined!" she moaned.

"No," Marla said firmly. "She's not ruined at all. Well," she added ruefully, "she's a sorry mess, that's for sure, but she's not permanently ruined. I've already been making phone calls, and I found an antique dealer that specializes in dolls and restoration. She said she can fix her up brand-new again. Clean her clothes, redo her hair, the works."

"This is our precious family heirloom doll," Kat said, anguished, lifting her puffy red eyes. "Gwen must have taken her out of the case. Why would she do that? Why?"

Marla shook her head sadly, cautiously watching Kat.

"We'll never know," my grandmother whispered, smoothing her hand down the doll's dress. "A secret gone forever. Gwen always loved her like we all have. My grandmother Anna would roll over in her grave if she could see her precious doll like this."

"We'll get her fixed up," Marla said. "I'll get Zach to drive me over to the antique dealer tomorrow so

she can get started right away. That will help —
I hope."

Grandma Kat didn't speak for a moment. Then
she said, "Nothing will help, but I appreciate all
you're doing for us, Marla."

There was a shout from outside, and the two
women jumped up and peered out the front
window.

"It's Zach and Preston in the yard," Marla said,
her voice tight. "They're back from the bridge."

"I'm going with you," Kat said. "Just for a moment.
I don't want to leave Gwen alone for long."

Within seconds both women hurried out the front
door and I was alone with the casket.

And the doll.

Creeping out from my dark corner, I couldn't bear
to look at Gwen dressed up in her Sunday best inside
the casket. I didn't want to see what death looked
like. It came too close last summer. I'd felt its fingers
clawing after me when I was sinking down to the
bottom of the bayou.

Instead I was drawn to the shoe box and Anna
Marie.

Without touching anything, I bent down to study
the grimy silk dress, all wet and wilted. Her eyelashes were stuck with tiny bits of dirt. She looked

distressed. In fact, her face appeared tormented, as though she was suffering. I'd swear those blue eyes were about to cry.

"Don't worry," I said softly. "Someday you will be beautiful again. I promise."

She just stared at me intently, as though willing my words to be true, and our eyes locked in a strange grip.

Wrenching my gaze away, I whipped my head toward the front door, wondering if I could escape before anyone saw me. I'd have to try the back door. Through the gauze curtains, I could see people in the front yard, more walking up the path, coming for the wake.

It was probably a stupid thing to do, but I couldn't help myself. Before I turned to sneak out the back door, I reached out and touched the beautiful doll, staring into its clear, sad eyes. My fingers barely brushed the texture of scalloped lace on her sleeves before a terrible shaking began.

My stomach heaved and I fell to my knees, like I was about to shatter into a million pieces. I wanted to cry, but I didn't dare make a peep. "Help me," I finally choked out.

From a tunnel of darkness the fireflies came zipping to my rescue. They flew frantically, as though

I'd done something very wrong, circling me, making me dizzy.

I don't think I was supposed to touch the doll.

The golden light blinded me and, instantly, I was sinking through the floors, spinning and whirling through a sinister gloom that squeezed my throat like a boa constrictor.

My arms whirled like a windmill out of control. I was positive I was going to die this time. I tried not to scream in case someone from the past could hear me, but terrified howls came out anyway. When I hit the staircase banister and landed with a thump, I was shrieking like a banshee.

CHAPTER SIXTEEN

Quickly, I cut off my screams and hyperventilated instead, trying to catch my breath. I swore I'd broken a couple of ribs this time, but when I got to my knees, I was breathing fine and nothing was sprained or bruised.

What was going on? I was slipping and careening through time like I was riding a demented roller coaster. "I want to go home," I whimpered from the floor.

It took a minute to get my bearings, but I was back in the original plantation mansion. Fading roses bloomed in the fibers of the carpet, worn down by decades of footsteps. I tried to remember where I'd seen it before. It was the same old-fashioned carpet in the upstairs hallway when I was crawling around right after Daphne died giving birth to a baby girl named Kat.

"So what time am I in now?" I said, my voice wobbly. "This carpet had to be newer in 1912 but it wasn't nearly this threadbare during Daphne and Hank's time."

Cold shivers ran down my neck. One of the bedroom doors was open just ahead. Late-afternoon sun spilled across the entrance in a shaft of pure gold.

A murmur came through the opening, and I finally got to my feet to tiptoe closer. An elderly woman with hair as thin as a spider's weave sat in a wheelchair facing the window. The sheer lacy drapes had been pulled open, showing off the lawns below. I could see the tops of the cypress swaying, and the murky bayou water just beyond.

A young woman knelt next to the wheelchair, and she was holding the old woman's hand. "Granny, you called me. You doing okay today? Can I get you something?"

"I'm perfectly fine, Kat. Quit fussing over me. 'Course, one never knows when an old woman like me is going to suddenly flee this earth. I might not wake up tomorrow, and that is why I need to give you something now. Before the wedding. It belonged to your mamma before she died, and I gave it to her on her wedding day as a family keepsake. Your mother was wonderful and beautiful and so talented. She — she never got to raise you, but I know she'd want you to have it." The elderly woman's voice broke.

"Dearest Granny, you've been like a mother to me. The best mother."

"You turning out so fine is all due to your daddy. I haven't been much use in this wheelchair."

"That's not true!"

"Pshaw," the old woman said, but she quickly grew more serious. "We've only managed to keep body and soul together due to Hank's hard work and tireless spirit. But that's neither here nor there. So here she is. I've been saving her for you all these years."

My eyes bugged out when the old woman placed Anna Marie, the beautiful porcelain doll, in the young woman's arms. The young woman named Kat. My own grandmother. I shook my head, trying to keep it all straight. Because I'd been time slipping all over the place. My grandmother wasn't a thirty-five-year-old mother grieving over her drowned daughter Gwen any longer. She was young, probably not much more than twenty, with bright eyes. She was wearing a cute green sundress that showed off her slim, suntanned arms. A diamond ring sparkled on her left hand.

"No more talk of leaving this world, Granny!" Kat chided, rising on her knees to kiss her grandmother's wrinkled cheek.

"I don't plan on it, darling girl. I'm going to see you safely married to that nice beau of yours."

"And I can't take your beautiful doll, either. You keep her — or give her to someone else in the family who can show her off. Where will I put her while Preston is finishing up college and we're living in a tiny apartment?"

"Well, who else am I going to give it to, unless my own granddaughter! I gave her to Daphne — your mother — on her wedding day, but she ended up back in my doll collection when she died. I need to give her to you before you take off and get married. To make sure Anna Marie stays in the family."

I tried to figure out what year it was. Miss Anna had to be at least eighty years old. I couldn't remember when my Grandma Kat was born.

Kat gave a warm laugh that filled the room. I recognized her laugh. The laugh of my very own grandmother. It hadn't changed since she was young. "Didn't your Uncle Edgar the adventurer bring you this doll from Africa or China or somewhere?"

"It was the Caribbean, actually, although Uncle Edgar traveled all over the world. He said she came from the Island of the Dolls."

"Sounds spooky," Kat said with a smile in her voice.

I could see her stroking the doll's silky hair and examining the beautiful clothing. She was perfect, in as fine a condition as when she was brand-new. But I also noticed that Miss Anna didn't answer Kat's question about the doll being a gift from Uncle Edgar. I knew why, and the knowledge gave me the creeps.

"She's beautiful, Grandmother. I'll treasure her always and pass her on to my daughter."

"I took care of her," Miss Anna said defensively. "Better than anybody else would."

Kat tilted her head. "That's a funny thing to say."

Miss Anna's gnarled fingers shook as she waved away her granddaughter's comment. "Never mind me. I'm just an old woman. I'm also bequeathing this house to you, my girl. Even though we had bad times and had to sell off most of the acreage, we managed to keep the house. Run-down as it is now." I wished I could see her face. It was hard to see the girl in black ringlets and a pinafore, digging up holes with Mister Lance, in this old woman now.

"You've sure had your share of hard times, Granny," Kat said quietly.

The elderly woman gave a snort. "My family was the most wealthy and respected family in St. Martinville Parish before the war and after the war. And I've spent most of my life watching it all disappear."

Gently, Kat reached out to stroke the arthritic, brown-spotted fingers gripping the rails of the wheelchair. "Tell me more, Grandmother."

Miss Anna cleared her throat. "I was the belle of the parish back in the days before the First World War. Married Charles Prevost, the most handsome man around. He fought in the trenches, worked so hard keeping this plantation going, then died early of a heart attack. Been gone for thirty years. After I lost Daphne, your daddy and I barely hung on to this place. Now the younger generation is moving away. Tearing down all the older homes. Don't care about history or family."

"Don't worry, Grandmother, I care. Very much. This house, the island, will always remain in the family, I promise."

"Just want to see you happily married now," Miss Anna said in a trembling voice. "And raise a family right here. I only hope I'll stick around long enough to hold your babies one day."

"You will, you will," Kat assured her, lifting her eyes. "Oh, my goodness! Who are *you*?"

I jumped when I realized that my Grandma Kat was staring directly at me through the doorway. My heart gave a distinct thud, loud as thunder in my ears. The next second, I dashed down the main staircase.

I ran and ran and ran, trying to get away, but for some queer reason I couldn't seem to leave the house. Racing into room after room, I doubled back when I heard Kat's footsteps behind me.

The front door knobs wouldn't turn, either, no matter how hard I twisted them. Next I ran to the back kitchen door, but I couldn't budge the dead bolt locked in place. Retracing my footsteps, I ran back down the hall, darting underneath the staircase into a closet filled with coats and umbrellas and hatboxes and the strong smell of mothballs. I closed the door and gripped the handle, positive Kat was going to haul me out any second.

Several long moments passed and nothing happened. Did I dare come out? Would Kat and the police be standing outside the closet waiting for me? What if I ended up in jail? I shuddered, holding in the tears and stroking the tender scar on my face, wishing the bizarre time slipping would stop.

Leaning against a rack of heavy winter coats, I closed my eyes. When I got home I was going to sleep for a week. My eyes flew open with a sudden realization. I'd touched all the doors in the house *and* the doorknobs over and over again, and yet I hadn't been ripped away. I hadn't fallen through the ceiling or floors into a new time period. Maybe I was really stuck this time!

Hours passed, but I didn't dare move. The light changed, too, the sliver of yellow growing darker under the door. Finally, I turned the knob and cracked the door an inch, hoping to feel the familiar jolt of time rushing past my ears, but nothing happened.

I said a quick prayer that once I crossed the closet threshold I'd be in the moldy, deserted house of my own time period once more. Tentatively, I pushed the door open a few more inches. It was early evening and the sun was setting. If I could escape the house and get back to the bayou, it would be the right time for the fireflies and then I could get out of here for good!

Relieved, I stepped through the door — and heard music. Wedding music.

I bit back a wave of emotion. The house appeared exactly the same as when I eavesdropped on Grandma Kat and the elderly Anna Normand Prevost. I hadn't gone anywhere. Or had I?

White wedding bells hung along the banister. The smell of rich food, lots of it, came from the direction of the kitchen. I heard the distinct notes of the Wedding March.

Kat, radiant in an ivory satin wedding dress, walked sedately down the main staircase, her hand clutched around an older man's arm. The man was her father, Hank, wearing a dark blue suit and smiling down at his daughter. It occurred to me that he was my great-grandfather.

A distant clamor came from the rear kitchen, but the music, the big rolling chords and melody of the Wedding March, drowned it out. The large front parlor was filled with guests, women dressed in summer frocks, the men in white shirts and ties and shiny black shoes.

Peering from under the staircase, I saw that Miss Anna was sitting in her wheelchair at the top of the stairs to observe the ceremony. She had a corsage pinned to her dress, pearl earrings dangling from her earlobes, and the thin strands of snowy white hair piled on top of her head.

I watched my Grandma Kat as a young woman smiling at a young man decked out in a fancy black wedding suit, a boutonniere in his lapel, standing next to a minister.

The young man winked at his bride, and a strange surge of wonder and happiness filled me. A flower girl tossed pink and yellow rose petals from a basket as Kat reached out to take her future husband's hand. Two gold rings sat on a red pillow waiting for the right moment.

While I listened to the minister's words as he married my grandparents, I wondered what I was doing here. Was I dreaming while I slept in the hall closet? And yet I could smell the heady scent of the flowers, the wedding food being prepared. My nose wrinkled. Something was burning in the kitchen. One of the caterers had likely spilled sauce on the stove's burner.

The minister pronounced Katherine Moret and Preston DuMonde husband and wife. The new bride and groom stepped toward each other, closed their eyes, and kissed. Seeing them made me squirm, but a peculiar lump formed in my throat.

When they finished kissing and opened their eyes, there was laughter on their lips. Happiness in their eyes.

My eyes burned again, but not from tears. Tendrils of smoke floated down the hall. Cooking oil was obviously burning. The reception menu must have contained *pain perdu*, and the chefs were frying bucket loads of dough.

My stomach growled as I leaned dreamily against the corner wall. I didn't know weddings could be so romantic and such fun. The next instant, a boy burst through the swinging doors of the kitchen and raced past the staircase. He nearly knocked me over as I crouched by the doorway for one final glimpse. It was time to find the fireflies. I'd stayed much too long. I'd get caught for sure as soon as the wedding music started up again and my grandparents walked down the aisle toward the doors.

But the boy's eyeballs were white, his face pale as a sheet as he raced into the main room. Gasping, he yelled, "Fire! Fire!"

In slow motion the room turned to stare at him. Disbelief registered on everyone's face. "Is this a joke?" someone murmured.

Preston DuMonde, my grandfather, pulled my grandmother Kat close and whispered in her ear. She smiled up at him, happiness written deep into her eyes. Their joy turned to shock as smoke began to pour down the hallway and seep into the parlor.

The wedding guests rose from their chairs as reality sank in. More shouting came from the kitchen. "Fire! Fire! Evacuate!" Behind me, there was the sound of pounding feet, doors opening and slamming.

"This way!" someone called as the foyer and great room filled with black smoke.

"No, out these doors!" another voice screamed.

Confusion ensued as wedding guests scrambled in several directions at once, pushing through the French parlor doors to the outside lawns. I flew behind a large potted fern, not wanting anyone to touch me, to see me. Why didn't I leave hours ago?

Seconds later, the rooms of the house turned dark and acrid. A burning sensation scraped at my nose and eyes and throat. Which meant I wasn't a ghost. I was really here, in the flesh.

People began to shout and scream as they ran, falling over chairs and rugs. Flower stands toppled, spilling dirt, scattering rose petals and chrysanthemums. Wedding bells tore off the banister railings as people shoved and jostled to flee the house.

The smoke grew thicker, and I couldn't see clearly any longer, so I dropped to the floor and started crawling. I worried that if someone touched me I'd be zapped to a different time period all over again. I was so *done* with all the bizarre time slipping. I wanted to go home now. More than I ever had before in my life.

My blood turned cold. Maybe I was supposed to save my grandmother? But that couldn't be right. She had survived the fire. She was still alive in the future. My future.

Still crawling on my hands and knees, I finally saw the front doors open and a dab of blue sky up ahead. Smoke roared out of the open doors as it sucked up oxygen. I heard the crackle of flames right behind me. The hallway was engulfed.

The fire department in Bayou Bridge was on Main Street far across the river. Were there fireboats and enough hose to reach the plantation house on the island? The house was more than a hundred years old, a pile of dry timber.

My grandmother's wedding day was ruined. She'd never mentioned that before. Then it occurred to me that she had never shown me a single wedding picture.

Wedding guests poured out the front door, stumbling, coughing, crying, and yelling. I kept crawling toward the door myself as black ash rained down. I was just about to reach the doorway when I heard Kat let out a scream.

"Grandmother!" she yelled. "My grandmother! She's upstairs on the landing! We need to get her!" The scene was so chaotic and confusing, nobody seemed to hear her, and nobody stopped to help.

I stumbled over a person lying in the hall. "Help me," the woman whispered in her pink suit and pearls. "I'm pretty sure I've broken my ankle and I can't walk."

"I'll help you," I told her, even though I was terrified to touch her. I didn't want to accidentally hurt her or take her through a time warp. As I reached out to push her across the slick floor toward safety, Preston DuMonde, my grandfather, scooped the woman up in his arms and carried her out to the front porch. As he heaved himself outside, he yelled, "Kat! Follow me! The door's right here!"

Horrified, I watched my grandmother ignore him. Instead, she clawed her way through the ash-drowned wedding guests and piles of wedding debris in the haze of smoke, heading in the opposite direction. My grandmother crouched on the first step of the wide staircase, holding an arm across her face against the billowing smoke. Orange flames licked the wooden banister. Ugly tendrils of fire reached for Kat's arms and legs as she crawled one step at a time upstairs to where the smoke was climbing, black and thick and blazing hot.

I staggered upward, staring through the banister railings. At the top of the stairs, Miss Anna sat slumped in her wheelchair. Was she already dead? It was crazy and stupid, but I couldn't stand by as they both burned to death. Leaping around a burning flower stand, I seized the banister to haul myself up.

The world turned black as I dropped through the floor, tumbling through time. My arms flailed like pinwheels. I wasn't going to survive the fall this time. It was going to kill me, knock me out forever. Tears seared my face as I screamed my head off, tumbling head over heels as I seemed to fall forever.

The descent to the bottom of the time chasm was slow and terrible. What if I never stopped? I screamed one last time for the only person who could help me. If I survived, I had to call my grandmother Kat in Baton Rouge.

She was the only person who could help me figure this out.

CHAPTER SEVENTEEN

After I slammed into the floor, my right hip hurt like crazy, as well as my ribs and elbows. I was going to be black and blue tomorrow, but I didn't think anything was broken. I squinted, bracing myself for blindness, but the world was still — the house utterly quiet.

The threadbare carpets were gone. The wedding bells had vanished, along with the old crystal chandelier that hung from the parlor ceiling with its pretty molded medallion.

The smoke was gone, too, as well as the black ash and hysterical wedding guests.

I was pretty sure this was what it felt like to be thrown from a roller coaster and dumped onto the asphalt at a state fair.

But I was alive. I hadn't burned to death. Wiping my hand across my nose, I swallowed and tasted smoke. Even though I'd time slipped again, I'd carried some of the past with me.

Rolling over onto my stomach, I jerked up into a sitting position. "Eww!"

Not only were the carpets gone, but there was no carpet at all. Just raw concrete. The floor was filthy. Dirt and dead bugs. Mildew grew in the corners of the empty living room — or what used to be the pretty parlor.

I narrowed my eyes. The staircase was in the wrong spot, and the main room was smaller. Light came through a doorway with rusty hinges, the door itself long gone.

A smaller room lay beyond. A window so dusty it let in little light. Empty spaces where the refrigerator and stove used to be. Gritty, peeling linoleum flooring. Black grease on the wall and a broken bulb hanging from a dirty yellowing ceiling.

Through a window, I spotted cypress trees beyond the overgrown, bramble-choked yard. Slowly, I trudged upstairs, passing bedrooms and a hall bathroom. It was the old plantation house, but different. Smaller, and now abandoned.

"Nobody's lived here for a long time." My voice echoed in the empty rooms.

I shook my head and tried to piece together the history of the house and my family. Time periods of this very house. Well, not this *exact* house, but the house that used to stand here. The plantation house *before the fire.* "This is the house that was rebuilt *after* the fire," I said out loud. "The house my mamma grew up in. The one Grandma Kat and my grandfather abandoned when they moved away after Gwen drowned."

I rubbed at my hot, scratchy eyes, and then raced downstairs and out the front door.

A setting sun burned red along the bayou. Fresh air never tasted so good on my raw throat. I brushed off the grit and cobwebs on my shorts and shirt, staring at the rickety front porch, the dormer windows, and the broken weathervane stuck in the middle of the roof.

The biggest question I still had was about Miss Anna. I'd seen her at twelve years old just like me in 1912. I'd seen a proper gray-haired woman holding a newborn baby while her daughter lay lifeless on the bed. And, finally, I'd seen an old woman in a wheelchair, stricken and crippled. She'd survived the death of her daughter and the death of her husband.

But had Miss Anna Normand Prevost survived the fire?

My sandals crunched along the dirt path as I peeked behind me every few steps. I wanted to see the beautiful, manicured plantation house of a hundred years ago. The trimmed lawns and rose garden, the stone paths and wraparound porch with rocking chairs and potted ferns. I wanted to see Mister Lance digging holes while Miss Anna gave him bossy directions. I wanted to see T-Paul's happy grin, and the ladies' early-century garden-party hats, gloves pulled up their slender arms.

Where had they all gone? Well, that was a silly question! They were all dead and buried. But where? Did they ever find the buried silver from the Civil War? Did Uncle Edgar ever marry Miss Sally? What sort of life did T-Paul have — or Dulcie and Miz Beatrice?

I wondered if my mamma would tell me. She didn't like talking about many things these days, especially not Bayou Bridge.

Dusk was settling and I tried to walk faster. Relief flooded my chest when I saw the lightning bugs dancing along the cattails. I swore they recognized me when they circled me inside their light.

Basking in the warm glow, I stepped across the planks.

I'd visited 1912 several times. Then again sometime

at the end of World War II when Daphne died during childbirth. Then I'd shot ahead to Gwen's wake, more than twenty years ago. Finally, I'd seen the early 1970s, when my grandmother got married.

I was halfway across the bridge, right in the middle of the river — when the fireflies abruptly disappeared — and I crashed into time once more. The strong wooden planks vanished beneath my feet, and I plunged past quivery pilings, shooting deep into the murky water. I screamed and my mouth filled with water. Instantly, I was choking, drowning. Water burned my lungs so bad I thought I'd throw up. A moment later, I *was* throwing up, retching my guts up, spinning and whirling in the thick, soupy, dark river.

I couldn't see a thing. Was I upside down? Where was the sky? Where were the trees?

I was gonna die all over again.

Some part of my brain was still working because the idea came to me that I needed to stop thrashing around. I tried not to panic but tilted my head back, hoping I could see the surface. My hair floated around me in slow motion. The bayou water was dark and sinister, but I could see a pale moon rising above a watery tree line. I tried to swim, pulling my arms to rise to the surface, but they were so heavy.

Like hundred-pound weights had been strapped to me. A monster trying to pull me to the bottom.

The water was cold, and I had no air left. Dropping like a rock hadn't given me a chance to catch any extra breath.

Behind my eyes, pain flashed like a knife slicing into my head.

Then something touched me, pulled at my hands, gripped and tugged at my arms. I panicked, a scream rising in my throat. There were monsters in the bayou! An alligator! I was dead for sure. Why was I so stupid to tempt fate?

All of a sudden, the monster pulling at me became human arms. Strong pale hands tugging and yanking and lifting. I swore my own arms were about to snap right out of the socket. Moments later, I was plunked down on the edge of the broken bridge. Water poured off me in puddles.

My lungs screamed in pain. My head hurt like I'd been pulverized in a grinder. My face throbbed and burned. Blood dripped down my shirt, and that's when I think I fainted.

Next thing I knew I was lying on some kind of bed, my clothes still drenched. Sirens wailed all around me, but there was so much water sloshing inside my skull I couldn't hear proper.

A woman's voice came out of the shadows. "Lie still, honey; we're going to get you to the hospital and patch you right up."

"Who're you?" I croaked.

"You're in an ambulance," she told me as she patted my hand. "I'm one of the paramedics and you're safe. Just close your eyes. I put some drops in your eyes so you don't get infection from the water. That's why you can't see too good. Try to relax; you're going to be just fine once we clean you up."

I tried to nod, but my head felt so heavy. Next came a pinch in my arm. "Ouch," I gasped, but the word came out funny, like I was talking from a mile away.

"That shot will help you relax, Larissa. Take some of the pain away, too. We're on the phone with the doctors at the hospital in St. Martinville." The woman leaned close. "You're a real trouper, and you're going to be fine."

I shook my head. I wanted my daddy. I wanted my mamma, but I couldn't get my lips to form the words.

The sirens kept going and rustling noises came from the paramedics as they moved around the ambulance.

Whispers came from the corner. "She's going to be scarred, you know."

"Yeah. Poor little thing. It's deep."

"She's lucky she's alive."

No! I wanted to scream. I knew I wasn't lucky at all.

The medicine made me feel like I was whirling on the ambulance cot. Why couldn't the fireflies have taken me back to the time before we moved to Bayou Bridge? If we'd stayed in Baton Rouge, this would never have happened. Instead I was reliving my own accident. But what did this have to do with Miss Anna and Grandma Kat?

"Not lucky," I finally croaked. My lips felt fat. I swear my body was sitting in molasses.

"You got yourself a good friend, *shar.*"

I shook my head. I didn't have any friends. All the kids at school were my enemies, and they always would be. Mamma said so.

"Don't shake your head at me!" the paramedic woman teased. "You surely do have a guardian angel. She called 911, and lucky for us we were right around the corner. She practically pulled you out of the water herself. And almost fell in trying to hang on to you before you sank to the bottom."

She had it all wrong. Nobody had helped me. It was the paramedics who saved my life, who'd dragged on my arms and wrenched me out of that miserable bayou.

The woman kept talking in a cheerful voice. "I'll

bet Alyson is your best friend. The other kids scattered, but she stayed with you and made the phone call. That's right, isn't it, Eric?"

"Yes, ma'am!" came a male voice in the direction of my feet.

"Yes, indeed. At least I think her name is Alyson. Got it here in my report. Said she's the sheriff's daughter. Probably knows a thing about first aid."

I kept shaking my head. Hadn't Alyson been the one to help *push* me off the bridge?

Alyson Granger had saved my life?

That was impossible.

But the paramedic woman said it was in the record.

Next thing I knew I was opening my eyes again and staring up at a thousand lightning bugs whirling in the air like a beautiful cloud of gold.

I sat up with a start, sucking in air. My throat felt fine. My eyes worked. I wasn't soaked through anymore, either. No blood, no headache. I was lying safely near the elephant ears, right by the town road. I was back in my own time.

Across the water, waves slapped against the broken pilings.

Feeling wobbly, I crawled down the rickety steps and fell face-first in the mud. I wanted to kiss the dirt.

I was alive. I hadn't drowned.

I lifted my hand and touched the scar on my face. It was still there. A ridge of white below my eye and nearly down to my chin. From a year ago. I'd slipped through time again.

What was happening to me?

CHAPTER EIGHTEEN

Streetlights flicked on one by one along Main Street as I ran home.

I pounded up the porch steps and burst through the screen door. "I gotta talk to Grandma Kat," I muttered, slamming the door behind me. Heck, she used to *live* on that island once. In the very house that was now rotting and smelly.

Somebody had to know what was going on, and the only person was my grandmother.

"Hey, Daddy? Mamma? Where are you?" I raced into the kitchen, but the place was empty. Nothing but a pile of dishes in the sink from lunch.

I pounded up the stairs and it was the same. Nobody around at all. An odd feeling punched me in the gut. Then the telephone rang.

I about jumped out of my skin, but it wasn't one of the antique phones along the back wall or the girl with the voice. It was the telephone in the kitchen. I breathed a sigh of relief and jumped downstairs two steps at a time so I could catch it before it stopped.

"Larissa, that you?" It was my daddy.

"Where are you?" I blurted out.

"Mamma should be there. She left the restaurant early — said she wanted to come home."

"No, she's not. Front door was unlocked, but no lights on. Mamma ain't here."

"You sure? She said she needed to come home and lie down."

"Nope. No one's here. Lights are off."

"Well, check upstairs. Help her out and I'll be home in a bit."

"Where you at?"

"Decided to make a quick trip to New Iberia to pick up some furniture I got at an estate sale last week."

"Hey —" I stopped, trying to figure out how to say my question.

"What?"

"Well, you know that house across the bayou? The one that's on that island?"

"Yeah," he said slowly. "That's where you got hurt

so bad, *shar*. I try *not* to think about it. Promise me you'll never go out there again."

I bit at my lips and didn't say anything. I couldn't make a promise like that. I'd been going almost every day for a week. "Um, wasn't there another house — like a big plantation-mansion sort of house long ago?"

"I believe I've heard something like that."

"I was wondering if we have any of the antique furniture from it. Stuff passed down, I mean. In the store or the storage shed. Something like that," I added casually.

"Don't think so, honey. You may not know this, but that original big house was destroyed in a fire a long time ago. So was everything in it."

"Everything?"

"Yep, think so. Really sad. Especially when we're in the antique business."

"Why *are* we in the antique business?" I asked him.

Daddy cleared his throat, and I could tell he wanted to stop talking. "Larissa, I gotta get on the road so I make it home before midnight. That's a good question for your mamma."

"All right," I said, feeling grumpy. "But you know Mamma doesn't talk much these days. She always acts like she's got chiggers biting her toes."

He laughed. "Well, help her out anyway, Larissa. Fix yourself some dinner, then get in your PJs, and I'll be home to tuck you in bed."

Before I could say another word, he hung up. I frowned and put the phone down with a bang. I felt mad all of a sudden, and my stomach was growling bad.

Before I went back upstairs to find Mamma — probably in the tub with the bathroom door closed and the radio on — I locked the front door. Then I turned on every single light in the house. The place was blazing by the time I got to my own bedroom. I'd probably get in trouble for wasting electricity, but Mamma never came out of the bath. The longer she took, the madder I got. Like she didn't care that I was home. I almost got stuck on the island all night long and nobody was even around to know or care. I was mad Daddy wasn't home. Mad that I was being ignored.

I had practically *died* today. What if I got stuck in the past? What if I never could get back? Sometimes I wondered if my parents would even miss me.

My throat still hurt from the smoke of the fire. I started coughing. Alarmed, I hurried to the bathroom, got a glass of water, and downed it, staring at myself in the mirror. My hair was a mess, my skin white as a ghost. I pulled up my sleeve and saw an ugly bruise on my elbow where I'd landed in the upstairs hall. The smoke inhalation, the bruises. I was really there, not just watching through a veil of time, but *really*, truly there.

Leaning forward, I ran a finger along the white scar, noticing black circles under my eyes. Soon as I touched it, the ridge of skin began to itch, so I rubbed at it. I didn't feel like fixing no food or talking to Mamma, but I figured I should tell her I was home. 'Course, usually she was screaming at me if I was late. And here it was, dark as pitch outside.

Finally, I flushed the toilet and switched off the bathroom light. "Mamma, I'm home," I said, pushing at the master bedroom door. "Been home for a while, so don't ground me. You feeling okay?" The last words gurgled in my throat. The master bedroom was dark, too. I flipped the switch on the wall.

Mamma wasn't lying on the bed at all. She wasn't sitting at her desk, either.

The bathroom was empty. Tub dry as a bone.

A queer dread started in the pit of my gut and ran straight up my throat. I raced back to the second floor of the store. "Mamma!" I called. "Mamma!" But I'd already gone through the entire house turning on lights. She wasn't anywhere.

Quickly, I unlocked the front door again and ran out onto the sidewalk. The other stores were closed, lights off for the night, except for the café way down Main. Grabbing the extra set of keys from the front desk, I locked the front door again and dashed down the sidewalk. Pushing my way into the café, I startled the hostess, a girl who looked like she was in college.

"Just looking for my mamma. You seen her?"

"You're the girl from the antique store, right?" she asked me.

I nodded, fighting the growing lump of fear in my throat.

"Haven't seen her since your family came in last week for dinner. Sorry."

I nodded again, my eyes darting around the room. It was easy to see all the tables. Verret's Café wasn't a very big place. A family sat in the corner, eating plate loads of food. Couple of teenagers wolfed down the cake-and-ice-cream Dessert Special.

Mamma couldn't go anywhere without a car, and Daddy had our only vehicle at the moment. My eyes watered as I ran back home. Once more I checked the whole house.

Mamma was definitely not here. I grabbed the phone again in the kitchen and dialed Daddy's cell number. "Daddy, I can't find her."

He sounded bewildered. "She's gotta be there. You know Mamma always curls up at night with a bowl of kettle corn and a diet soda for her television dramas."

"I checked everywhere. Twice. Even went down to Verret's Café. Every place else is closed up. It's dark, Daddy. And it's getting late."

"Hmm, what time is it?" he murmured as I checked the kitchen clock on the stove.

"Almost nine thirty," I whispered.

"Maybe she went to visit someone and forgot to leave a note. I'll get home fast as I can, but I bet she'll turn up. Just sit tight, and don't worry, Larissa."

"Okay," I said as we hung up for the second time in an hour.

But I knew something was wrong. Felt it deep inside my stomach all the way down to my toes. "Mamma, where are you?" I said into the silence. The house — the store — was so quiet.

A new idea popped into my head and I rushed back upstairs, searching her closet and the dresser. Mamma's house and car keys were sitting there on her key ring. So was her purse. She wouldn't go anywhere without those two items. Even if she went for a walk she always took them. If they were still here was that a good sign or a bad sign?

I opened the back door and went into the yard, but it was empty, too. Just weeds, no porch or chairs for sitting. The telephone pole was like a giant hovering in the darkness outside the fence line. I shivered and ran back inside, locking up again.

"Mamma left without locking the front door," I reminded myself. That unnerved me. My mamma *never* did that.

A pounding started behind my eyes, and Daddy wouldn't be home for a while.

I paced the floor, circling the furniture. I didn't want to do the nightly round of locking up and putting things away like I always did. Having all the lights on was a comfort, although small.

Prickles of cold kept running up and down my arms and back.

Finally, I forced myself to close up the two rolltop desks. Straightened a shelf of books. Picked up a pile of spilled old *Life* magazines.

"Where are you, Mamma?" I asked into the silence.

When I reached the doll case I crouched down, gripping my knees to stop them from trembling. "Oh!" I sucked in my breath. The lock to the case was undone, the sliding glass door ajar.

Horror filled me. *The porcelain doll, Anna Marie, was*

gone. Her usual spot on the shelf was bare. Crawling over, I pulled open the glass door and searched just to be sure I wasn't seeing things. The doll hadn't fallen down onto the lower ledge. She hadn't been taken out and placed somewhere else. I'd have seen her as I searched for Mamma the last hour.

I sat back on my heels, trying to figure it out.

The doll had disappeared.

Just like Mamma.

CHAPTER NINETEEN

Three seconds later, the telephone began to ring.

My knees were wobbling as I zeroed in on an ugly green phone from the 1950s that probably weighed twenty pounds. I snatched it up, my hands sweaty.

"Larissa, that you?"

It was her, of course. "Yeah, I'm here. What do you want?" All at once I got plain, spittin' mad. This girl was so mysterious all the time. "Tell me what's going on or don't ever call me again," I told her fiercely.

"You sound upset. What's happened? Did — did — your mamma disappear?"

"How do you know that?" I yelled into the receiver. "Where is she? Tell me right now!"

"I'm sorry, but I can't. There are funny rules about this calling business."

"It's all some big joke to you, isn't it?"

"No, no, I promise!" She sounded frantic. "Whatever you do, don't hang up on me!"

I whirled around and a receiver fell off one of the stick phones, dangling on its frayed cord. I slammed it back in place. "Give me one good reason and maybe I'll think about it."

"I could give you a whole bunch of reasons, but I can't. Every time I tell you too much, the connection cuts out." She paused to let that sink in.

"Is that why every time you start giving me information I need — you suddenly disappear?"

"Exactly. If I say too much, it might affect history. If something different happened than what was supposed to, it could be terrible. I can only give you hints. You've got to have faith in yourself. The more you believe in something, the better chance you have it will come true."

"I guess that does make sense," I said slowly.

"Right now you gotta think hard," she went on. "You have all the answers, you just don't know it. And you need the doll most of all. It's got the last clue."

I shook my head. "Nope. The doll doesn't have any clue. I've seen that doll my whole life and it doesn't have anything on it."

The girl lowered her voice. "It's not where you *can* see it."

"For your information, the doll is gone, too. How can I find it if somebody came into the store and stole her?" The front doors were unlocked when I got home, and neither of my parents had been here. The doll was rare and in almost perfect condition, except for the tiny chip on her chin. She was valuable, especially to a doll collector. Mamma had drilled that into me for years.

A lightbulb came on in my head. "The doll is *with* Mamma, isn't it? She's the one who took it from the case! But wait. That still doesn't make sense. My mother isn't a person who just takes off without a note or a phone call — or her purse. Especially at night. With a baby coming."

The baby. Maybe Mamma had gone to the hospital.

I dropped the telephone and ran to find the calendar Mamma kept on her bureau. I flipped the months backward and forward, counting the weeks she'd already crossed off. "The baby isn't supposed to get here for five more weeks."

Early babies weren't good. That had happened way too many times in our family already. This baby had to make it. She had to!

"Oh, golly, the telephone!" I raced back and

shoved the receiver to my ear. "Hello, hello, you still there?"

The line was dead.

"Dang it!" I yelled. Now I wouldn't learn what she meant by the doll and the clue. Maybe she'd said too much already. The last thing she'd said was, "The clue is not where you *can* see it." Our connection had probably been cut at that moment, and I hadn't realized it when I ran off to find Mamma's calendar.

I stared at the rows of phones. The fact that the girl could call me at all was nothing short of a miracle. I was beginning to understand that she only had a limited amount of time and never wasted it by giving me details I could figure out on my own.

Bounding downstairs, I grabbed the phone book to find the number to the hospital in St. Martinville to see if Maddie Renaud had checked herself in. She hadn't. Then I called the hospital in New Iberia. She wasn't there, either.

So if Mamma wasn't at the hospital having the baby, where was she?

Finally, I grabbed the kitchen phone and punched in Mamma's cell phone number. I couldn't believe I'd forgotten to do that the very first thing.

As I held the phone to my ear and listened to it ring, I slowly walked back upstairs. When I stood at the master bedroom door, a faint ringing was coming from Mamma's purse.

A wedge of emotion lodged in my throat. Mamma's cell phone was sitting inside the pocket of her purse, merrily ringing away. Mamma had left the house, but she hadn't gone willingly. I looked up the phone number for the sheriff's office and started dialing.

CHAPTER TWENTY

Sheriff Granger and Daddy pulled up to the curb at the very same time. "We'll find Mamma, *shar,*" my father told me quietly as he hugged me hard.

Sheriff Granger asked a million questions. When was the last time we'd seen Mamma? He wanted to know where I'd been and who I'd called so far. I showed them Mamma's purse and phone still sitting on the dresser. And I told them about calling the hospitals.

Sheriff Granger called the hospitals himself just to be sure Admissions hadn't given me the runaround while Daddy called the neighbors and a few of our best customers.

I sat on the edge of a velvet settee and rubbed at

my scar while I listened to them. I didn't tell either one of them about the deserted house. Or the fireflies. Or the girl calling on the antique telephone. They wouldn't believe me anyway. They'd think I'd gone off the deep end.

Maybe I *was* losing my mind. Maybe something was wrong with me, even more than a horrible scar. I got up to get a tissue for my watering eyes when the front doorbell jangled.

Alyson Granger and her mamma came through, their arms laden with a casserole and rolls and a chocolate pound cake. Mrs. Granger said, "Larissa, child, show me where your kitchen is. These things are hot."

"Well, the pound cake isn't," Alyson added.

I was so shocked I didn't say a word. Just pointed, and then followed them past the front desk. Mrs. Granger set the covered dish on the stove and the basket of rolls on the counter. Alyson put the cake on the table, moving the bowl of apples that always sat there.

"Now, I know this is nothing fancy," Mrs. Granger said. "But I had a sneaking suspicion you and your daddy probably haven't eaten any supper. So I brought over part of our supper. And we hadn't yet cut the cake."

"You didn't have to bring over your own meal," I whispered.

Mrs. Granger tsked her tongue. "My husband said your daddy barely got home from traveling tonight, and you've been alone for hours. Least we can do. It was actually Alyson's idea." She smiled at her daughter, and I felt my face turn red. Alyson was staring at our collection of refrigerator magnets like they were the most interesting thing she'd seen in a year.

"I know you're frantic over your mamma, Larissa." Mrs. Granger put her arm around my shoulder. "But we'll find her."

I nodded without speaking. That's what everybody said, soon as they saw me. Like I wouldn't believe it unless they told me. But how did they *really* know? Mamma could be anywhere. Hurt, kidnapped. Maybe she even ran away. I knew she had been so unhappy the last year. She'd hate knowing Mrs. Granger was in her kitchen. With my archenemy, Alyson.

At least, I'd always thought she was my biggest enemy. I glanced at her out of the corner of my eye. Once more I could hear the paramedic's voice telling me Alyson Granger had tried to pull me out of the bayou and called 911.

"I feel a little sick to my stomach," I said softly.

"Don't know if I can eat any supper. But, thank you, Mrs. Granger. Sure appreciate your thoughtfulness."

She briskly picked up her pot holders. "That's what friends are for. Let's just put it all in the fridge for your dinner tomorrow. It'll keep just fine."

Friends? Were she and my mamma friends? I never thought so. But folks didn't bring dinner over at ten o'clock at night and hug you tight if they weren't trying to be your friend.

I could smell the scent of yeast dough and laundry soap on Mrs. Granger's skin when she hugged me, and found it strangely soothing. "Let's go see what the sheriff's found out," she said, slipping her arm through mine and taking Alyson's arm with her other hand.

After she gave her husband a few suggestions of names to call, the clocks in the store began to chime eleven. Mrs. Granger made hot coffee for my daddy. His eyes were bloodshot, and he kept running a hand through his ragged hair as he got up and down off a chair between telephone calls. He hadn't shaved this morning, either, and he looked scruffy after the long day and a night on the road.

After that, Mrs. Granger made hot chocolate with marshmallows for me and Alyson even though it was summertime. She said it was "a comfort drink."

After two or three sips, mine turned cold on a table doily. Alyson drank hers down, then walked around the store, taking in the tea sets and jewelry boxes and crates of old magazines.

I watched her like a hawk stares at a mouse. Not because I thought she'd steal something, but because it was so strange to see Alyson Granger in our antique store.

She caught me staring. "Someday I want to decorate my house in antiques. I love these small blue plates with the edge of ivy and flowers. Do you know where they're from?"

"They came from an estate sale in New Orleans a few months ago," I told her. "They're early-century Wedgwood from England."

I kept gawking as she examined a set of china dancing girls next, trying to remember details from that terrible night a year ago. My memory swam with a hundred voices and images, but I didn't remember Alyson hanging on to me along the pilings.

I'd lived the horrible experience all over again when I'd time slipped, but for the first time I finally remembered the woman in the ambulance holding bandages to my face as she talked about my accident.

I didn't want to be grateful to Alyson. I'd spent a year hating her. I didn't want to consider that I'd been wrong or look at her in a whole new way. I rubbed at the scar as my eyes burned. Maybe I was the person who had misjudged and hated unfairly.

Alyson perched on the edge of the sofa nervously. "I'm real sorry," she said softly. "I hope they find your mamma."

A jumble of thoughts and words were stuck in my throat like glue. "Thanks," I finally muttered, noticing that she didn't try to reassure me that Mamma would come home like all the grown-ups did.

"Um," Alyson said, shifting uneasily. "Make sure you reheat the casserole at three hundred and fifty degrees."

It seemed such a silly, meaningless thing to say I almost giggled. I thought I was the only one who said things like that. I raised my face, gulping down my shyness. "Did you really do those things that day?"

Alyson lifted her eyebrows. "What day are you talking about?"

"The day I got this," I answered, pointing to the jagged white line across my cheek. I brushed the hair off my face and felt myself get braver. "The scar from the bridge."

Her face fell. "That's why you hate me, isn't it? I tried a hundred times to say I was sorry, but . . ." Her voice trailed off. "I felt awful you ended up falling into the water. We never meant that to happen. We really didn't. I know that's hard to believe, but it is the truth. I *am* sorry, Larissa. Every time I see you I want to talk to you. Like the other day when I got you from the island in my brother's boat — but everything I wanted to say sounded stupid in my head. And, well, I guess I'm a year too late."

"It's never too late," I heard myself say, and all at once I realized it was true. If Alyson had never meant to hurt me — and that day truly was an accident — maybe I had to rethink all my hateful feelings. Maybe it wasn't too late to forgive, either. Alyson brushed at her eyes, turning her head toward her father so I wouldn't see them watering. His gold sheriff's badge glinted in the glow of the Tiffany lamps as he spoke into his cell phone.

"So it was you who called 911?" I asked, not wanting to stop the conversation.

She frowned again, clearly puzzled. "Yeah, didn't you know that already?"

"Not until — not until recently."

Alyson looked surprised. " 'Course I did. Most of

the other kids got scared when you actually fell in. I was terrified you were gonna drown. Never been so scared in all my life. If you died, we'd all be killers and go to jail."

I couldn't help it. I snorted, and then laughed, remembering all the times I'd wished she and Tara would go to heck and never come back.

Alyson cracked a smile. "Tara helped me hold you to the pilings while I used her cell phone to call for an ambulance, and then she ran home. Tara — her family — well, let's just say, she's not as bad as you think."

I was so surprised at this information I didn't know how to react. Tara had tried to pull me out, too? I wasn't ready to forgive Tara Doucet, but maybe that was something I needed to think about.

"Did you see any alligators under the water? I was actually more scared of gators than of you drowning once we got you to the piling."

This whole conversation was surreal. "All I remember is the pain. Water pulling me under. My arms aching something fierce."

"For so long I wished I could go back in time and do that day all over again. I'd been here at your store, you know. With my mamma, for the first time."

"You were? I don't remember that."

"Yeah, I saw your doll collection upstairs. I wanted to hold that pretty porcelain doll. The really old one that's not for sale?"

Something started to nag at my brain, but I couldn't think what it was.

"You had it that day on the bridge," Alyson added. "Remember?"

I reared back, blinking in surprise. "I had what?"

"That beautiful doll. Tara just wanted to look at it. But you were being stingy about letting us hold it for even a minute."

I gripped the edge of the couch. "That's because I wasn't supposed to take it out of the case. My mamma would have tanned my hide and grounded me for a year. It's a family heirloom."

"That must be why your folks don't want to sell it."

Memories tugged at the edges of my mind, but just then, Sheriff Granger hung up the phone and pursed his lips, shaking his head.

"No one's seen her," Daddy said, sounding defeated.

The sheriff scratched the back of his neck. "We'll file a missing persons report, but I can't begin a search party until twenty-four hours have passed.

Since your wife is an adult she could just be off somewhere with a friend — or just went away for a while on her own. I'm sorry, Luke. We'll have to sit tight until tomorrow. But I'm betting she'll show up."

Daddy hunched his shoulders, shaking his head. "This is not like Maddie. If there'd been an accident, wouldn't we know?"

His words hung in the air. Sheriff Granger looked sorry for him and didn't speak at first.

"But she didn't take her purse," I said. "If there was an accident, nobody would know who she was."

Sheriff Granger pursed his lips again, and I knew I was right. "The hospitals say nobody fitting her description has come in tonight."

Daddy made a choking sound and got up, striding across the room and then slamming the door of the kitchen behind him.

Tears crashed down my face. My throat was so tight I couldn't breathe. Twenty-four hours might be too late. Anything could happen in twenty-four hours.

After the Grangers left, I put on my pajamas and brushed my hair. Wind blew at the trees like an invisible hand was shaking the limbs. Mamma was out there somewhere — alone.

Daddy shuffled into my bedroom. It was long after midnight, but I couldn't get my mind to stop imagining all the bad things that could happen. "Get into bed now, *shar,*" he said. After I crawled in, he pulled a blanket over my shoulders. "Sleep, Larissa. That's all you can do right now," he whispered, his voice scratchy. "Things'll look better in the morning."

After he closed the bedroom door, I stared at the shadows on my ceiling. The next instant, I sat up with a jerk. I'd forgotten to call my grandmother Kat. I wondered if Daddy had contacted her. I thought about running downstairs to ask him, but I was afraid to bother him. I was afraid to see him crying. Maybe he'd wait to see if Mamma came home on her own before worrying Grandma Kat.

Deep in my gut, I knew Mamma wasn't coming home on her own. She was gone because of the house on the island. Because of all the bad things that had happened in the past. My alarm clock ticked on my nightstand. Past one o'clock now. I balled my fists into my still-burning eyes, residue from the smoke at the Normand plantation house. I couldn't stop thinking about Miss Anna trapped in her wheelchair at the top of the stairs while flames raged around her. Daphne dying in childbirth, Gwen in her casket, me in the ambulance. They all had to be connected, but how?

When I woke a few hours later, dawn was creeping under the blinds. My body felt slow as a slug. A dream caught at the edge of my brain. Alyson and I had never finished our conversation before Mrs. Granger hustled her home. She'd told me that I'd taken the doll out of the locked glass case the day of my accident. Even though I didn't remember that part, her words had worked at my mind all night.

Pressing my eyelids, I walked through each scene from the past step by step. I replayed Gwen lying in a casket, Grandma Kat's friend Marla bringing in Anna Marie all muddy and wet from the bayou. I pictured Miss Anna giving the young, about-to-be-married Kat the doll to keep as an inheritance. Miss Anna crying when Hank handed her the doll from the mantle in Daphne's bedroom after she died.

Where was the doll during the wedding? Had Anna Marie been there or upstairs in the doll case? Squeezing my eyes tighter, I went back into my memory of hiding under the staircase during the wedding ceremony. I scanned the wedding guests all dressed up in their seats, the wedding bell decorations, heard the wedding music. Behind my eyes, I saw my grandmother and grandfather kissing and smiling at each other, heard the clapping of their friends and family. And I smelled the smoke burning in my nose all over again.

My eyes roved the scene over and over again, searching for details. There on the mantle above the fireplace — behind the minister in his black robes. Among the flowers and wedding bells, Anna Marie had been nestled prim and proper in all the wedding tulle loveliness. That exquisite doll had been smiling her secret little smile and gazing out at the world with her piercing blue eyes.

The doll had been at the scene of every single tragedy.

But did that mean anything? Sunrise lightened my bedroom, and I opened my eyes. The doll being inside the house wasn't unusual. She belonged to the family. She'd been passed down to every generation. I'd inherit her one day, too. She was just a doll. Nothing strange about that.

"You're dreaming crazy things," I told myself.

I'd time slipped through four generations since Miss Anna was a girl. Her daughter, Daphne. Her granddaughter, Kat. And her great-granddaughter Gwen. I'd even relived my own accident. Chills crept up my spine as I realized that every single generation had a terrible tragedy associated with it.

And every time a tragedy happened, the doll had been there, watching. Smiling her perfect, disturbing smile.

CHAPTER TWENTY-ONE

When I woke for the second time, it was broad daylight, and I was upside down on the bed with the blanket twisted around my toes. I ran straight into Daddy's room, but he was nowhere in sight. Just a damp towel in a heap on the bathroom floor.

When I got downstairs, he was eating grits cooked in the microwave. Blech. He looked as bad as he had the previous night with his bloodshot eyes. He was in a clean shirt, but he still hadn't shaved and looked as grubby as a ditch digger.

"We opening up the store?" I asked.

"Don't know," he said, gulping down a demitasse of coffee. "I'm going to nose around the property, inspect the sheds. Then go down Main and talk to some of the neighbors that live behind us. Someone's got to have seen her leaving."

"She didn't take anything with her," I said. "No money, no nothing."

"Which means she can't have gone far, right?" he said hopefully.

I chewed on my lips. "Did you — did you guys —"

He set his cup in the sink. Stared me straight in the eye. "Did we what? Spit it out, Larissa."

I gulped and tried to speak. "I was just wondering if you guys had another fight."

"You mean an argument between me and Mamma?" He looked pained. "Is it that bad?"

I shrugged and tried to find my cereal in the cupboard. The box was empty, but I wasn't hungry.

Daddy put his hands on my shoulders. "No, we didn't have a fight yesterday, Larissa."

I peeked up at him from under my long hair. "I'm worried about the baby."

"Me, too, honey. Me, too." He paused and held out his hands. "Come here."

I ran into his arms and felt sobs heaving in my chest. I didn't want to cry, but I couldn't help it.

"I'm so sorry," he said. "I should have had you come curl up with me last night. I'm only thinking about myself and not about how worried you must be."

"Is it okay if I call Grandma Kat?"

My daddy let out a groan. "Of course! I was going to call her last night, but it got so late I hated to wake her and have her worrying all night. Or have her driving over without any sleep. Will you talk to her while I get out and do some asking around?"

I nodded and he kissed the top of my head. "I'll be back soon. Then we'll open shop for a few hours. But I don't —" He stopped.

"What, Daddy?"

"Nothing, honey. Don't worry. We'll find her."

He'd said those reassuring words again, but what if we *didn't* find Mamma? What if she was hurt? The baby could die. She could die. Mamma had never come home last night. Which meant something terrible had happened to her. But maybe she'd left on her own. What if she'd wanted to leave us and she was gone for good? That was just as bad.

I found Grandma Kat's phone number on the pad next to the calendar and dialed. She picked up on the second ring. "Good morning, baby doll. How are you today?"

I couldn't even answer her. "Mamma's missing," I blurted out.

I heard her take a sudden breath. "What are you talking about? Where's your daddy?"

"He's out looking for her. She never came home last night. The sheriff was even here —"

"I'll be there fast as I can," she said. "And I'll pack a bag."

My grandmother lived in Baton Rouge, almost two hours away.

Glancing at the clock every two minutes, I tried to eat something, but nothing was appetizing. Leftover gumbo in the fridge had congealed grease on top. I shut the door and nibbled on a cracker.

I tried to get the store ready by going through the morning rituals, but Daddy wasn't here and everything felt wrong. Everything *was* wrong.

Next, I riffled through Mamma's purse looking for clues. I slipped my fingers around her keys, studied her driver's license, and found a few dollar bills in her wallet plus a few crumpled old receipts.

After that, I sat on the floor in front of the doll case and stared at the empty spot left by Anna Marie. I thought about the doll's icy blue eyes and how I used to get the heebie-jeebies. But a doll can't *look* at you. They're made of porcelain and cloth and plastic. They're not alive.

I couldn't get past the knowledge that the doll didn't really belong to my family. Anna Marie rightfully belonged to Dulcie. That fact made me squirm inside, like I had worms in my gut. Guilt on my shoulders. Going clear back to my great-great-grandmother Miss Anna.

I paced the floor a hundred times. Stood in front of the wall of telephones and willed the girl to call me and explain what was happening. Total silence. "Where are you?" I shouted, and then stormed into my bedroom.

Halfheartedly, I made my bed, then went to the bureau and poked through my earrings and bracelets. I picked up a necklace I didn't wear very often because I didn't want to accidentally lose it. My grandmother Kat had given it to me for my twelfth birthday a few months ago. A simple gold chain with a gold heart on it, but the chain was tarnished, the heart plain and simple. She'd said it was very old and told me to take care of it. I needed something to do while I waited, so I put the gold heart around my neck and fastened the clasp. I touched the heart while I stood before the mirror. The antique necklace made me look grown-up. Took the focus off my scar, too, which was never a bad thing.

An hour later, Grandma Kat's car screeched to a stop in front of the antique store. She barreled through the door, dropped her overnight bag, and picked me up in her arms all in one scoop. She was tall and ramrod straight with long dark hair that came out of a Clairol bottle. I wrapped my arms around her neck as her own arms held me tight and close. She was still strong enough to carry me to one of the ratty, overstuffed sofas sitting in a corner that no customer ever purchased. One of the sofas we used ourselves when we wanted to squirrel away with a book on a rainy day.

We curled up together in the corner, and Grandma Kat pulled an afghan over us, keeping us tight like a cocoon. Then she whispered in my hair and rubbed my back.

"Mamma is gonna be okay, isn't she?" I hadn't believed anyone else, but I knew if my grandmother said it was all right, it would be.

Grandma Kat pressed a hand over her heart and looked straight into my eyes with her dark green ones. "Yes, she is, Larissa, I'm feeling that right here. I think Maddie needs us to find her because something bad *could* happen. I'm not saying it will, only that I can't explain the strange feeling I'm having. Maybe I'm just superstitious, but there it is. Or maybe I'm just getting old."

"You're not old," I told her.

She gave me a lopsided grin. "Well, that's debatable."

I couldn't help staring at her, trying to see the young woman underneath the wrinkles. She'd been strong and gentle and kind then, too. She'd raced upstairs in her beautiful white wedding gown with the lace train and white tulle veil to save her grandmother despite the flames and smoke. Despite the fact that *she* could have died. And now, despite her strength and unwavering hope, I could tell she'd been crying on the drive across Highway 10. Her eyes were puffy and the lines around her mouth seemed deeper than usual.

I filled her in on Daddy and the sheriff and the missing persons report.

"Maddie disappearing like this does not fit with what I know about my daughter," my grandmother said. "She had a reason. And if we can figure out the reason, we'll know where to find her."

"That seems too easy."

"Well, it sounds easy, but figuring it out might take some time. Tell me what's been going on around here lately."

I fidgeted and chewed my lips. Should I tell her about the strange phone calls? The cloud of fireflies that helped me slip through time?

"The doll's missing," I said, blurting out the next thing that popped into my head.

Grandma Kat's eyebrows jumped. "Show me."

I grabbed her hand and we hurried upstairs to the doll collection. The empty space was still there. Part of me had been hoping I'd imagined the missing doll because I'd been so scared. Or it had been too dark to see her. I crossed my fingers that Anna Marie would be sitting in her usual spot, pretty as a picture.

But she wasn't. The only thing left was the cardboard sign saying NOT FOR SALE.

"So your mamma took the doll with her?" Grandma Kat said thoughtfully.

"That's all I can figure out. She was the only one with a key to the lock."

"I see," my grandmother said in a low voice. "There's a reason she took Anna Marie, and if we can figure out why, we'll know where your mamma is."

Grandma Kat was right, but my brain was bursting with so much the last few days, it was all a jumble. Seemed like I should know where Mamma was, but my fears had thrown a wall up, blocking me from figuring it out.

"Let's get us some tea in the kitchen, Larissa, honey."

I arranged several chocolate-chip cookies on a plate. Cookies that Grandma Kat had grabbed from her freezer and brought with her. When the teakettle began to whistle, she steeped the raspberry tea bags in our cups. I was dying to ask her a whole slew of questions about the Normand plantation house and what Miss Anna was like, although I had to pretend I didn't know her name.

After we sat down at the table, I asked, "What was it like growing up in that old house on the island? Who built it and lived there first?"

"Oh, my, you're talking ancient family history." Grandma Kat blew across her cup. "Let's see. You actually come from a family that came over straight from France with their life savings. They bought up a few hundred acres and started a sugarcane planta-tion long before the war, probably twenty years at least, in the 1840s. Sugarcane took off and made them a lot of money, and they bought many hundreds more acres. They built a big mansion house right there on the bayou. Several generations lived there over more than a hundred years."

"That's a long time ago," I said, eating up the plate of cookies one at a time.

"Barges came up the river to load the cane and take it from there up the Mississippi. Of course, there were parties and balls and I heard once that one of your great-great-great-grandfathers was even mayor of Bayou Bridge — back when this town was much bigger and very important in the cane industry. When the Normand sugarcane plantation fell apart, the town shrunk. Land got sold off. Subdivided. People left for other places or other businesses."

"So Bayou Bridge wasn't always this small?" I fiddled with my tea as it grew cold, wanting a glass of milk, but I didn't want my grandmother to stop talking. I still couldn't get the image of her in the ivory wedding dress out of my mind, her young face aglow with happiness.

"Nope," she said, getting up to freshen her own cup. "Lots of happiness and wealth out on the island, but lots of sadness, too. Especially after the war."

I studied her, knowing some of it. "What do you mean? What happened?"

"Well, bad times started with my grandmother, actually. Miz Anna Normand. She was the belle of the county, but in the first years as a newlywed she contracted polio, which put her in a wheelchair for the rest of her life."

"How awful," I said.

"I never knew her then, of course, but she used to tell me stories about her youth. That she was a bit of a hellion. Sassy, bossy, demanding." Grandma Kat gave a faint smile. "She used to tell me stories about her Uncle Edgar, too. She adored him. I think everyone did. He gave her a pony once, and by golly, that pony used to throw her every time she tried to ride her. She suffered lots of stitches and a couple of broken bones. But she married well. A handsome young man named Charles Prevost — my grandfather — who had money and combined his sugarcane farm with the Normand plantation. They had a daughter named Daphne, but couldn't have any other children because Anna was too ill from the polio. Bad luck — or tragedy — seemed to follow her and Charles. The sugarcane didn't do so well, especially during the Depression. Then they had several bad weather years. One year a hurricane came right up Bayou Teche and destroyed the crops just before harvest. They sold off parcels of the farm up and down Bayou Teche, year after year, to make ends meet. She told me once how happy they were when Daphne married a fine gentleman who had big plans for reviving the sugarcane. Henry Moret hired a new foreman, experimented with new farm equipment and planting rotations, but it didn't last long at all. While they were still young, Daphne died during the birth of their second child — and the baby —" She broke off and her eyes got misty. "Miz Anna said it about killed her when she lost Daphne after everything else that had gone bad in her life."

I set down my last half-eaten cookie. "That baby was you, wasn't it?"

Grandma Kat nodded. "Daphne and Henry Moret were my parents. I had an older brother, but when my daddy finally gave up the farm after most of the land was gone, my brother moved to New Orleans and opened a real estate office. Your great-uncle, William. He left Bayou Bridge behind and never looked back. He let me have the old plantation house, which was wearing out by this time, let me tell you. It survived three wars, several hurricanes, famine, disease, and death, but it was still standing when I got married —" She broke off again and wiped at her eyes. "Oh, my, this is all old history, Larissa. Doesn't matter anymore. Life goes on, it always does, and we make the best of things and keep putting one foot in front of the other. Even when it seems impossible some days."

"What happened?" I begged. I wanted to hear her tell me. I wanted to know if what I'd seen was truly real.

Grandma Kat grabbed a tissue box off the fridge and blew her nose. "Look at me getting all sentimental and weepy. Well! The beautiful plantation home burned down when I was getting married to my sweetheart, Preston DuMonde, your granddaddy, may he rest in peace."

"You mean the whole house burned to the ground?"

"Pretty much. The fire department in those days was a long ways off across the bayou, and it just went up too fast. A kitchen fire, unfortunately. I mean, I know it's just a house, but it was also a piece of history dating back to 1840. And my family home. Worst part was my grandmother Anna."

"What happened?" I was intensely curious. This was part of the story I did not know. I closed my eyes, conjuring up the smoke and the screams of the wedding guests. Miss Anna in her wheelchair at the top of the stairs as Kat fought the smoke one step at a time in her wedding gown to save her.

"I'm afraid the last tragedy of her life was her own. She died from the fire. Inhaling all that smoke was too much for her lungs, which were weakened from the polio. She was gone by the time we got her out of the house. Had to lay her down right on the front lawn. She would have hated that. All the wedding guests, firemen, and police swarming the place. It was the best day of my life marrying your grandfather — and truly the most awful day of my life."

I shivered, tears stinging my eyes. "I'm so sorry, Grandma. To have the house burn down and your own grandma dying on your wedding day sounds like the worst thing in the world."

She patted my arm, smiling through her own tears. "Nothing to be sorry for. I'm sure it doesn't mean much to you."

I gulped past my swollen throat. She was wrong about that. It meant too much to me.

"Goodness," Grandma Kat went on. "It happened so many years ago, although I miss her stubborn, crotchety ways. Anna Normand Prevost would have been your great-great-grandmother. She was born at the turn of the century. The year 1900 right on the nose."

I thought of Mister Lance and digging for old buried silver in the backyard. "Do you know what happened to Mister —" I stopped and cleared my throat, thinking of Dulcie and her mother as well. But there was no way I could speak their names. I wasn't supposed to know them.

"Who, honey?"

"Oh, nobody," I said carelessly, wiping at my nose. "I'm sorry your wedding day was ruined," I added, changing the subject back again.

"Fortunately, I had a very happy forty years with your grandfather. He was a fine man, and didn't mind that I was — oh, listen to me go on and on."

"Didn't mind what?" I asked as my grandmother suddenly pulled her hands off her teacup and into her lap. Heat burned my cheek as I touched the scar along my face, pulling my hair over to hide it.

Something clicked inside my head. Grandma Kat always wore long-sleeved shirts with collars. Even in the heat of summer.

I reached out to grab her hand. At first, she resisted, and then she let me pull back her sleeve. The skin on her arms was wrinkled, like you might expect with someone going on seventy years old, but her skin had an abnormal shiny texture. I always thought she got her wrinkles early, but now I knew that the marks up and down her arms weren't old-age wrinkles at all. "You were burned in the fire, Grandma Kat. On your wedding day."

She nodded slowly, sadly. "I tried to save Miz Anna, and I was devastated when I couldn't." She shook her head like she wanted to shake away the horrific memories. "But we rebuilt the house and raised our own girls there. The place was smaller, of course, much smaller, but I put in the same-style staircase with a banister. Didn't get the big wrap-around porch like in the old days, but our little porch was good enough for sitting on hot evenings with a glass of lemonade and a book."

"And then you lost — I mean Gwen —"

Her eyes went distant as she gazed off across the kitchen as though seeing the past all over again on the other side of the room. "Yes, my oldest daughter, your aunt Gwen, was drowned on our very own bridge during a lightning storm." My grandmother reached over to stroke my face and I tugged away, not wanting her to look at the hateful scar. "We almost lost you in nearly the same way. I couldn't believe it. Like history repeating itself."

History repeating itself. Why did that phrase sock me in the gut? But I wished she wouldn't talk about my accident. Some days, I wished I could disappear into a hole.

Grandma Kat took my chin in her gentle fingers and forced me to turn my eyes toward her. "No, you look at me, Larissa Renaud. I know that living with the accident and the scar hasn't been easy this past year. But that scar will fade."

"No, it won't!" I was surprised at how loud I said the words.

She grasped both my hands and wouldn't let go. "Believe what I'm telling you, darling girl." Then Grandma Kat quickly rolled up both of her long sleeves and I saw her strange skin, the shocking white patches, and ugly flaps of skin that didn't quite lay right. She pulled down her collar and I could see burn scars along her neckline and throat, too.

"But at least your face is okay!" I cried out. My cheeks heated up at how petty my words sounded when she was so badly burned her whole life. "This scar is the first thing everybody sees. I'm ugly and I always will be."

"That scar *will* fade," Grandma Kat went on, ignoring my outburst. "It's not as large and ugly as you think. You're *allowing* it to be bigger and take over your life, Larissa Renaud. You are a better person than that. So many people love you, Larissa. And that scar doesn't make a bit of difference in their love and affection. You can't shut your mamma out or your friends here in Bayou Bridge."

"But Mamma drives me crazy about it!"

"Whooeee, she drives *me* crazy about it, too! But, Larissa, you've got to understand that losing Gwen hurt your mamma bad. Every time she looks at you, she remembers the sister she adored, dying on that bridge. She doesn't say it or show it, but she's terrified she's going to lose you."

"She shouldn't be. I ain't goin' nowhere! Unless it's to get away from her!"

My grandmother gave me a grin, and I felt my lips tug upward.

"Scars inside and outside both fade with time. That's one of the harsh aspects of time — and the beauty of time, too. You've got to believe that. Just like we've got to believe that your mamma is out there somewhere. She's just waiting for us to find her." Grandma Kat leaned back, staring hard at the ceiling. "So what is Maddie doing that's so darn important she left the house last night without taking a single practical item with her — except that doll?"

"The doll," I whispered. The doll that was always everywhere — until now.

"My grandmother Anna gave me that doll before I got married. She said she wanted it to stay a family heirloom. Anna Marie has been well taken care of. Although," Grandma Kat added, "she's not the sort of doll you play with, is she?"

"Have you ever noticed —" I stopped and licked my lips. "That the doll was always around whenever a family tragedy happened?"

"Of course the doll was around. Why wouldn't she be? A family possession is always in the house. Especially when it's passed from one generation to another."

"But," I said slowly, "something horrible happened every single generation."

My grandmother poured more tea and blew on it. "Every family has tragedies. It just seems like ours has had more than its share."

Later that afternoon, it was officially twenty-four hours since Mamma had gone missing. Sheriff Granger organized a search party, recruiting volunteers from all over town. Dozens of people showed up within an hour, ready to spread out and search. I was standing at the store window as folks showed up with flashlights and water bottles, wearing hiking boots. I had no idea so many people cared about our family.

After talking to my grandmother, I knew I needed to organize my own search party. A party of one — me. Because finally, after hours of wracking my brain, I was pretty sure I knew where Mamma had gone. And I was going to find her and bring her home. Along with the doll.

The girl on the telephone had told me that the doll had a clue. So finding the doll was almost as important as finding Mamma. I was the one who could find Mamma faster than anybody. Because I was going to search places nobody else would think of looking in first.

While Daddy was outside with Sheriff Granger dividing the neighbors and townsfolk into small groups and giving instructions, I sneaked out onto the porch to make my way to the river. Before I could get down the first step, Alyson Granger showed up. A girl who couldn't seem to leave me alone.

CHAPTER TWENTY-TWO

"What are you doing following me?" I said, trying to push past her.

"I'm not following you. I came to be part of the search party. I even brought our dog, Beau. Daddy told me to."

She had a German shepherd on a leash. A beautiful dog with black and brown markings and a star on its forehead. I put my hands behind my back so I wouldn't pet it even though I was dying to. I'd always wanted a dog, but my parents said it was impossible. Too many breakable things in the antique store. And furniture wouldn't sell with dog drool on it.

"He's trained, too," Alyson added. "At the police academy in Lafayette. Daddy got him from a friend of his when Beau retired. Isn't that funny, a dog retiring? But he's the best dog ever. And really good at finding things — and people."

"That's awesome," I said, taking a step backward so Beau couldn't start licking my face.

Alyson became very chatty. "So where are you going to start? Which group have you been assigned to?"

"Um, I haven't. Yet. I, um, gotta do something first. I'll be right back."

"I'll wait here on your porch," Alyson said, reaching down to stroke Beau's head.

I scurried back inside the store, then ducked out the back door and ran around the side of the house. I had to get away from Alyson. She'd ruin all my plans.

Skirting the backyard of the neighboring house, I was out of sight within a minute and running headlong toward the river road.

It was getting on to early evening. A crazy time for starting a search party because it was going to be dark soon, but it was the perfect time for me because of the fireflies.

The day had been hotter and muggier than usual. My shirt stuck to my skin. My hair clung like glue to my neck. And my fingers felt slimy with sweat. Even the gold heart necklace was sticking to the folds of my neck.

I flew down the road, kicking up dust, and I was at

the broken bridge in ten minutes flat. Throwing a glance behind me, I gazed across the moving water and swallowed hard. It still freaked me out to cross the bridge, even as the fireflies swarmed up over the elephant ears. Like they were happy to see me, like they wanted to see me. What if the magic disappeared and I crashed into the river and drowned this time like Gwen? Or tore up my face permanently and became a hideous monster?

I sucked in a gulp of air, wiping my hands on my shorts, and stepped out along the planks, allowing the fireflies to swirl me up in their column of light and carry me to safety. As soon as I reached the opposite bank and jumped onto the dirt path, I heard a shout.

There was Alyson standing on the far side of the bridge, right where the planks had crashed into the water from the lightning storm, their jagged nails lying underwater, waiting for a victim. "Larissa, what are you doing?" she yelled. "Where you going?"

I stopped, frozen. Then, pretending I hadn't seen her, I darted up the path toward the empty house in the cypress grove.

"Larissa!" Alyson screamed, but her voice grew faint as I ran.

I clenched my jaw when I got to the end of the

path, and then groaned. I was hoping it would be the mildewed house my mamma had been raised in, the house that was rebuilt after the fire. I'd had the gut feeling I'd find my mother hiding out in Gwen's old bedroom with the doll. Instead, the majestic Normand Mansion rose before me under a perfect blue sky.

I'd time slipped again.

Wedging myself into the woods, I followed the curve of the meadow to the back of the house, looking for the family or gardeners.

Not a sign of life, and eerily quiet under the hot sun.

"So where is everybody?" Guess I'd picked a bad day. But how did I know what was a bad day or a good day — or what I was supposed to be doing here anyway?

I shook my head, gnats flying into my mouth and eyes. Swatting them away, I spotted movement down by the barns and sheds. I drew closer, careful not to make any noise.

Three women were crossing the lawns toward the barn. No, not three women. Two women and a girl. Dulcie and Miz Beatrice. But who was the other adult?

The trees grew thicker on the far side of the island. Water sparkled through the branches where the

Bayou Teche twisted and turned just like a snake. Fortunately, I could stay hidden more easily at the rear of the house.

The women hurried, their backs hunched over, furtive-like. What was going on?

Darting through the trees, I found myself behind the row of old slave shacks. Most houses from the pre–Civil War days still had slave shacks on the property. Decrepit square boxes with four walls and three or four steps up to the front door, beaten by sun and rain and barely standing.

When this was a huge, working plantation, there were probably lots of these houses lined up along the bayou side of the island. The occupants would have had the river for washing and some privacy from the main house.

Now there were only about six shacks left, silent and dark. None of the windows had glass. Most front doors were off their hinges, creaking in the light breeze.

Miz Beatrice and Dulcie and the strange older woman hurried up the steps of one of the slave shacks. I crept closer, keeping my head down. Underneath the window ledge, I heard the murmur of voices.

"You sure Miz Normand don't know I'm here?" said an unfamiliar woman's voice.

"'Course she don't know, Aunt Delphine," said Miz Beatrice. "Although it's my afternoon off, and I can visit my great-aunt if I want to. But I'm not a fool," she added. "Except I keep gettin' taken for a fool by that Miss Anna. She's got a black heart."

"Now, now," Aunt Delphine said. "Remember your Christian manners. She's a little girl and black hearts take time to develop."

"You're kinder than I am, dear aunt," Miz Beatrice admitted. "Every nice thing Dulcie does for that girl goes unnoticed or un-thanked, and some days I want to give her a piece of my mind."

"Sometimes little rich girls don't know how blessed they truly is," Aunt Delphine said. "They take life and privilege for granted. That's all they've known. Servants are there to take care of them, not be their best friend," she added wisely but sadly.

Miz Beatrice sniffed. "Dulcie, show her the doll."

The doll? I stifled a gasp and tried not to move.

"Here, Aunt Delphine," Dulcie said timidly. "Mister Edgar gave her to me, and I wanted to show you how marvelous she is."

"Mister Edgar gave her to you?" Aunt Delphine said in her soft, older voice. "I've heard that man is generous to family and servant alike. She is mighty pretty, Dulcie girl. I'll bet you be lovin' on this doll every single day!" The woman gave a low whistle. "Real porcelain and decked out like a princess."

I heard rustling as if the woman was fingering the petticoats and ribbons. But why bring the doll out here to show it off?

Miz Beatrice spoke up again. "I'm sure the doll was very expensive. It was a *gift*, too — but Dulcie ain't seen her since the minute Mister Edgar gave it to her all wrapped up in a white box."

"What happened then?" Aunt Delphine asked. "I don't understand what you talkin' about."

"Soon as Dulcie unwrapped the box and everybody oohed and aahed, Miss Anna says she wants to hold her. Then she wants to see all the doll's fine clothes. Then she wants to put her with the rest of her doll collection. Said Dulcie could visit any time she'd like, but that it was better if she was with the rest of the dolls so she didn't get dirty or lost. As if my Dulcie don't know how to appreciate fine things!"

"Now, now," Aunt Delphine said calmly. "So you're saying Miss Anna basically took Dulcie's gift from her?"

"Yes, ma'am, that's right," Dulcie added in a fierce whisper. I pictured the servant girl in her work dress, boots on her feet, hair tied under a cap. The doll was the only thing of value she'd ever received in her whole life. "She horned in and snapped her out of my arms within five minutes, easy as you please!"

Miz Beatrice spoke again. "The doll has been locked up in a cabinet twenty-four hours of the day ever since. Does Dulcie ever get to take her out or hold her — never! Miss Anna says Dulcie can have her when she leaves service or gets married, but that may never happen. It ain't right to take her gift, and I'll bet my last quarter Miss Anna Normand forgets her promise."

"Oh, dear me," Aunt Delphine said. "I'm so sorry, darlin' Dulcie."

"Every time I clean Miss Anna's room I ask permission to look at her." Dulcie's voice cracked, and I winced at the pain in her voice. "I ask to take her out of the case — even for just five minutes — and she's always got an excuse. She's busy. Or my hands are too dirty even though I scrub 'em ten times a day."

"So how'd you get the doll out of the cabinet to show her to me?" Aunt Delphine asked.

"Miz Julianna and Miss Anna are out for the day shopping in New Iberia," Dulcie said.

Her mother added, "We ain't got much time, and you gotta get back to your boat before they come home."

"And you need to get this doll back into the locked

cabinet before anybody suspects anything," the older woman said.

"Do you have any idea what this doll is worth and if we could ever afford to have your relatives ship us one?" Miz Beatrice asked. "I've been saving my nickels for years and thought it couldn't hurt to ask."

I chewed on my fingernails as I listened to them. So Aunt Delphine was originally from the Caribbean islands?

"Let me see her," Aunt Delphine said. "Mister Edgar said he'd bought her when he was traveling in the islands?"

"That's right," Dulcie told her.

I heard more rustling and then the elderly Delphine whistled. "Good Lord, do you know where she comes from?"

"We just said the islands," Miz Beatrice said with a hint of impatience.

"My dear niece, look at this mark on the bottom of her left foot! That's the stamp of the doll makers from the Island of the Dolls."

"That's right!" Dulcie repeated. "Mister Edgar said she'd come from the Island of the Dolls. What does that mean?"

My ears strained to hear as their voices grew more secretive.

"The Island of the Dolls has the most exciting and dangerous dolls in the world," Aunt Delphine went on in a hushed tone.

"Why are they dangerous?" Miz Beatrice asked apprehensively.

Aunt Delphine said, "She's certainly a beauty, right down to the pearls in her ringlets and her perfectly molded toes. But when the doll has a certified stamp from the Island of the Dolls, it means she's most likely got a spirit inside. A powerful spirit."

Dulcie piped up. "What does that mean?"

"If the spirit is a good one, the doll can bring luck and a good life to its owner. If not — well — let's just say anything could happen. Dolls from that island have been known to do crazy things to their evil owners. If you believe the stories, of course."

"Of course," Miz Beatrice said drily.

Her aunt clucked her tongue. "I'm just telling you what I know, child!"

"Maybe you don't want to own this doll," Dulcie's mother told her.

"Not necessarily," Aunt Delphine said. "For someone with a good heart, like our Dulcie, the doll could bring some schooling or a good man down the road. Now that Miss Anna took her — well, let's just say that I hate to see what happens to the girl. *If* she don't give her back. That's all I'm sayin'. Blessings and good fortune need to be shared and passed around. That's why kindness is so powerful. I hate curses and avoid them like the plague, but only time will tell what kind of a spirit this doll got when she was created. She's special, all right. But those island dolls can be tricky, too."

There was shocked silence from Dulcie and her mother. Crawling outside the little shack in the twilight, I peeked through a crack in the doorway. I was glad I was wearing my sneakers that didn't make any noise. I just *had* to see what they were doing.

There was barely enough light shining through the two inches of space to make out the three female figures. Aunt Delphine was tiny, shorter than Dulcie, with dark skin and fine features. I could see the whites of her eyes and the diamond pattern on her dress. Black boots neatly tied up, a collar of tatted thread around her neck.

Aunt Delphine gently brought the doll to her bosom, inspecting her perfect porcelain face. "Mister Edgar chose well. This doll *is* powerful. She's got a strong spirit. I can tell from her eyes. Them eyes practically watch you talking, don't they?" She chuckled thoughtfully. "She has a soul with a strong will. The doll can make things happen. And if the owner of the doll — the original owner — has been thwarted, there's no telling what could happen."

"That sounds ominous," Miz Beatrice said, wringing her hands.

Aunt Delphine shook her head. "Doesn't have to be. You'll just have to admire her from afar, sweet Dulcie, and keep on being the good girl you are. You'll reap God's blessings. I believe that with all my heart. Even when we live a hard life of endless work, you can be happy and contented inside. Will you remember that when I'm dead and gone?"

Dulcie nodded soberly, blinking her eyes. "Yes, ma'am."

The three of them crossed the floor of the shack, and I hurriedly backed up and raced for the trees. The door creaked open. Footsteps tramped down the stairs and the three women crossed the lawns back to the house.

My throat swelled up as Dulcie clutched the doll tight to her chest. Her face was next to Anna Marie's cheek like she was whispering love into her ear. Like she knew she might never get to hold her treasure ever again.

CHAPTER TWENTY-THREE

It was foolish, but I raced toward the house, following Dulcie and her mamma after they bid Aunt Delphine good-bye on the path to the banks of the bayou.

I tiptoed up the porch steps and accidentally brushed one of the rocking chairs, setting it in motion. The chair creaked back and forth and I stood stock-still, hoping nobody would hear it.

The back door had lace curtains on the inside, but when I cupped my hands against the glass I couldn't see anybody in the hall. Gently, I turned the knob and slipped inside. Sometimes I couldn't figure out if I was the ghost or they all were. The memory of Miss Anna reaching through decades of time to touch me with her fingers haunted me.

I was walking into somebody's house that didn't even exist anymore — or did it exist in another dimension? The family was all dead now. This wasn't real anymore, right? But reality kept doing very strange things.

The air smelled like lemon oil and roses.

An antique table and hat rack gleamed with fresh polish to my left. Except they weren't antiques. They were brand-new in 1912. I peeked into the sitting room. Cushiony sofas and settees were arranged in cozy groupings. Tables with Victorian lamps and lace doilies. A baby grand piano positioned inside the bay window overlooked a rose garden. Pathways of stone and wrought-iron benches sloped down to the lawn.

All at once, footsteps treaded softly on the carpeted stairs. Voices came from the foyer. Hugging the wall, I crept forward.

Every day of my life I'd seen that antique doll in her glass case. Her icy blue eyes following me, as though she was deliberating something — or planning her next move. Those eyes had imprinted on my brain. And now I knew she had come from the Island of the Dolls with a soul. A soul that had the potential for evil. No wonder she always gave me the creeps.

Goose bumps crawled up my neck as I remembered all the times Anna Marie seemed to be alert and aware of me. Times I'd have sworn she had moved just a little bit. It was all real. She was real. Something inside her *was* watching me and thinking and cursing my family for more than a hundred years.

Now I knew why I was here. Why I was a witness to five generations of tragedy and heartache. The doll was still in my family. The curse was alive and well.

I shivered. I had to get out of here. I couldn't get stuck in 1912. Arrested for trespassing or hauled off to jail. Or worse.

Miz Beatrice harrumphed as she and Dulcie came around from the kitchen and headed for the stairs. I dove under the stairwell. "Now let's get this doll back into Miss Anna's doll case before we're both kicked out of this house. Gotta get supper going, too. It's so hot I'm taking the easy way out tonight. Cold left-over ham and salads. Hope T-Paul didn't eat that last lemon icebox pie I saved for tonight."

Their voices faded as they thumped their way upstairs, skirts swishing.

My palms were sweating as I slinked around the corner, stepping light as a whisper up the carpeted steps. On the second-floor hall, closed doors lined the walls. One opened door revealed a bedroom and an adjoining bathroom that was fancier than I expected, with a tub and sink and decorative tile on the floor.

Up another half landing, a maid rushed past, her arms full of clean sheets. She didn't glance down to see me sneaking past a table full of fresh-cut roses ready for arranging in a huge vase, which was a stroke of luck.

I ducked down when Miz Beatrice glanced over her shoulder. As soon as Dulcie and her mother entered the bedroom, I leaped across the hall and peeked through the open door.

They were standing in Miss Anna's bedroom. All done up in pink chintz and flouncy drapes. A vanity table was piled high with hairbrushes and toiletries.

Miz Beatrice stroked the doll's delicate pink silk dress. "She is certainly the nicest thing you ever did possess, my girl."

Dulcie's eyes watered. "Mister Edgar gave it to me, fair and square," she said wistfully.

"I'm sorry to say, you'll probably never own anything else quite like it. And we've been loyal, hardworking employees."

"Miss Anna's got so *many* dolls."

"That she does," Miz Beatrice agreed.

Miz Beatrice took a key out of her skirt pocket and quickly opened the lock to the doll case. Slowly, Dulcie placed Anna Marie next to a row of glamorous dolls decked out in satins and jewelry. I felt a pang of loss myself.

"She's so busy riding her new pony, she pays no attention to her doll collection," Miz Beatrice added. "How many does one girl need? She's got at least three dozen. And you with nary a one to your name now."

The next moment, Dulcie was quietly sobbing. "She's so beautiful, Mamma!"

I still recalled the look of pure joy on her face and the thrill in her eyes when Uncle Edgar gave Dulcie the doll.

Miz Beatrice's voice was strained. "Don't keep fretting, my girl. Life ain't fair, but you can hold your head high. We've done nothing wrong by showing her off to your great-aunt Delphine. I suppose it's a bad thing to admit, but I'll secretly laugh if the doll refuses to let Miss Anna hold her. Maybe the porcelain will stick to the shelf like glue. Serve her right when she took her from you in front of everyone at the party, then traipsed off to the trees, giggling."

"Mamma?"

"Yes, Dulcie?"

"Did you see Miss Anna's face when she came back from the woods that day?"

I froze behind the door. She was talking about the same afternoon Anna saw me hiding in the shrubbery and touched me.

"Her face was so white I'd-a sworn on a Bible she'd seen a ghost!" Miz Beatrice burst out. "Well, maybe she did. Maybe that doll's 'spirit' or 'soul' or whatever is already alive and playing tricks on her!"

"Maybe so," Dulcie said quietly, wrapping a finger around Anna Marie's glossy curls as she sat on the shelf.

"Time's up, my girl," Miz Beatrice said briskly. Striding across the room, she locked up the doll case and tucked the key into a small drawer that pulled out of a jewelry box. Dulcie stared daggers at the jewelry box and her anguish seemed to radiate. "Come on, Dulcie," her mother told her. "If we don't leave now, Sarah will see us when she comes down from doing up the master's bedroom."

Dulcie's eyes filled with tears as she blew a kiss to the doll, and then brushed a final finger along the glass case. "Good-bye," she choked out.

An ache pressed deep in my chest like I had a hundred-pound weight on me. Quick as I could, I tiptoed down the staircase, slipped out the back door, and ran for the trees. I was moving so fast, I fell straight into a big bush and collapsed. Rolling over, I gazed back at the house, breathing hard.

My brain was going a hundred miles an hour with so many wild thoughts as sweat trickled down my face. The doll *was* cursed. The doll was at every scene of tragedy in my family for five generations. She'd cursed every one of us. Even the day I'd fallen into the bayou — because I had a secret I'd never told my parents — not even Shelby Jayne.

I'd taken Anna Marie out of the doll case that day. Stolen the key from my mamma's purse, opened the lock on the glass case, and put her in my backpack before school. I'd been mad at Mamma for never letting me look at her. Never letting me play with her. Always saying no. Always being grumpy and sad and ornery.

The doll had been with me the day I fell off the bridge and gouged up my face forever.

Now, at this very moment, the doll was with Mamma. For some reason, she'd taken her when she left the house yesterday. What Mamma didn't know was that the doll was dangerous. That the doll might try to hurt her. Or even kill her.

Not only could the doll's curse hurt Mamma, but my baby sister who wasn't even born yet. I felt a whimper in the back of my throat. A terrible realization dawned on me.

Miss Anna had lost her daughter, Daphne. Then lost her own life in the fire.

Grandma Kat had almost been killed in the mansion fire. Then she lost her daughter Gwen.

If not for Alyson saving me, I had come dangerously close to drowning.

There was a pattern. I had to find Mamma and stop the doll — before history repeated again with a new and terrible tragedy.

I was almost certain Mamma was the next target — along with my unborn baby sister.

CHAPTER TWENTY-FOUR

When I climbed out of the bushes and dusted myself off, Dulcie was standing right in front of me, staring at me with her dark brown eyes. "Who're you?" she whispered.

My throat turned bone dry. "Um." Nothing else would come out.

Dulcie rubbed at her head with her thin fingers, clearly puzzled. The faded calico dress she wore had probably been washed two hundred times. She'd taken off her white work cap, and black curls surrounded her heart-shaped face. "You ain't got hardly any clothes on," she added.

I tugged at my shorts and tank top. "Um, I guess so."

She gave me a small smile. "'Course, it's so hot, you're probably cooler than me. But your mamma lets you out of the house lookin' like that?" She folded her arms across her chest, her voice rising in a thick accent.

I couldn't help being happy around her, and her smile deepened right back at me. Another day, a different time, and I think we'd have made friends right then and there.

Dulcie lowered her voice. "Why are you here on the island? I was standing at the upstairs hall window when I saw you running across the grass."

"I'm — I — it's hard to explain," I finally said. "But it's a matter of life and death." Unexpectedly, my words echoed those of the girl on the phone.

She listened to me thoughtfully, sadness behind her eyes, but curiosity, too. "Are you magic? A witch?"

I shook my head. "Neither. But one day my mamma's gonna live in that house. And right now, I'm looking for her, and I thought she might be here. Because she's in danger."

Dulcie bit at her lips, nodding as though she understood. "I'm sorry."

"Because of your doll," I added in a low voice.

"What are you talkin' about? How could your

mamma be in danger because of my doll — I mean Miss Anna's doll?" She made a face, and then her eyes welled up.

"You love that doll, don't you?" I asked softly.

She sucked in her breath. " 'Course I do. I'll love her until I die. But how do *you* know about the doll?" She reached out to jab me with her finger — before I could stop her.

"Ouch!" I said as she poked me hard. Instantly, I fell over and hit the ground, the world spinning like a roller coaster. I lay there, staring up through the limbs of the cypress, until the dizziness stopped. When I scrambled to my feet, Dulcie was gone. The plantation mansion was gone, too. In its place stood the neglected moldy house rebuilt after the fire.

I was back in my own time at last. Fast as I could, I raced toward the house. I was positive now that Mamma was here. It was the first place I thought of after I talked to Grandma Kat.

But after running in and out of every room and up and down the staircase, there was no sign she'd ever been there. I'd been so sure! Now what should I do?

I slammed the rickety front door shut and hurried down the path to the bayou. Mamma couldn't have come across the water. There was no boat at the dock and no fireflies for her. There was no boat and no fireflies for me now, either. I was stuck.

A moment later, I noticed a faint outline of footsteps next to mine on the dirt path. The trees shaded the path just enough that the ground stayed damp when it rained. I studied the prints, then put my foot next to one to compare. Slightly bigger. Not a man's footprint, but a woman's size. Wearing sandals. They had to be Mamma's. So she *had* come out here, but where was she now?

All at once, Alyson Granger emerged from the trees. That girl had followed me. I just *knew* she would! I took a good look at her feet, but she was wearing sneakers like I was, which made a completely different print in the damp dirt than the suspicious ones I'd just been studying.

For once I was grateful to see her, elated even. And she had Beau, the German shepherd, with her.

"One of these days, Larissa Renaud," Alyson said as she led me around the curve of the island to where she'd hidden her brother's rowboat and we climbed inside. "You got some explaining to do."

Beau licked my hand as he sat on the floor of the boat and panted, his tongue lolling out of his mouth. "There's one more place I plan on going," I told Alyson straight out. "And you can't come with me. It's private."

She pulled on the oars, her expression serious. "Can I come some other time?"

"Maybe," I said, trying not to look at her so I wouldn't change my mind. "Well, probably," I added, thinking about how she'd saved my life. Guess I owed her enough to be nice to her. This was the second time she'd rescued me from the deserted island when the fireflies had disappeared.

After Mamma was found, the doll's soul destroyed, and my baby sister safe, I'd find Alyson Granger and talk to her like a real person. Maybe even like a friend.

As soon as the boat bumped the shore, I jumped out, tossed the line around a piling, and yelled, "Gotta go!"

"You sure you know what you're doing?"

"Yep! And don't follow me, okay?"

I could sense her eyes on my back as I ran, not toward town, but in the other direction. To Bayou Bridge Cemetery.

I was scared and I was elated. I knew Mamma might go to the deserted house on the island — and I was right. Had she slept there overnight? I wondered. Was she scared? I couldn't figure out why she'd stayed out all night, or why she hadn't returned home. Didn't she realize we'd be worried sick?

As soon as I got to the cemetery gates, fresh chills crawled along my arms. Dusk settled, shadows filling the corners. Night was coming on. I didn't want to be here, but I had to come, even if it meant finding Mamma sleeping among the tombstones.

Now where was that grave? I'd only been here once before — on Gwen's birthday with my mother almost a year ago. We'd brought flowers. Daisies and yellow roses, which Mamma said had been Gwen's favorite.

Following the winding paths as the graveyard sloped down toward a copse of trees by the water was the older section of the cemetery. The part of the graveyard that was full. A minute later, I spotted a pair of stone angel wings peeking out from behind a granite family tomb circled by a small wrought-iron fence. Some other family had been buried together inside that fence decades ago, but Gwen was on the outside, alone, by herself. Being here made me melancholy. I could only imagine how it made Mamma crazy inside her heart.

I reached the angel and touched the cold stone, gazing across the sloping grass hills and headstones. She was nowhere in sight and I felt like bawling. I was *so* sure she'd be here. That Mamma would come to her sister's grave — because the doll had once belonged to Gwen.

"Oh, Mamma!" I whimpered. "Where are you?"

Darkness expanded, wind tore through the trees, and my knees dropped into the tall, uncut grass. Goose bumps prickled my arms as I watched the sinking orange sun.

Gwen's grave was long past twenty years old now.

The doll had cursed her and killed her. And then it struck me. If it weren't for Alyson Granger, I'd be dead, too. Alyson had defied the curse, had hung on to me with all her might so I wouldn't drown. Suddenly, I had a whole lot of questions to ask the sheriff's daughter, my archenemy, who wasn't my enemy any longer. An extraordinary realization.

I peered at Gwen's name, the dates of her birth and death. Mamma had grieved for her older sister since she was nine years old. I choked back a sob. I was the big sister now, and I had a little sister to save. A sister I hadn't even met yet.

The only way to save her was to defy the curse. Defy the doll's malevolent soul from the Island of the Dolls. The Normand, Prevost, Moret, and DuMonde tragedies were going to stop with me. No Renaud tragedies, if I could help it. I didn't want Mamma or my little sister buried here next to Gwen.

Tears burned my throat as I thought about Grandma Kat, who had never known her mother. She was horribly scarred trying to save her wheelchair-bound grandmother and then barely saved herself as her family's home was destroyed. Later, she lost her daughter. How did my grandmother survive so much? How could she still be happy? All of a sudden I wished she was with me right now.

I was circling the angel, searching for clues, when my foot sank into a freshly dug hill of earth to one side of the gravestone. My heart thudded so loud, my ears popped. I yanked out my foot, shook off the dirt, and then dropped to my knees, shoveling dirt away fast as I could. Underneath the earth about twelve inches was a bulky item wrapped in a blanket.

"What is this?" I muttered. Snatching up the bundle, I quickly unwrapped the cloth. Inside was the doll, Anna Marie. I was so shocked, I nearly dropped her.

She was in perfect shape. Not a mark or grass stain on her. "Mamma?" I whispered, darting glances around the graveyard. I was terrified of who, or what, might hear me.

Then my brain clicked. *"You need the doll . . . it's got the last clue. . . ."*

My pulse raced. It was time to destroy the doll. Even now, in the twilight, the icy blue eyes fixed their stare on me. I'd have sworn on a Bible her eyes were moving all on their own. Anna Marie was waiting to see what I would do. No, she was laughing at me.

I needed to destroy her for the evil she'd wreaked for a hundred years. The wickedness she'd inflicted on *me*.

Wishing I had a flashlight, I spread out the small blanket. I laid Anna Marie on top and wanted to tear her to pieces. Rip off her hair. Rip off her arms and legs. Tear the beautiful clothes and lace and ribbons into shreds.

"I hate you," I told her calmly.

Anna Marie's face was deceptively serene, while her eyes stared daggers into mine.

"You need the doll."

"It's your lucky day," I said in a cold voice. "Guess I need you in one piece."

"Not where you can see it . . ."

Slowly, I undressed her, searching for the final clue.

Finally, I found it slipped under layers of lace and chemise, down inside her petticoat.

"Got it!" I cried, glancing around to see if anyone heard me. There was a single streetlight over by the trees, but I still felt vulnerable.

I unrolled the tiny piece of paper, relief washing over me. Here was the final clue.

But the very instant I began to read the words, the letters twisted and turned on the page. Each letter became a black-eyed red snake that writhed and wiggled, shriveling up on the paper. Then the clue caught on fire. Yellow-and-blue flames licked straight up the paper.

"Ah!" I screamed, dropping it as heat burned my fingers. The clue turned to a heap of black ashes in the grass. A sob wrenched from my throat. "No! I need that note!"

I picked up Anna Marie and shook her, hard as I could. The perfect ringlets flew around her head. Her eyes rolled back. I wanted to throw her as hard as I could, but I knew if I hurled the doll against the angel's wings I'd smash the porcelain. "Stop it, stop it!" I yelled at her. "You destroyed the clue! You — you!"

Tossing her onto the blanket, I paced the grave site. I'd been outwitted by a doll.

Stiffly, I walked around the angel wings, fuming and frustrated. "Oh!" The words I'd read before they started to burn hovered before my eyes. My instincts had been right. *The doll is cursed — and you must figure out how to break the curse.*

Picking Anna Marie up again, I smoothed down her rumpled dress. "You *wanted* me to smash you because you didn't want me to find the note. But I'd already figured it out. I didn't need that note at all."

The doll smiled at me, unflustered. She was cool and harsh to the end. "Crushing you won't destroy the curse," I said with a groan. "The soul you have inside you is alive and well." Eerily, she seemed to nod at me, and her eyelashes fluttered.

"Even if your beautiful porcelain body is shattered and gone, the soul is still alive," I said. "You'll continue to torment my family. Because we stole you over a hundred years ago."

It wasn't enough to find the doll or the hidden clue. I had to find another way to banish the soul. When I figured that out, I'd truly save my mamma and my unborn sister.

CHAPTER TWENTY-FIVE

Cursed dolls, magical fireflies, time slipping. The whole thing was insane. I had to talk to someone — and Alyson Granger was not it. She might turn me in to her sheriff daddy, who'd put me in a jail cell. Or a mental hospital.

Wrapping the doll back up in its blanket, I rushed home. I needed a telephone bad.

More streetlights flickered on. Down a couple of the side streets, I caught sight of searchers waving flashlights in the distance. A knot of tears stuck in my throat. "Where are you, Mamma? Where did you go *after* the graveyard?"

I tried not to picture Mamma falling into the bayou where the bridge was broken. I'd been right about her going to her old house and to Gwen's grave. I just had to figure out where she was *now.*

As soon as I walked in the door, Grandma Kat seized me in her arms. "Where have you been, Larissa? We've been frantic. After Sheriff Granger let the search parties loose, we turned around and you were gone!"

"I'm sorry," I apologized. "I — I went looking for Mamma, too."

The lines running down my grandmother's face made her seem ancient and sad. Some of them, I finally recognized, were burn scars. I'd never known. I'd always thought she was beautiful. My Grandma Kat had always been cheerful and loving. She never let her scars make her angry or miserable like mine had. I couldn't help staring at her in wonder.

"Don't know what I'd do without you, Larissa. You're my only grandchild." Her voice broke as she hugged me tight. Her cheek was soft next to my face, a balm against my own hot white scar. "I'm so relieved and grateful you're here. Now why in the world would you go looking for your mamma? There's a whole search party out across town."

"I went to the cemetery," I said slowly. "To Gwen's grave."

Grandma Kat's face crumpled and she took my hands in hers. "You are a very wise girl, Larissa. Oh,

Maddie," she added, staring through the window of the store. "What are you thinking? Why don't you let us know where you are?"

"I haven't figured it out yet, but I know she *was* at the cemetery."

"How do you know that, and what have you got in that blanket?"

"It's the doll, Anna Marie. She was buried next to Gwen's grave."

My grandmother blinked. "You're absolutely right. Maddie must have been at Gwen's grave. Which means she can't be far off. But why do you suppose she left the doll at the graveyard?"

I didn't say anything, but I was pretty sure Mamma had figured out that there was something wrong with Anna Marie. She left the doll for us — for me — to find. So that I would know she was okay, wherever she was.

"I'm going to put this doll back in the case and lock it up again," I said, lying straight out to my grandmother. I didn't want her taking Anna Marie away. Not yet. I still had to figure out how to break the curse, and that was going to be the hardest part of all.

"I'm not letting you out of my sight, either. You're grounded to the house."

"But —"

Grandma Kat put up a hand. "No buts. Now go into the kitchen and eat something. We got all that good food the Grangers brought. A few of your kind neighbors dropped off some decadent desserts. It's a good thing I'm pacing miles across these floorboards."

"Can I at least make a phone call?"

She gave me a quizzical look, but nodded. "Yes, but come back down in ten minutes."

Gripping the doll, I sprinted upstairs and went straight to the wall of phones.

"Ring!" I commanded. "You have to call me. I don't know where else to go to find Mamma. And I don't know how to fix the doll. You have to help me."

I stopped, staring at each old-fashioned phone in turn. The voice on the phone had started all this. She'd given me hints all along, and now she'd deserted me. The girl knew the history. She knew the antique store. She knew my family. And the girl on the phone knew about the doll. Why else had she told me to trust the fireflies and follow them?

"Ring!" I said one more time. My voice died out. The second floor was so quiet I could have heard a pin drop. The girl on the phone had also told me that she could only say so much. She couldn't tell me what I had to do. I had to figure it out on my own.

The past and the present were going on all around me. All the time. Maybe the future was, too. The girl said she had to be careful not to change history.

I held the doll up again. "It was you all these years. And you're more alive than ever. Heck, you even burned up the note right in my fingers! Which means you won't let me destroy you . . . which means that isn't the answer."

I paced the floor, one slow step at a time, the doll's cold blue eyes following me. "Something else is the key to fixing this. To stopping your soul from cursing us forever."

I dropped into one of the armchairs, placing Anna Marie on my knees. "If someone put a sick soul inside of you on that island, then that means I have to cure you," I whispered. "And curing takes healing. Like a doctor." Even as I said the words, I knew it was true. I knew that was the answer. "But how? You're so strong and you've been so vicious for so long. So who can heal — Miz Mirage!" The answer came to me like a gasp of air. Why hadn't I already thought of the *traiteur*? Shelby's mamma, Miz Mirage, the healer, was exactly what I needed.

I wrapped up Anna Marie in the blanket again. I couldn't stand to see her face any longer. Especially not her eyes. They were too real, too human.

My next problem was getting out to Miz Mirage's house in the swamp without a boat. Shelby always met me at the town piers and we rowed out together. I slapped my forehead, feeling slow. "Alyson Granger."

Heat raced along my scar as I left the bundle that contained the doll on the bed. I was afraid of her. I wanted to bury her in one of our old chests. Lock it up and throw it away. But I needed her.

My fingers dropped from my cheek to my neck. Rubbing the skin along my throat, I felt the hard beat of my pulse. Something was missing. The gold heart necklace! It wasn't there.

"Oh, no!" I cried, clutching at my shirt. Quickly, I stripped down, shaking out my top, searching the floor. The necklace wasn't here. I'd lost my grand-mother's heirloom. She'd trusted me, and I'd been careless.

I went up and down the stairs, searched my par-ents' room, the entire second floor, but there was no sign of it. Perhaps I'd lost it at the graveyard when I was digging up the doll. Or it might have fallen when I was on the island earlier today. I thought about all the places I'd been: tramping across the lawns, down to the water, inside the groves of cypress, along the dirt path. It could be anywhere!

My throat tightened as pounding footsteps came up the stairs.

Grandma Kat flew into my room. "Just got a call from Sheriff Granger. He put out an all-points bulletin on Maddie. A few hours later, they found your mamma at the airport in New Orleans. She tried to buy a ticket to go to Martinique — one of the islands in the Caribbean."

My jaw dropped and I almost fell to the floor.

That meant that Mamma *did* know about the doll, just as I suspected.

Grandma Kat sank down onto the bed next to me. "Why in the world would Maddie want to fly clear down there?"

I bit my lips and shook my head, playing ignorant.

Grandma Kat reached over to pick up the bundle lying on my bed. "What's this?" she asked, removing the folds of the blanket to reveal the doll hidden inside.

I swallowed, watching my grandmother study Anna Marie. "That's how I found her at Gwen's grave."

"What an exquisite creature she is. My grandmother told me the doll had come from the Caribbean from her Uncle Edgar. Maddie probably heard me say that when she was growing up. But how strange that she would try to fly there on her own — now? Five weeks before the baby is due. How strange!"

The doll at the grave — the airport — it meant that Mamma *knew.* I didn't know how she knew because I'd only figured it out myself, but there was no doubt in my mind.

"Oh, my," Grandma Kat said sharply, holding a hand to her chest. *"Look at her eyes."*

Anna Marie's cold blue eyes were watching us, the pupils turning first to me, then to my grandmother. The black lashes closed and opened again.

"Okay, that's enough!" Grandma Kat snapped. She folded the blanket around the doll again and plopped it on the dresser. "We're letting our imaginations get away with us. We just moved her — or her eyes got broken sitting in the graveyard. Maybe somebody stepped on her accidentally."

I knew that wasn't true, but my grandmother was trying to be sensible and realistic. She didn't believe in time slipping or magical dolls. But that's also why I loved her. She made me feel safe.

"Katherine!" my daddy yelled, stomping up the stairs. "Kat! Larissa!"

We rushed out of my bedroom and down to the second floor.

Daddy lunged across the top step of the stairs, and his face was positively wild.

"What's going on, Luke?" Grandma Kat said. "Surely they didn't let Maddie on that airplane!"

"No, an ambulance transported her to the hospital in New Orleans. She's gone into early labor. I'm leaving now."

"I'm coming, too," my grandmother said firmly. "Maddie needs her mother."

"But what about Larissa?" Daddy said. "We're more than three hours away and could be there all night. Especially . . ." His voice trailed off and I knew what he was thinking. The baby was coming five weeks early. What if something happened to Mamma or the baby — again? He didn't want me there.

I gulped back a wedge of emotion. Daddy was worried because the baby was coming early. But *I* knew they were in a danger even greater than that. Mamma had just spent the last thirty hours or so with the doll. The doll knew the baby was coming. Maybe this dratted doll had caused Mamma to go into early labor. I had no time to lose in breaking the curse.

"I'll call Alyson and stay with them," I said. "Mrs. Granger offered."

Relief swept over Daddy's face. "That's right. A perfect solution. Pack a few things real quick, Larissa.

Your grandmother and I will drop you off on the way out of town."

Within twenty minutes I was on the front porch of the Granger house with a backpack of clean underwear, a toothbrush, my pillow, and Anna Marie tucked inside a fresh blanket, out of sight.

Daddy kissed me good-bye, and Grandma Kat held me tight. "Everything's gonna be all right," she said in my ear. "We found her. We'll call you soon as we get there."

Mrs. Granger led me inside. The house was hot, stifling. I broke into an instant sweat. "I'm sorry to say that the air conditioner broke down right before dinner. All the kids are sleeping outside on the back lawn tonight. Hope you don't mind, Larissa. We got a tent set up and sleeping bags all ready to go for you girls to have some privacy. Plus, my famous potato salad and corn fritters for supper as well as homemade ice cream to cool everyone off."

"Thank you, ma'am," I said, feeling self-conscious while Alyson flitted nervously about.

It felt strange to be here. Archenemies thrown together during a crisis. Nobody but me knew how bad the crisis actually was.

Beau came up and started licking my hand. I crouched down to pet him, smelling his doggy smell as his wet nose sniffled up my arm.

"He likes you," Alyson said.

I liked him, too. He was big and solid and would knock me over if I let him. After a minute of him nudging at my hand to keep stroking him, I crouched down and put my face into the fur along his neck. Someday, maybe I could have a dog like him, too. He sniffed along my cheek and his tongue sandpapered the ridge of my scar. I sat back, startled, but it didn't hurt.

"You can come visit him any time," Alyson added. "Let's go set up our sleeping bags."

"Popcorn and a movie coming!" sang out Mrs. Granger. Alyson's two younger brothers started horsing around, throwing pillows at each other.

Alyson rolled her eyes. "They're showing off for you, Larissa. They do that every time company comes." She took my hand and led me out to the back lawn. "We got us our own private tent."

After we unrolled our sleeping bags, I asked, "Alyson, do you know the way out to Miz Mirage's place?"

"Yeah, I think so. I canoe in the bayou all the time, actually."

"I was surprised when I saw you with a boat that first time."

"Well, Tara isn't really an outdoor girl, so I don't go out on the water too often. It's sort of a secret thing I like." She busily straightened her pillow, her voice dropping. "You'd probably rather be out there with Shelby Jayne than me, huh?"

I shrugged. "She's with her grandmother in Paris for a couple of weeks, actually."

"Then why you asking?"

"Because I have to go out there. Tonight. And I need you to take me."

CHAPTER TWENTY-SIX

Alyson blinked her pale eyes. "You crazy? Like now?"

"Does your daddy have any lanterns?" I asked.

"Yeah. We go camping a lot out at Lake Fausse Pointe State Park." I could see her mind going. "I guess it's not that late. Not completely dark yet. And since I live on this side of town, I'm closer to Miz Mirage than where you live. We could probably be back in an hour."

"We could put the boat in at the broken bridge, right?"

"Why do you want to go out there?" Alyson asked.

"Because of her." I pulled the bundle from my backpack and pulled back a corner.

"Oooh, she's beautiful!" Alyson reached for her, but I snatched her back. Alyson looked startled. "I'm not going to hurt her."

"I know," I said. "But *she* might hurt *you*. I can't take that chance."

Alyson raised her eyebrows. "What in the world are you talking about?"

I didn't answer, just said, "We've got to hurry. My mamma and my baby sister might die before I can get to Miz Mirage's house."

Alyson widened her eyes. "I can't believe you just said that."

"I'm serious. It's a matter of life and death." Everything the girl on the phone had said had come true so far. The realization made me terrified.

"You're serious, huh?" Alyson stepped outside the tent and I followed, waiting while she zipped up the flap door. "I'll go talk to my mamma and meet you at the side of the house."

I returned the doll to my backpack and slipped my arms through the straps. Took Alyson forever to come back. Finally, she returned and led me out to the side yard, handing me an oar to her brother's boat. "We both gotta row. We'll get there in half the time."

Within minutes, we were at the bayou banks.

Alyson had two lanterns lit, one for each end of the rowboat. A bright yellow moon was rising slowly above the cypress on the far shore.

"I'm glad the moon is almost full," Alyson said. "I can see the lay of the land, and the lanterns will help us steer clear of branches or gators."

"Alligators?" I said with a gulp.

"They'll stay on the far side of the bayou," Alyson assured me. "But they're easy to spot at night with their red eyes."

"Your mamma okay with this?" I'd figured we'd have to flat-out lie to her or sneak away.

Alyson made a face. "She argued with me and I told her it was a matter of life and death — that you had to see Miz Mirage or your mamma might get sick. I told her we couldn't call her up — we had to see her in person."

"Thank you, Alyson," I said, grateful once again.

"Well, my mamma said we got one hour and then she'll send out the Search and Rescue team if we're not back. I got my cell phone, in case of trouble. If we didn't have a phone, she'd say no for sure. She's got Miz Mirage's phone number, too. I go frogging with my daddy all the time, so she knows I know how to row at night and I know where I'm going."

"Never knew you were a tomboy. Or a daddy's girl."

Alyson made another funny face as she pushed the boat into the water. It slipped along the bank, and I got into the front so she could steer from behind. I obeyed her commands, rowing first on the right, then the left. The water was glassy, not a ripple of a breeze, and we cut through it quickly. The giant trees stood motionless along the shorelines. Frozen black silhouettes without a breath of wind. Hot and still as a painting.

The woods grew denser as we left the edge of town. The trees thickened, their branches touching overhead. Sawed-off cypress stumps rose out of the low-water areas. We passed a beaver dam and there were rustlings in the brush.

"Mice. Rabbits," Alyson said.

"What about snakes?"

"Keep one eye on the trees overhead. They don't bother us unless we mess with their territory. Now, if we were frog hunting, that'd be a different story. We'd be closer to the banks."

The buzzing of cicadas was thunderous at night and razor sharp. Frogs belched like they'd eaten too many flies, and the crickets were singing so loud I could hardly form a thought. "It's like the trees are alive," I said as I pushed my oar through the water.

"It is," Alyson said, and I heard the grin in her voice. The next moment, she said, "Hey, we're here."

We came around a thicket of tupelo, and bumped against the bank of a small inlet. Elephant ears burst in profusion along the bank. The glow of yellow lights spilled through a window just ahead. My heart galloped into high gear.

Dropping the oar under my wooden seat, I jumped out first, toes sinking into soft, damp earth. Alyson tossed me the rope and I tied it around the creaking dock piling.

As we walked to the front door, Alyson grabbed my arm, and I could tell she was nervous. I'd been here several times to have a sleepover with Shelby Jayne. I knew Miz Allemond but Alyson didn't, and the stories about *traiteurs* never really went away.

"Sorry," she said, dropping my arm and lifting her head.

"It's okay," I told her.

"Maybe I should just wait in the boat. The moonlight makes it so light you can practically see everything. Plus it's hot — and stuff."

I knew she was making up excuses, but before I could respond, the front door opened.

"Thought I heard voices," Miz Mirage said. The lightbulb behind her burned bright, and her hair was a halo of wild black curls.

Alyson's hand crept toward mine again, clutching it in a death grip.

"Come on in, girls," Miz Mirage said before I could open my mouth.

The door swung wide, and I pulled Alyson over a split plank on the porch. I could see the whites of Alyson's eyes gazing around the house: the wood stove spilling over with ashes from the winter, drying Spanish moss on racks, and a live owl sitting on top of the bookshelves blinking its yellow eyes. The smell of something spicy and wonderful filled the air.

Miz Mirage was as beautiful and mysterious as ever. Her thick black hair was tangled and wind-blown like she'd been outside all day in the garden or fishing, but she was smiling as she pulled us into the kitchen.

"What do I owe the pleasure of an evening visit from one of my favorite people, Larissa?" she asked. "I apologize for the mess. Shelby Jayne will kill me if I don't get this place cleaned up by the time she returns from her grandmother Phoebe's. It's easy to let my projects take over the house — and to forget my chores."

She waved a hand toward the sink filled with dishes from at least three days. The counters were cluttered with all sorts of odds and ends and stacks of mail, vases of wildflowers, and boxes and groceries. "I've been tending some pets for a few folks. Plus working on a new shrimp recipe. More paprika, that's the secret. Plus I've been growing some new varieties of peppers and onions."

"Smells good," I said, nervous to be here without Shelby.

"Sit down. Both of you. You're Sheriff Granger's daughter, ain't you?" she said to Alyson, who whispered, "Yes, ma'am."

In two seconds we were at the kitchen table with bowls of steaming shrimp gumbo, a basket of homemade bread, and spoons.

Gingerly, I dipped my spoon and blew on the thick, hot stew.

"Here's some cold milk, too." Miz Mirage sat at the table and studied us while we tried to eat. After a few minutes, Miz Mirage shook her head, earrings chiming against her neck. "You surely got me curious, Larissa Renaud. What you got in that backpack?"

"I — well — this is going to sound really strange —" I started.

"I've heard lots of peculiar things in my time. Probably most of it much more peculiar than what you got in there."

"Okay." I unzipped the backpack, bringing out the bulky blanket. When I folded it back, revealing the beautiful porcelain doll, Miz Mirage sucked in a breath.

No sooner had I stood Anna Marie up on the tablecloth, her silks and ribbons pooling out around her, than Miz Mirage's telephone rang.

"Ah!" I practically jumped to the ceiling.

Snatching up the receiver, Miz Mirage said hello, and then glanced over at us. "Yes, they are," she said. "Yes. Oh, dear. I see. Of course. Yes, I'll do that myself." She hung up and turned to face us. "That was your mamma, Alyson. Checking to make sure you arrived safely. But also to tell Larissa that she needs to get home fast as she can. Your grandmother called from the hospital."

My stomach started to hurt. "It's my mamma, isn't it?"

"Yes, Larissa, I'm afraid so. Your grandmother is on her way back home to get you. She says you need to go to the hospital in New Orleans with her."

The scar on my face seemed to catch fire. I touched the long white ridge and jerked back like I'd been burned. "Mamma's bad off, isn't she? Are she and the baby going to die?" I started shaking. I was cold and hot all at once and my stomach turned nauseous. "I think I'm gonna throw up."

"No, you aren't!" snapped Miz Mirage. "Breathe, Larissa. Slow breaths." With flying fingers, she fixed me a drink of something white and chalky. "Drink this," she said, rubbing my back. "Take some deep breaths. Slow and steady. Good girl. You're gonna be fine."

"Is the baby already born? What's happening?"

"I don't know a lot of details, but the baby was born early and she's not well. Your mamma is very, very sick, and they're worried about both of them. They had to take her into emergency surgery. I'm so sorry, darling girl."

"No," I whispered, holding my hands to my burning face. I was going to lose both my mamma and my sister in one fell swoop.

"Now, Larissa Renaud," Miz Mirage said fiercely. "Tell me what is wrong with that dreadful doll!"

When my eyes dropped to the table, a shock wave ran through me. The glass of medicine fell from my hand and shattered on the floor.

Anna Marie's blue eyes had turned a fiery red. Her mouth was curved into a wicked smile. She was staring at all of us, her eyes flickering back and forth.

"This doll ain't got a happy soul inside," Miz Mirage said evenly. "Where did you get her?"

I shuddered with cold and sweat and fear. "Our antique store. She's been in my family for a century."

"When did she first come to your family?"

"In — in, um, 1912."

"Good Lord Almighty." Miz Mirage sank onto a kitchen stool, running a hand through her tangled hair. "Who created her? Who bought her?"

"Uncle Edgar, my great-great-grandmother Anna Normand's uncle. He got her from the Island of the Dolls in the Caribbean."

"Well, Uncle Edgar Normand was a fool! Don't he know nothing?"

"Um, wouldn't he be dead by now?" Alyson asked, glancing between me and Miz Mirage. "You're all talking like he's still alive."

Nobody answered her as we all stared at each other.

Mirage straightened. "He was probably an ignorant fool and didn't do it on purpose. Got caught up in the island magic. But those doll makers, they liked to fiddle with souls and magic." Miz Mirage eyed me. "So you mean to tell me you're related to the old Normand family?"

I nodded, unable to speak. The room was still spinning, but my stomach was settling.

Mirage shook her head like she was shaking out cobwebs. "Okay, right, I already knew that. Because of Gwen." Her voice turned tender. "I'm just putting it all together. I used to visit them out on the island practically every day when I was a girl, although it's not the original plantation house. For some reason it was rebuilt, long before I was born, but I can't remember why now."

"There was a fire," I whispered, and then I went on to tell her about Miss Anna dying in the fire in her wheelchair, her whole life of bad luck and losing the plantation and her only child, Daphne. Then I told her about my grandmother Kat's burns.

"A family curse brought on by a doll infused with a soul and mind of her own," Mirage said thoughtfully. "Both you and Gwen, too . . ." Her voice trailed off, and her eyes grew misty.

Alyson's jaw was practically on the floor. "Should I call my mamma to come get us?"

Miz Mirage gave her a quick hug around the shoulders. "No, you're both gonna be fine." She turned back to inspect the doll. "I know your grandma Kat, of course. She was Gwen's mamma, and Gwen was my best friend. I know this doll, too, but I've never seen her like this. The soul that came to life has grown stronger. Good Lord, it's been how many generations now?" She counted on her fingers. "Five generations suffering tragedy after tragedy." Her voice broke, and she walked to the sink, staring through the curtains into the backyard as moonlight fell and lit up the blue bottle tree. "Even you, Larissa, falling into the bayou. How strange and coincidental is that? And now Maddie and the baby," she added, her voice low. "Gwen's little sister ran away to escape the tragedy and pain, but she took the source with her. All this time, the curse has been in her possession."

I tried not to cry, but tears were burning so hot I thought my eyeballs would catch on fire. "Mamma and the baby are in a bad way, aren't they? The curse is still going! The doll is going to kill them, too!"

Miz Mirage pressed a hand to her eyes as though struggling to stay calm. "I'm not going to lie to you, Larissa. Yes, they are in a bad way. Your daddy and grandma thought you ought to be there to be able to say — I mean, when — your mamma comes out of surgery." Tears fell from her face and she wiped them away. Coming closer, she took my hand and squeezed it hard.

"Was it a girl for sure? Do I have a little sister?"

"You sure do, honey. Miz Kat said she's beautiful. Just like you. Your daddy named her Emilie."

The lump in my throat swelled. "I'm not beautiful at all. This scar makes me ugly, and I always will be. That doll did this to me, too."

"Well, you ought to know better than that, Miss Larissa. Beauty ain't skin deep and never was. Most folks don't even notice that tiny scar, or if they do, it soon disappears when they get to know the real person Larissa Renaud is. Only person who sees it all big and ugly and hateful is you, darling girl."

"And my mamma," I said slowly.

"Your mamma is like I used to be. Heartbroken over Gwen. She's letting it eat away at her heart. But that might be the doll as well, working its hateful curse on her."

"We've got to stop the curse!" I cried, jumping to my feet. "But how am I going to do that in the next few minutes? Mamma might be dying right this second!" Impulsively, I smacked the doll across the table. I wanted to tear her hair out strand by strand. Etch scars into the perfect, beautiful, porcelain face.

Miz Mirage grabbed me and held me tight. "Ssh, ssh, everything *will* be all right. You gotta believe it, my girl." She stroked my hair, smelling like garlic and cinnamon and pet owl. Then she knelt down and dried my tears with her fingers. "That's where we are in luck, Larissa. This doll don't need a curse undone. That poor soul caught inside her needs healing. And you are gonna help me do just that right now."

"You mean, I can save Mamma and my baby sister?"

"Absolutely, sweet girl. Now let's get to work. No time to lose." Mirage opened up her cupboards and brought out a wooden box. She sat in her chair, setting down the box and lifting the lid.

"I heard about the healing spell you did for Livie Mouton," I said.

"You know Livie's family?"

"Well, she's a year older than me, but I know her mamma woke up last summer after a terrible coma. She recently had a painting in an art show."

Miz Mirage's gaze made me feel warm and loved. She reached out to stroke my face, brushing back my hair. "This doll isn't sick, but there's jealousy and envy and hate inside of her. We're going to heal that and bring out a healthy spirit as well as love."

"What are you going to do?"

Alyson was still quiet as a mouse. Her eyes bugged out of their sockets, but she didn't say a word.

"I've got some healing oils to start with, Larissa.

Lavender and cinnamon and frankincense." She brought out a small ceramic cup and a tiny silver spoon. "Gently stir these together."

Miz Mirage poured three drops of each oil into the creamy white cup and I stirred them together, smelling the strong woodsy frankincense, the perfumed cinnamon, the flowers of a lavender bush. The aroma was powerful and calming and sweet as quiet thickened in the kitchen.

"Look at the doll," Alyson blurted out.

I jumped when she said that, but when I gazed down at Anna Marie, her eyes were no longer twitching and red, but the icy blue of her gaze was still intense and eerie.

"Now rub this concoction on the doll's arms and neck and throat," Miz Mirage said.

Tentatively, I touched the beautiful porcelain skin. She was cold, too, but her neck and face were on fire. I snatched my hand back. "She's burning up hot!"

"That's good," Mirage assured me. "The soul — whatever it is inside her — is gathering itself, getting ready to fly off."

I finished putting the healing oils onto Anna Marie, and I felt myself getting calmer and stronger and more peaceful, too. I started talking to the doll as though she could hear me. "Everything is going to be fine. You don't have to be angry any longer. You don't have to inflict hateful curses on my family. Miss Anna was wrong to take you, wrong to steal you, and wrong to treat Dulcie so badly. You are supposed to bring joy and happiness, not inflict pain and suffering and death. And . . . and you're supposed to be returned to your rightful owner." I let out a surprised gasp. "I never meant to say that!"

"You're doing splendidly, Larissa," Miz Mirage said. "You're saying what is meant to be said after a hundred years."

"The words just spilled out, but how can I return her to her rightful owner? That's impossible. Dulcie is long gone, and who knows where her descendants might be? Maybe halfway across the country."

Anna Marie's eyes widened as though she could hear me. Then she snapped them shut, almost as though she was asleep. Her brow furrowed, angry and tight and frustrated.

"Keep going, Larissa," Miz Mirage said softly. "You know what to do."

I chewed on my lips, touching each perfect finger on the doll's hands, caressing her glossy yellow curls. It was weird, but I knew I had to talk to her like she could hear me. Like she was alive. Because in so many ways, she *was* alive. "To the soul inside you from the Island of the Dolls. Return to your ancestors. You are no longer bound by this doll's body, by this world and its pain and suffering. Go in peace and love. Go back home."

Nothing happened. I could tell that nothing was happening. "What else should I say?" I asked Miz Mirage. "I don't know what else to do!"

"Dig deep into your heart, Larissa. Don't be afraid, I'm right here," she added, squeezing my hand across the table.

I swallowed past the knot in my throat, the worry over Mamma so sick in the hospital. Tried to choke back the fear that I'd never see my new sister; that she was too little and too sick, and she'd die before I could ever hold her. I thought about how I hated the doll and the soul trapped inside it, cursing my family. I hated the fact that I was scarred for the rest of my life. Every time I gazed in the mirrors at home, I wanted to throw them across the room. Just like my yearning to shatter the doll.

A new thought grew inside my mind. The doll *knew* I hated her. She knew I wanted to destroy her. That's why the curse wouldn't leave, why it was sitting inside the beautiful porcelain body. Behind those hateful, cold, blue eyes.

I took a deep breath and let it out, tears stinging the back of my throat. Instead of all the hate and anger I had inside of *me*, I tried to think about everything Grandma Kat had told me about letting go. About not letting the scar determine who I was for the rest of my life. To not become a scared, ugly girl hiding from the world. Tears ran down my face as I held Anna Marie in my lap, cradling her in my arms. Alyson smiled over at me, tears filling her own eyes as she watched me cry. I didn't want to be the scarred, angry girl in town anymore. Or the ugly daughter hiding away in my bedroom at home. I wanted to be loved for who I was, unconditionally. And suddenly, I knew what I had to say.

"Dear Anna Marie," I said softly, gazing into her pretty blue eyes. She stared right back as though she were truly listening. "I forgive you for hurting my family. I forgive you for hurting me. You probably didn't realize how strong and powerful you were. Envy and jealousy that got out of control. That took over your heart. I forgive you, and I love the beautiful doll you can be. Please, please let love heal *you*, too."

Instantly, Miz Mirage flew out of her chair and flung open the kitchen door to the backyard. Abruptly I stood, the chair falling over as I witnessed the most wondrous miracle.

A swarm of fireflies hovered around the blue bottle tree, whirling around the yard and the porch, as if they were waiting to come in. As if they'd been waiting for Miz Mirage to open up the house. Within seconds, hundreds of lightning bugs flew into the kitchen, dancing and spinning and sending out tiny rays of golden light. The light was warm and wonderful and full of joy. Tears streamed down my face as I clasped Anna Marie to my chest and held her tight and loved her.

"There!" Miz Mirage cried out, flinging her hands toward the black sky studded with stars. "Go! Fly! There is the path that will take you back home."

But she wasn't ordering the lightning bugs to leave. She was talking to the doll's cursed soul, that unhappy spirit that had caused so much misery.

The fireflies filled the kitchen and the swamp island with love and tenderness. It was so astonishing, and so powerful, I never wanted it to end. Across the room, enclosed by the cloud of fireflies, Alyson's face was shining, too. We raised our arms to bask in the light, whirling and dancing around the kitchen together, as I held the beautiful porcelain doll aloft.

Outside, the blue bottle tree trembled ferociously. The bottles clattered together and bobbed on their branches as the tormented spirit whooshed out of

Anna Marie and flew through the door, disappearing into the night.

I gazed across the yard as the blue bottles swayed together and then slowly stopped, one by one.

There was utter silence in the kitchen.

"It's done," Miz Mirage whispered as the fireflies flew out the door in a stream of magical light, disappearing among the cypress and elephant ears.

I cleared my parched throat. "Will the spirit know the way home back to the islands? It won't get lost, will it?"

Miz Mirage slumped into her chair. She looked exhausted. I was exhausted. Like I'd just run a hundred miles and performed a thousand push-ups. Mentally, it felt like I'd just done a year's worth of homework all in one night. "Don't worry, Larissa. The soul knows where to go after this life. Someone who has been waiting for her will lead her home."

"Really, truly?" I choked up again, and I realized I was still clutching the doll to my chest. She felt warm and cozy in my arms.

Miz Mirage smiled behind her own tears. "It's over, darling girl. You did it. You've been brave and wise and good, Larissa Renaud. I'm so proud of you." She put her arms around me, and when I pressed my face into her neck, fresh tears came bursting out.

My mamma was safe. My baby sister, Emilie, was safe.

Alyson scooted closer and we fixed our eyes on the lace and ribbons and jaunty hat. The doll was dressed just like Miz Julianna and Miss Anna and Miss Sally Blanchard. Like all the proper ladies of the early century. Her eyes were a soft, pretty blue. Her mouth looked relaxed and gentle.

Anna Marie was just a doll again. A doll of porcelain and finery and dark eyelashes. The spirit had been driven out. Or put to rest. Or taken home. Whatever it was called.

The antique doll was only a doll once more. A doll without the power to hurt my family ever again.

CHAPTER TWENTY-SEVEN

A month later, Mamma and me and Grandma Kat pulled up in front of a small brown house in St. Martinville. Grandma was driving and she cut the engine while we gazed at the small, older homes and neighborhood. The grass was mowed neat and tidy, and a blue Chevy sat in the driveway.

Daddy was home tending Emilie, and Mamma's health was better than in a year. She held my hand tight in hers and leaned over to brush my hair out of my eyes, straightening the jeweled butterfly clip she'd given me for the occasion. I had to admit I liked the clip, and I liked her fingers on my hair. Plus, the pretty clip made my boring straight hair so much fancier.

Having Emilie home and healthy had softened Mamma. Her face wasn't so tense and angry. She was smiling more and letting me bathe and dress my little sister. I'd even heard her singing soft lullabies, which was completely *not* like my mamma at all. Me and Daddy would hear her coming down the stairs and smile at each other.

"I'm kind of nervous — are you?" Mamma asked, biting her lips.

I nodded, holding tight to the bag on my lap that held the case with the doll, Anna Marie, inside. "Thank you for helping me find Dulcie's great-granddaughter, Mamma."

She didn't open the car door yet. Just grasped my hand in hers. "You are a generous person, Larissa. You're doing the right thing by giving Anna Marie to the family who rightfully owns her. She should have been handed down in Dulcie's family all these generations, not ours. Would have saved so much grief and heartache and tragedy." She glanced over at Grandma Kat. "She's an exquisite doll, but there was always something about her that bothered me. I could never pinpoint what it was; that's why I left her in the doll case and never sold her. She was a family heirloom, but she always gave me a slithery, bad feeling."

"I felt it, too," I said.

"I know you did, I could tell. And it got worse the last month. Remember when I asked you if you'd been messing around with the doll?"

"Oh, yeah," I said slowly. "I forgot about that."

"One night when you and your daddy were in the kitchen making popcorn, I passed the doll case on my way to bed, and Anna Marie's eyes followed me straight across the room. I thought for sure I was seeing things. Or a trick of a mirror on one of the bureaus."

"What did you do?"

"I started testing her at different times of the day. I'd catch her watching me, and her eyes were actually moving. One day I even screamed out loud when you and Daddy were gone. I sat down in front of her one time and she smiled at me. It wasn't no nice smile, either. That's when I knew there was something inside of her. And I had the realization that *she* knew *I* knew it. I started researching where she came from when you and Daddy thought I'd gone to bed. Once I knew a bit of her history, I knew I had to go to the Caribbean and find the Island of the Dolls for myself and talk to some of the doll makers."

"That was so dangerous, Maddie," Grandma Kat said, making a tsking sound with her tongue.

Mamma kept staring out the windshield. "I wasn't thinking straight, that's for sure. The doll started to play mind tricks on me. I felt like she knew what I was thinking. I had to go before I got so close to my due date the airlines wouldn't let me on the plane. And I knew if I told you where I was going, you'd stop me. I should have left a note, but I was so afraid. That doll got so bold with her wicked stares. I was terrified of what she might do. I had no idea you were thinking the same things, Larissa."

My mamma had done a brave thing. Maybe foolish, just like me, but brave. She'd been trying to take care of me. I bumped my shoulder against Grandma Kat, enjoying the warm coziness as I sat between them both in Grandma Kat's ancient Lincoln with the bench seat. "You sure you don't mind giving her away? After all, Miss Anna gave her to you personally."

My grandmother shook her head. "Anna Marie wasn't my grandmother's doll to give. It's a sad, sad story, but today feels like it's going to be extra special. Although I don't think it'll beat when your mamma and baby sister were able to come home from the hospital. All thanks to you, Larissa."

"It was Miz Mirage, really."

Grandma Kat shook her head. "Larissa, you were brave enough to know you needed to go to her. You were smart enough to find the doll at Gwen's grave in the first place."

Mamma kissed the back of my hand. "I left home so fast I forgot my phone and purse, but I had my I.D. and some money in my pocket, so I made some calls to the airlines and St. Martinique airport from a pay phone down Main. Then I caught a ride to the island with Mr. Boudreaux, who was just leaving the town dock to go fishing. But the evil was getting worse, and I was sick physically as well as had this horrible feeling inside. I had to leave Anna Marie behind at the cemetery, or she would have killed me on the airplane. I knew someone would eventually go to Gwen's grave site, and I figured that was the safest place."

"It took me a while to figure out where to look for you, but I finally did," I told her.

"Well, now," Grandma Kat said, consulting a paper with the address. "We'd better get up to that front door or they'll wonder what we're all doing sitting in this car in the heat. Dulcie's descendant is a woman named Sophie Cambray."

"I wish the doll was going to a girl like me," I told her. "Not an old lady."

Mamma let out a laugh as she shut the car door, and then tugged me up the porch steps. "Do the honors, my girl."

I pressed the doorbell, feeling the weight of the bag with the doll in my other hand. Almost as soon as I heard it ring, the door flew open.

A young woman stood there wearing a floured apron, a mass of dark curls, and pearl earrings. "You're early! I barely got the first batch of brownies in the oven. I'm Sophie, please come in."

She led us to a small front room where sunshine poured in the windows. I noticed that there were daisies from the front garden on the end tables next to a sagging sofa that had seen better days. She was young enough that the little house made me wonder if she and her husband might be college students. The duplex was small, yet cozy, and smelled delicious, like chocolate. "I'm Sophie," she said again, untying her apron and balling it up in her fists like she was nervous.

Grandma Kat extended her hand. "I'm Katherine DuMonde. We spoke on the phone. I grew up in the old Normand-Prevost house on the island. This is my daughter, Maddie, and Larissa, my granddaughter."

"Pleased to meet you all." Sophie gestured for us to sit. I perched on the edge of a chair and studied a collection of glass cats on the mantle. Through the window I could see kids playing a game of tag football. A group of girls in shorts sat on a lawn across the street talking and pretending not to watch the boys. A man drove by pedaling a bicycle, a toddler sitting in the back with a miniature bike helmet on his head.

"My grandmother told me that *her* mamma worked at the Normand plantation when she was a girl. My great-grandmother was Dulcie Lamar. Those were different times, weren't they?"

Grandma Kat nodded. "They surely were. Like a different world. But really only a couple of generations ago — at least for me, since I've got a few decades on you!" She laughed and Sophie seemed to relax. I relaxed more, too. Everybody always liked my Grandma Kat.

"I read in the newspaper this morning that the house out there is going to be bulldozed," Sophie asked. "Is that true?"

"Yes, we got a call a couple of weeks ago," Grandma Kat said. "It's been sitting empty for more than twenty years and there's been quite a bit of vandalism. Folks wandering through and squatting and making a mess of the place. Teenagers, too. It's not safe anymore. Some kids spent the night recently, and one of them fell through the staircase and broke his leg. It's infested, too, with all sorts of bugs and critters."

I noticed Mamma turn away to peer out the window. Like she didn't want to hear them talk about it. I got an unexpected shiver as if I was seeing inside my mamma's heart. She didn't want the house condemned and destroyed. It was her childhood home. The home she'd grown up in with her sister, Gwen. Taking down the house meant taking away all the memories of Gwen in the house. I was glad Shelby Jayne had found Gwen's old scrapbook hidden in the cupboard upstairs. Mamma had it in a safe spot now. I wondered how often she took it out to pore over its pages.

Sophie lowered her eyes. "Must be hard to hear that about a place that was your home."

"It is," Grandma Kat admitted. "But we don't have funds to fix the place up. Actually, it needs to be torn down. There's no way to make repairs to get it livable again. Somebody will have to start over — if the land ever sells. Needs a whole new bridge, too, and that will cost a pretty penny. So the place will probably be left empty."

"A piece of history lost, too," Sophie said. "Which is sad. I love history. I was a history major at the community college in New Iberia." A buzzer rang from the kitchen and the young woman jumped up. "Oh, that's the brownies I made for y'all."

"You really didn't need to," Mamma said, finally turning from the window.

Sophie brushed her hands at the air. "I don't need much of an excuse to make my mamma's famous brownies with white chocolate chips. Besides, my husband loves them and he'll polish off the pan tonight."

A couple minutes later she was back with a plate of warm brownies dripping with icing and glasses of sweet tea. "They're messy, but you won't care once you taste them."

I held a big chocolate square on my lap on a napkin and pinched off pieces as it cooled. It was delicious. "Mamma, you should get the recipe."

Mamma said, "It's probably a secret family recipe."

" 'Course not!" Sophie said lightly. "I'll write it out for you."

I studied her under my eyelashes, wondering how old she was. Not old at all, but out of college, married. I wondered if she had kids, but there wasn't any sign of children. No toys or diapers lying around.

"I was just glad I got off work a bit early today so this worked out perfect."

"Speaking of family secrets . . ." Grandma Kat started.

Sophie's forehead wrinkled as she set down her glass of tea. "I wasn't quite sure what you were talking about on the phone, Mrs. DuMonde."

"Please call me Kat."

Sophie blushed. "Yes, ma'am."

"Well, it's about your great-grandmother Dulcie. She was the same age as my grandmother Anna. They were both girls of about twelve when Anna's uncle came to visit. A man named Edgar Normand, a sea captain — whose father had ties to bootlegging during the Civil War, no less! Uncle Edgar always brought gifts for the family when he visited Louisiana. He was generous, and treated the servants well, too. This particular year, I believe it was 1912, he gave a special gift to your great-grandmother Dulcie."

Sophie's eyes opened wide. "That was very kind of him, but how would you even know that? It was so long ago, and she didn't leave a diary or anything."

Grandma Kat turned to me. "Show her, Larissa."

I pulled out the box and opened the lid. As I lifted out Anna Marie, her petticoats and crinolines made a soft shushing noise. I showed her to Sophie, smoothing the ribbons on her hat.

"She's beautiful!" Sophie exclaimed. "And she's in perfect condition."

"A doll makes a fine gift for any girl that age," Grandma Kat said gently.

"She is perfect, except for a tiny chip on her chin," Mamma finally spoke from her chair.

"But you can hardly see it," I added.

"She's worth a great deal," Mamma added. "My husband and I own Bayou Bridge Antiques."

"Why didn't you sell her a long time ago?"

Mamma shook her head. "I couldn't bear to sell her because she was my sister's doll. My sister drowned in the Bayou Teche when she was a girl."

Sophie's expression turned tender as she studied Grandma Kat's and Mamma's face. "I'm so sorry. I can imagine why you'd want to keep her."

Mamma took a gulp of her tea as Grandma Kat leaned forward, blinking back emotion. "But don't you see, Sophie? We've had the doll in our family all these years, over a hundred years, and yet the doll was never ours to sell. She never belonged to us. She belonged to Dulcie. She belongs to your family. She's rightfully yours."

"I'm not sure I understand . . ." Sophie said.

"Uncle Edgar gave the doll to Dulcie, and Miss Anna Normand took her. She was jealous of your great-grandmother."

"How could she be jealous of a servant girl whose grandparents used to be slaves? That doesn't make much sense."

Grandma Kat lifted her shoulders. "Some things we'll never truly know, but when we recently learned the story, we wanted to make things right."

I could see Miss Anna in my mind, Dulcie and her mamma, and the doll collection in Anna's fancy bedroom. I knew the details of how it all happened, but I'd never tell. I'd never breathe a word.

I realized Sophie's eyes were on me. "I don't feel right taking your doll, Larissa. Seems like you should have her. Especially since your own mamma and grandma have kept her so special all these years."

I shook my head. "I don't want her. I can't have her. No!" I thrust the doll into Sophie's arms and stepped back. "Please. You have to take her. It's the only way to make things right."

Sophie searched my face, frowning, and her dark eyes were so much like Dulcie's it took my breath away. I'd never forget when Dulcie caught me in the bushes and the awareness I'd had that we'd have been friends if times had been different. "Will you tell me her story sometime?" Sophie asked.

I shrugged and wiped my sweaty palms on my shorts.

"Please?" she asked again, her soulful eyes keeping a hold on mine, like she knew I had a secret.

"Maybe," I whispered.

"Thank you." I think Sophie understood that there was more to the story than we were letting on. When she gazed down into the lovely porcelain face, she added, "I don't think this doll should ever be sold. She's a true heirloom, isn't she?"

"We best be going now," Grandma Kat said.

"Wait!" Sophie said. "Please, don't go yet. I have something I want to show you, and I just remembered it." She walked down the hall for a moment and returned, holding a simple chain necklace with a gold heart on it. "I don't know much about Dulcie Lamar, but this was something she possessed that was passed down through the generations, too, just like the doll. I got it from my grandmother a few years ago. I've always wondered where the necklace came from. They were dirt-poor back when she was growing up during the Depression. I can see why Dulcie and my grandmother would have treasured it, even though it's not worth that much now. A nice little necklace for a girl. What makes it valuable is how old it is."

My necklace! The one that went missing the day I wore it to the island that last time! It must have come

332

undone and fallen into the grass or dirt — right before Dulcie poked me with her finger to see if I was real. Dulcie had found it and saved it all these years. Tears pricked my eyelids. That strange, brief connection with Dulcie had lasted her whole life.

Sophie gave me a quick look. "Have you seen this before, Larissa?"

I didn't know what to say. There were no words to explain. Time was colliding again, in new and bizarre ways.

Grandma Kat spoke up. "May I see that necklace?"

"Of course." Sophie handed over the delicate chain, tarnished with age, but the gold heart had been polished and it shone under the sun coming through the window. "Looks like a friendship bracelet of some kind, don't you think?"

"I agree," Grandma Kat said, staring straight at me. "My grandmother Miss Anna Normand had a necklace like this. She gave it to me and I gave it to my granddaughter, Larissa, as a keepsake only a few months ago on her twelfth birthday."

"Just like this?" Sophie said, her eyes seeing more than I wanted her to. "What a coincidence."

I still couldn't talk. My brain buzzed with so many thoughts I was dizzy. I shook my head, trying not to let the lump in my throat grow even bigger.

"I'm fairly sure that's a story we'll never truly know," Grandma Kat said, gazing at me with her piercing eyes.

The room grew quiet and Mamma finally rose to her feet. "Thank you so much for seeing us, Sophie. And thank you for the delicious brownies."

"My pleasure." Sophie touched my hand, pressing the necklace into my palm with her warm fingers. "I have a feeling this belongs to you, Miss Larissa Renaud," she whispered. "I want you to have it. Seems like a good exchange for the porcelain doll, don't you think?"

I moved my chin up and down, unable to speak. The next instant, Sophie put her arms around me and hugged me tight. "Thank you," she whispered in my ear. "I'm so glad we met."

"Me, too," I said, my voice choking.

When we broke apart, Sophie pointed her finger at the corner of the sofa where the porcelain doll was sitting regally in her lace and ribbons. "Look, seems like she is smiling. It's odd, but the doll looked quite unhappy when you first pulled her out of the box. You were holding her in your chair over there by the window, and I noticed. But now she's happy, don't you think?"

"Definitely," I said, my heart so full I thought it would burst.

Sophie stroked the blond curls and ran a hand down the silk dress. The doll was smiling gently, not maliciously. Her eyes had lost the stormy, contemptuous stare. She'd been purged of the cursed soul. She *was* smiling, and I breathed the biggest sigh of relief of my life.

CHAPTER TWENTY-EIGHT

Two weeks later, bulldozers arrived on the island.
Alyson called me up to talk about it. "I can't believe they're really pulling it down. They're tearing everything apart like it's a bunch of sticks. It's so sad. Makes me want to cry."

From afar, I'd already seen the walls crumple in and the roof collapse, but it hurt to hear Alyson say the words out loud. "I didn't want to go and watch, but I had to. It's like a piece of history lost. A piece of my family."

The whole island had been cordoned off. No public allowed due to falling chimneys and crashing bricks. There were warning signs and yellow Caution tape. Tractors with clawed arms taking bites out of the house. In the Bayou Teche, huge flatbed boats sat ready to carry the torn lumber and roofing away. An enormous pile of debris. It came down so fast I had cried, although I didn't admit that to Alyson. I watched from a distance on the path with Mamma and Grandma Kat. They both were wiping their eyes but didn't speak a single word.

I'd never see the house again. I'd never see 1912 again. Even the fireflies had disappeared, leaving me lonely and melancholy.

The next day I tried to get back into a routine. I offered to open the store by myself while Mamma took care of Emilie. It wasn't the same because I was used to Daddy walking the store with me, checking on the price stickers while I dusted and made sure no stray books had floated off behind a lamp or inside a desk drawer.

I had just turned the Bayou Bridge Antique Store sign to OPEN when Grandma Kat rang on the phone by the cash register. "Larissa! Get your mamma and the baby and get yourself out here to the bayou! Pronto! It's an emergency!"

Her frantic tone startled me. "What about the store? Daddy's gone to Napoleonville — he's picking up a truckload of antiques from an estate sale. I'm in charge."

"I know! That's why I said to bring the baby!"

I'd never heard my grandmother like this before. Excited, nervous, worried, all at once.

"But —"

"Emilie is almost six weeks old and healthy, and there ain't no reason she can't come, too."

"But where are you?"

"Waiting for you at the bank by the bridge. Didn't I say that already?"

She snapped her cell phone shut, and I almost dropped the dead receiver I was holding. My grandmother had never acted like this in her life.

When I told Mamma she gave me an odd look. "Grandma Kat really said that? Guess we better get on over there and see what all the fuss is about."

While Mamma strapped Emilie into the stroller and covered her with blankets and a sunbonnet, I locked up the register and the front door, quickly flipping the CLOSED sign out.

We hurried down the sidewalk, past the bakery and post office and Verret's Café and the town square where a bunch of kids were lounging around on the lawn.

It was hard pushing the baby stroller on the dirt road, but Emilie fell asleep, her pink cheeks jiggling as we went over the washboard ruts.

"Is this too much walking, Mamma?" I asked.

"I'm fine, Larissa, truly. Better than I've been in a long time. It was like there was something strong and powerful and wicked holding me down. Making me angry and hateful all the time. I'm sorry for so much of the past year, Larissa, for so many unkind things I said to you."

"Were you scared? That night in the hospital? So far away in New Orleans?"

She reached over to take my hand in hers, and we pushed the stroller together. "I don't want to scare you, but I felt like there was something trying to kill me and Emilie. As if we were being yanked away from this world. I can't even explain, it sounds so crazy now. Thank goodness I was in the best hospital in the state."

A minute later, we got to the broken bridge. Through the trees I could see backhoes and the steel flatbed boat piled high with the ruins of Mamma's childhood home. I tried to speak, knowing the sight had to bother her, but no words came out. Her face was impassive, but I could see her jaw tighten and her knuckles whiten on the stroller handle.

Rays of sunlight sparked across the water like golden firefly lights. I knew I'd never see the fireflies again. The time of the fireflies was over and they were gone. The past was dead and buried. Nobody would ever know who had lived here for so many generations. Miz Julianna and Miss Anna and Dulcie and Mister Lance and Uncle Edgar and Daphne and Gwen had been swallowed by time. Not I or anybody else would ever see the old plantation house rising out of the cypress grove again.

A pang throbbed in my heart and my eyes watered so bad I kept rubbing at them.

Mamma fussed over Emilie, sticking a binky in her mouth to keep her asleep, and said, "How are we going to get over to the island if we don't have a boat?"

"We could borrow Alyson's rowboat."

Mamma gave me one of her looks. "No way I'm taking a baby in a rowboat — even if it's only a couple hundred yards across."

"Where's Grandma Kat?" I asked. "She said she was right here at the bridge."

A drop of sweat trickled down Mamma's brow. My hair burned on my neck under the sun. My question was answered two seconds later when a skiff came roaring down the bayou, hugging the shoreline. Grandma Kat stood next to Sheriff Granger, who was at the wheel.

"What is going on?" Mamma asked when my grandmother threw us the towline to wrap around the piling while we boarded.

Grandma Kat's face had a strange expression. "I'm not sure, Maddie, but the sheriff called and said there was trouble when they pulled the old house down."

Mamma's eyes darted toward Sheriff Granger. "What sort of trouble?"

He pushed his hat back off his forehead. "When the main portion of the house came down, the brick chimney toppled into one of those hundred-and-fifty-year-old trees in the grove, busting up so many of the main limbs it killed the tree, unfortunately. The bulldozers had to take the tree down, which put them behind. Otherwise, they'd have cleared out of here today. The barge is ready to haul all this out of here, but they gotta chainsaw up the tree and get another boat to take it down to the sawmill."

Mamma shaded her eyes. "So what's the problem?"

"Oh, Maddie, get in the boat!" Grandma Kat burst out. "You have to see it to believe it! I'm so impatient I'm about to jump out of my skin, but I wanted you girls here with me. I just wish Preston were still alive."

I climbed into the boat and sat on one of the cushioned seats while Sheriff Granger helped Mamma in with Emilie and the stroller. "Didn't Alyson come with you?" I asked.

"Another time," he said, smiling at me. "But she's dying to know what's going on."

The wind whipped my hair as we crossed in about sixty seconds flat. Then we were climbing out, and the engine of the barge lying along the shoreline was so loud I covered my ears. As we walked down the path and entered the clearing, a pile of concrete rubble, broken drywall, and insulation littered the foundation where the house used to be. A lump rose in my throat.

Grandma Kat pulled on my arm. "Over here. Watch your step. There's broken glass, too."

"I'll wait here with Emilie," Mamma said.

"You sure?" my grandmother asked.

"I am sure," Mamma said firmly.

Sheriff Granger put a folding chair down for Mamma and stayed with her. "You two go on," he said. "You don't need me any longer."

The backhoe turned off the machine and it grew quiet, like they were waiting for us to leave so they could get on with hauling out the last of the wreckage.

With the house torn down, the island felt like a graveyard. My gut felt jumpy and sort of sick.

Grandma Kat clasped my hand tight in hers. "Let's cross over here, Larissa. All this used to be lawn back in the day."

I nodded. I knew that. I'd seen it with my own eyes.

All of a sudden we came up to one of the big oaks that had been knocked over. Branches were everywhere. The trunk was huge, sprawled along the perimeter of the cypress grove. Its roots were humongous, like thick, giant veins sticking into the air. Clods of dirt and mud and spiderwebs clung to the gnarly underside.

Grandma Kat stopped at the deep, wide hole the tree had left when it was knocked clean out of the earth.

"Don't touch anything," one of the workmen said. "Might be unstable, although that tree ain't goin' nowhere until we chainsaw it up into pieces."

"How old do you think this tree is?" Grandma Kat asked.

"At least a hundred and fifty years. Probably dates back before the war even, which would make it closer to two hundred years old."

My grandmother nodded. "That's what I was thinking."

"Why'd you drag us out here to look at a tree, Grandma?" Seeing the beautiful, ancient oak uprooted made my eyes prickle. I was surprised at my reaction. My heart had a deep hole, too, and I wanted to cry a little bit.

Grandma Kat pulled me to her side. "Look down into that hole, my girl."

I leaned over. Roots as thick as my wrist criss-crossed deep into the earth. Then smaller roots, a whole web of them, as they spread even deeper into the ground. Many had been cut, though, and there were pieces of root lying all over the ragged grass, too.

Then I saw it. A wooden box buried down inside the ground. A chest with leather straps and a padlock.

Images of Mister Lance in his suspenders swam in front of my eyes. I got so dizzy I almost fell over.

"Steady, Larissa," Grandma Kat said.

"It looks like a treasure box!" I breathed.

"You think maybe all those rumors and gossip since the war weren't just rumors and gossip?"

My heart beat with a hundred emotions. "What if there's truly something inside?"

"Only one way to find out." She motioned to one of the tree specialists, who came over and spent several minutes pulling up the chest.

"How long has it been there?" I asked him.

The man said, "From the looks of things, this box was buried under the tree when it was first planted. All these years, decades and decades, the tree has been growing taller and bigger. Even if you dug around it, you'd have never found it."

"Guess the person who buried this wooden chest didn't want anyone finding it."

"That'd be my estimation," the man said as a second man helped him heft the chest up onto the dirt. "It's pretty heavy, actually," he added, stepping back.

"Ingenious way to bury your family treasure," Grandma Kat said with approval. "If there's anything of value actually inside. Maybe it was already confiscated and the location forgotten — or the person who buried it died somewhere else."

"Or nobody believed him," I spoke up.

My grandmother lifted her head. "You got a guess as to who that might be?"

I rubbed at my scar. "Nope. Somebody who lived before Miss Anna's time, but probably somebody like Uncle Edgar, who was rich. Maybe his own father. The Yankees came and took over the house during the war, so they buried the family gold so the soldiers wouldn't get their hands on it."

"Okay, I can't stand it," Grandma Kat said. "Young man, will you do me the pleasure of taking your shovel to that padlock? I don't assume the key is anywhere nearby."

Two whacks with a shovel and the archaic padlock shattered.

I knelt on the dirt with my grandmother as she lifted the stiff, dirt-drenched lid. The wood of the box began to splinter, rotting after so long, but the inside of the chest was lined with a decaying royal-blue velvet.

Nestled inside the box was a second slim mahogany box with gorgeous floral etchings. Grandma Kat lifted it out and opened the lid on its rusty hinges. "Oh, my Lord in heaven, Larissa, will you look at that!" Gently lifting the layers of tableware, she counted out loud. "Twelve sets of silver!"

I stared at twelve forks and knives and spoons anchored by ribbons of burgundy.

"Look, these are tiny cocktail forks," Grandma Kat went on. "And big soup spoons. And a whole set of serving spoons. How large they are! Real silver, not plated. Real silver, Larissa. Only the best for those sugarcane farmers before the war. It's got to be worth a fortune."

I peered into the bottom of the old chest and saw rotting velvet pouches shredding with age. "Look, Grandma, look! Silver coins and gold coins," I breathed. "Piles of them. Falling out of their pouches!"

With shaking hands, my grandmother retrieved one, holding it under the sun in her palm. "Perfectly minted," she whispered. "The etchings still deep, as though they were never used. This is Confederate gold and silver, minted in the early days of the war."

I bent my head, the coins sparkling under the sun. "It says Confederate States of America! 1861 and 1862. So many of them."

Grandma Kat grabbed me up in a huge hug and we rocked back and forth for the longest time as she wept with shock and joy. Our knees got grass-stained. Perspiration dribbled down our faces. My grandmother closed her eyes, and I was pretty sure I knew what she was thinking because I was dreaming the very same thing.

I was picturing the beautiful plantation mansion towering above the rise of the ground. Perfect emerald lawns rolling down to the water once again. The broken bridge crossing the Bayou Teche rebuilt, wide enough for a car this time.

"The silver and the coins were here all this time," Grandma Kat whispered in awe. "All during those years of tragedy and death. When we lost hundreds of acres of farmland. When the house burned to the ground. When we had to move away. Your parents barely scraping by."

"The rumors weren't just gossip, then. Uncle Edgar talked about it, didn't he?"

"That's what my grandmother Anna always said. But I also heard that Uncle Edgar was just a dreamer. A wanderer with a fat bank account, so what did he care about digging up the whole island to find some long-lost family forks!" Grandma Kat rocked back on her heels in wonder. "Sometimes we don't know what's right under our noses until it looks like all is lost. Not until all *is* lost does something wonderful rise out of the ashes."

"Or rises up from the ground!" I couldn't help adding.

Grandma Kat gave a big, wonderful laugh, and Mamma was suddenly next to me, holding Emilie in her arms. She fell to her knees, putting a hand against her mouth. "What does it all mean?"

"It means," my grandmother said, her voice shaking, "that the family curse is finally over."

"Just weeks after Dulcie got her doll back," I added. "Our family finally gets a real home. On our very own island."

Grandma Kat's eyes were misty. "It means the past has caught up with the future. Our ancestors were watching out for us all along."

Emilie, my baby sister, who had almost died trying

to come into this world, gurgled at me. I bent to kiss her tiny puckered mouth. Then she gave me the sweetest cherub smile, and I laughed while my mamma wept and my grandmother wiped tears from the corners of her eyes.

Our lives were going to change in so many ways I could hardly take it in. I reached up to touch the raised line of skin along my scar, tears filling my eyes. I wanted it to shrink. I wanted it to go away. But miracles could happen. Maybe I was dwelling on it too much. Torturing myself. Wanting to suffer when I didn't need to.

Grandma Kat let out another cry. "There's something else!" she said, moving aside the mound of old coins.

Underneath the bags of old coins was a beautiful old-fashioned mirror. My grandmother held it up to the sunshine, and light reflected off the gilded edges and the glass smudged with age.

"Look at this gorgeous handle, Larissa. It's not very big, but ladies used to keep these on their dressing tables. I wonder if a woman, not a man, buried this box."

"It appears that way, doesn't it?" Mamma said. "Burying not only the coins, but the silverware and this mirror. This mirror must have been valuable to want to hide it. The woman didn't want to lose her precious possession to wartime scavengers."

"I think you're right, Maddie," Grandma Kat said. "There must be some way to find out who buried these things and what happened to her. Here, Larissa, why don't you hold the mirror?"

The curved oval with the dainty handle was just big enough for the reflection of my face. Wisps of hair fell across my eyes in the old glass. Slowly, I pushed the hair away. Prickles ran down my neck. The girl who had owned this was my ancestor. How old was she, and what was her name?

I'd always had a love/hate relationship with the stuff in the store. Mostly junk, I always figured. But sometimes there were true treasures. Like this mirror. Family heirlooms from the past — antiques — took on new meaning.

My whole life changed again, the past and present colliding once more.

I took a breath, turning the handle between my fingers so I could see my profile better. Sudden, happy tears bit at my eyes as I realized that the scar was fading and shrinking. It was still there, but not so huge. Not so ugly anymore. Maybe the scar wasn't as horrible as I'd always thought, just as Grandma Kat and Miz Mirage had told me.

As Daddy always said, the scar showed what I'd been through. What my family had endured. It proved our strength and our love. The scar was part of me and always would be, helping to make me into the person I was becoming, but still only a small part of who I was deep inside.

"Can I keep this mirror?" I asked as I gazed into the glass, barely recognizing myself anymore.

Grandma Kat kissed the scar on my cheek. "Yes, Larissa, you keep it. I hope it always reminds you of just how beautiful you are."

There was one thing I was still curious about as I rocked back on my heels under the shade of the cypress grove. "Do you know what happened to Uncle Edgar? Did Miss Anna ever say?"

"She did, actually," Grandma Kat said. "He was her favorite uncle *and* drove every woman in the parish crazy with his handsome looks and exciting travel stories. But when he came back to Louisiana for the last time, he finally married a woman by the name of Sally Blanchard. They had only one child, and I'd have to look up the genealogy records to remember if it was a boy or a girl; I can't recall at the moment. He took Miss Sally as a bride, to Paris. They had a flat on the Seine, but they also spent their days traveling to

Africa and South America and sailing the South Pacific.

"Finally, Uncle Edgar built Sally a villa in the countryside and that's where they spent their last days. Together and very happy indeed."

EPILOGUE

Three days later, the telephone rang. I jumped a mile high, bumping my head on the shelf I was polishing with lemon oil.

It was a blistering July day. Shelby Jayne and I had big plans for a sleepover. We were going to cook outdoors while the blue bottle tree shimmered in the bayou breeze.

Shelby said she also had some fancy finger sandwiches her grandmother taught her how to make, and I was bringing ingredients to create Sophie's decadent brownie recipe.

We planned to stay up late, watch movies, and play with Mister Possum Boudreaux and Miss Silla Wheezy, Shelby's cats. Miss Silla was going to have kittens soon, and Mamma said I could pick the best of the litter. She'd finally consented to letting me have a pet — but not a pet as big as a German shepherd like Beau.

Tomorrow I had a lunch date with Alyson Granger at Verret's Café. A lunch date — like we were teenagers. I was hoping Alyson and Shelby would one day be friends, too. I had so much to tell both of them.

The phone kept ringing and nobody answered it.

Finally, I glared at the bank of telephones on the back wall. One of the old pink Princess phones from the 1980s was jiggling like there was an earthquake. Slowly, I walked over, swallowing hard. I lifted the receiver to my ear. "Hello?"

"It's you, Larissa!" the girl cried out in relief. "I wanted to try to call you one last time, and I got it to work." Her voice quieted. "You did it. You followed the fireflies and found the clues. You saved your family, and you should be proud."

All at once, my ears started ringing in a very peculiar way. I finally recognized the voice. The voice that had started everything. The voice that kept me searching and questioning and never giving up. I don't know why I didn't realize it earlier. Probably because it wasn't a little girl's voice, but a girl who was growing up. A girl more sure of herself, stronger. A girl who was happy.

Understanding dawned on me in a dozen different ways. "*You're* the person who moves things around the store at night. Not because you're a ghost, but because you live here, in the future. Time *does* slip in a parallel dimension, the past, the present, and the future. That's why you said you had to be so careful about not changing history. *You* were the one who put the note inside the doll so I would know for sure what I had to do."

"I knew you could do it all along." She paused. "Have you ever thought about calling your old phone number, just to see if your younger self might answer?"

I felt fireflies fluttering at my insides as I listened to her. I couldn't say another word because I'd finally figured out what had been happening all along.

"I can't talk anymore," she said softly. "But I think you know why."

"Yes —" I put a hand on the wall to keep from falling over. "It was silly to think this was some sort of joke when everything came true."

"It never was, Larissa. You know that already. And you know the truth."

"Yes," I whispered. "But — but — can you tell me how old you are?"

"Almost sixteen," she answered. "We're living in the new house on the island now, so I had to call while you still lived at the antique store. I'm not sure you ever really *needed* me to call, but I did just in case. Because not calling meant Emilie might have died. And Mamma. Maybe you, too."

"You mean *ME*," I choked out. "Because — *you are really me.*"

The girl never acknowledged that I had guessed correctly at last. There was only silence as the connection was cut and she was gone, the telephone cord dangling unplugged in my hand.

I replaced the receiver, sinking to the floor. I touched my cheek, the thin line of the white scar. It was still there, but I didn't notice it so much anymore. It was finally fading. Fading like all sad and sorrowful things finally do when there's hope.

The girl on the phone was me all this time. Four years from now I would somehow figure out a way to telephone the past — to make sure that there *was* a future.

A future that was filled with so much light and possibility — and Mamma and Emilie — a future where I was surrounded by everything and everyone I loved.

ACKNOWLEDGMENTS

I'm dedicating this book to my baby brother and his sons, because this is the story I struggled to write in fits and starts and pieces here and there during his final six-month fight with brain cancer. A story of family and history and the generations of love that link us all together. Kendall was a huge book lover his entire life, as well as guitarist, singer, and songwriter, who organized his first band in high school and later, on board the various naval ships where he served as Chief Electronic Technician. He got to travel the world and loved it, but mostly he wanted to be a husband and father, and looked forward to retiring and making his family his first priority. I adored listening to his navy adventures and travel stories, and will miss those and his music most of all.

My love goes especially to my husband and my sons, as well as my brothers, sisters, in-laws, nieces, nephews, and my mother for all the encouragement and support you've given me as I pursued this writing dream for so many years — um, make that decades.

I'm blessed to work with exceptional book-loving people, and I want to thank Tracey Adams, Josh Adams, Quinlan Lee, and the Adams Lit family for being my cheerleaders, confidants, and friends, and for keeping me sane during all the highs and lows of drafting, revisions, copyedits, marketing, new ideas, and craziness. I'm blessed and pure *lucky* to have you all in my corner.

Thank you, Lisa Sandell, for always knowing just how to lift me up and spur me on to do my best work. You are a generous editor and an inspiring friend in my life.

Special thanks and love go to Carolee Dean, my long-time writing partner, friend, and a writer of unaccountable talent. Thank you for more than a decade of lunches and chats, brainstorming and cheers.

Thank you to the Scholastic team who works so hard on my behalf: editorial assistant Jennifer Ung, associate editor Jody Corbett, copy editor Monique Vescia, production editor Starr Baer, and book designer Elizabeth B. Parisi. Every single time I open up the first copies hot off the press, I'm stunned and transfixed by how gorgeous every single book is, inside and out.

I'd like to shower hearts on the huge Scholastic Book Fair and Book Club teams around the country, working so hard to bring my books to schools, kids, and readers. Thank you to the Fairs and Clubs editorial team for loving all the story ideas Lisa and I have sent across your desks.

Wow, Erin McGuire, I think you've outdone yourself this time on the cover artwork. It's dazzling and perfectly magical.

Last of all, thank you, dear readers all around the world, for your emails and kudos and love. It's an honor to know my books make a difference in your lives, and it's a privilege to write for you.

ABOUT THE AUTHOR

Kimberley Griffiths Little is the author of *The Healing Spell*, *Circle of Secrets*, and *When the Butterflies Came*, as well as a dozen short stories that have appeared in numerous publications, and the critically acclaimed novels *Breakaway*, *Enchanted Runner*, and *The Last Snake Runner*. She is a winner of the Southwest Book Award, the Whitney Award, and has been included in the Bank Street College Best Books of the Year list.

She grew up reading a book a day and scribbling stories, while dreaming of seeing her name in the library card catalog one day. In her opinion, the perfect Louisiana meal is gumbo and rice, topped off with warm beignets, although crawfish étouffée runs a close second.

Kimberley lives in a solar adobe house near the banks of the Rio Grande in New Mexico with her husband and children.